D0348615

SKYE KATHLEEN MOODY

RAIN DANCE

WORLDWIDE.

TORONTO • NEW YORK • LONDON
AMSTERDAM • PARIS • SYDNEY • HAMBURG
STOCKHOLM • ATHENS • TOKYO • MILAN
MADRID • WARSAW • BUDAPEST • AUCKLAND

In loving memory of my father,
Robert Arthur Moody

RAIN DANCE

A Worldwide Mystery/July 1998

First published by St. Martin's Press, Incorporated.

ISBN 0-373-26278-7

Printed In U.S.A.

The author is grateful for generous contributions and support from St. Martin's editor Kelley Ragland and literary agent Pam Ahearn. For their kind and unsparing critique, the author thanks her sisters, Suzie Hockett and Elizabeth Speten; and for research assistance and the ride to the Gitchee Gummee Motel, Ann Munro.

Both *National Geographic* and the World Wildlife Federation provided valuable research material, especially the comprehensive findings of U.S. Fish and Wildlife agents Chris Servheen and Judy A. Mills, authors of "The Asian Trade in Bears and Bear Parts," published by the World Wildlife Fund. Also, Washington State Department of Fish and Game provided enlightening assistance.

This novel couldn't have been completed without the unconditional support of my mother and stepfather, Donna and Dick Kelly. Many others contributed to this story's long journey to publication, and toward each of them I feel gratitude, especially to Paul Rodenhauser, M.D., lovable spouse and reality base.

Humankind has not woven the web of life.
We are but one thread within it.
Whatever we do to the web,
we do to ourselves.
All things are bound together.
All things connect.
Whatever befalls the Earth
also befalls the children of the Earth.

—Chief Seattle

The ocean has no compassion, no law,
no memory.

—Conrad

ONE

Her Big Swim

ON THE EVE of vernal equinox, an angry squalling sea cast up the remains of Madge Leroux. Turbulent surf flung them onto rocks at Point Danger jetty, a half mile north of Ozone Beach, Washington. Beachcombers who found the corpse at first thought they had stumbled over a snarl of fragile driftwood. But it was the balance of Madge Leroux, widowed timber queen, whose husband's logging empire had in one generation stripped bare ten percent of the Olympic Peninsula's evergreen forests.

There was a hole in her head the size and shape of a .38 bullet. A little old lady ought to go more peacefully. But this particular L.O.L. had more enemies than a hake has scales. In view of her reputation, how she came to die made a sort of perverted sense.

It was murder. Consider: An autopsy revealed the seventy-four-year-old Madge had enjoyed superior health and well-being before this violence triggered organic decay and bloating. The bullet had pierced the skull, burst and frazzled the cortex, made a pass at the frontal lobe, and exited just above the right eyeball. When found, the corpse's hands and feet were tightly bound with sturdy hemp sailor's cord. It's kind of hard to shoot yourself in the back of the head, especially when you're tied up. It wasn't suicide.

The beachcombers were tourists from Tokyo. They'd never seen living seaweed before, let alone a human corpse. Except on sushi—seaweed that is—and then it was dried, and that looked different. So they told the Harbor County sheriff before he released them to their tour group. They weren't much help.

According to the sheriff's report, Madge had disappeared from her estate near Ozone Beach some three full days before her remains were discovered. Her only living relative, the notorious bachelor-cum-crackhead Parker Leroux, Jr., reported that his mother (Madge) had gone beachcombing one moonlit night and never returned. Fearing she'd been kidnapped for ransom, as heir apparents must constantly dread, Parker hesitated to contact the authorities. No use infuriating the kidnappers. He awaited their instructions. Days passed with no news of the timber queen; then, just as the son decided to notify the sheriff's office, Madge's remains washed ashore. Quirky coincidence.

A tearful Parker eulogized to the news media: "Mother frequently beachcombed at night," he lamented on live television, "especially during storms. She believed negative ions shot off the turbulence and penetrated everything. She believed these negative ions would preserve her veneer, thus, whenever a good storm hit, she headed straight for the beach. She claimed the shelling was best then, too.

"The night Mother disappeared," Leroux added between appropriate emotive pauses, "we had one heck of a storm down here. So go figure. Anyhow, it's business as usual at Leroux Timber Corporation. Beyond that, I have no comment."

Servants at the Leroux estate, interviewed by the sheriff himself, supported the son's description of Madge's queer habits. A maid reported that the only item missing from the house was Madge's little pearl pink overnight case, which she always carried on beachcombing expeditions because it had a washable vinyl interior. That was all anybody knew. At least anybody who was talking.

Roy Ball, the Harbor County sheriff, had unofficially ruled a "death by misadventure" within five hours of the body's discovery. A case of beachcombing gone sour, Ball opined. But here was the rub: Madge Leroux's remains had washed up on coastal beaches owned by the United States Department of the Interior. Specifically, Madge had come ashore on the Ozone Beach National Park and Bio-Diversity Sanctuary, an ecological nirvana under the jurisdiction of the DOI's Fish and Wildlife Service. Thus, what Ball thought really didn't carry that much weight. This was indisputably a case for Fish and Wildlife agents.

Madge Leroux would have wanted that.

TWO

Pelicans

IT WAS ONE of those dense gray drizzly mornings Seattle normally reserves for tourists. A thick fog shrouded Puget Sound. You could hear foghorns but you couldn't see the ships in Elliott Bay with fog this low and languid. Over Seattle, the sun was a UFO.

If it's true that raindrops are angels' tears, mused Venus Diamond, there must be a long tragedy in heaven. Her lymph nodes ached from the dampness. Misty rain had been falling nonstop for three days, since the morning she'd stepped off a Singapore Airlines flight and presented her passport at immigration, having nothing to declare at customs besides a horrendous case of airplane legs and malaria fever. Adding insult to these injuries came the worst trans-Pacific jet lag she'd ever experienced. The fog in her head precisely matched the fog in the streets, and she navigated Pike Street with less authority than the Three Blind Mice.

It was still early morning; the fog and drizzle might lift by midday, creating what natives call a "sun break," a rent in the pall through which sunlight leaks briefly, revealing wondrous natural beauty, including that sublime scoop of ice cream called Mount Rainier, the snowcapped Olympics and Cascades, Puget Sound's sparkling saltwater inlets, emerald islands, and amidst it all, Seattle's soaring urban skyline, bustling Pike Place Market, and careening hillclimb streets. The fog sometimes lifts, the rain might pause, but a real native never tells tourists that. Seattle has a reputation to uphold, Venus reminded herself. The drizzling Emerald City. Oz on a slant.

Guessing a signal light's message, Venus crossed Third Avenue and walked one block to Union Street. She paused at a *latte* stand on the corner, purchased a double hazelnut shooter with a lid on, then moved deeper into the heart of the fog-shrouded metropolis, past animate figures she could barely make out but instinctively knew were other humans on other missions. They too must be late for work.

Soaring majestically above the deep harbor, puncturing the fog, the art deco Bumbershoot Building marked the exact center of downtown. Venus went in, crossed the expansive pink granite lobby, avoiding the umbrella shakers, and entered a crowded elevator. Rising up forty-three floors rankled the jet lag, but the malaria fever seemed almost manageable this morning. Now sole occupant of the elevator car, she felt her forehead. One-oh-one or two. Not bad. She might live after all. At the forty-third floor, she stepped out of the elevator into the foyer of the United States Department of the Interior's regional headquarters. DOI paid dearly for this celestial western-view perch in the Bumbershoot. On this dim morning, having view windows was about as useful as owning a surfboard in Nome.

No one noticed her entrance. Anyone brave enough to focus on her this morning might be startled by the jaundice, and the enormous rheumy green eyes. The fever had burned off most of her hair; the barber in the Bumbershoot's lobby had finished the job, slicking back the tattered remains into a ragged James Dean. She'd lost twenty pounds she couldn't spare and if you saw her sideways you might think she wasn't there at all. So no one noticed her entrance. This morning she generated about as much electricity as a firefly in a casket.

She passed Oly Olson's office on tiptoe, because she knew what he was doing in there and wanted no part of it. In her own small office, Venus put the *latte* down on the glass table she used as a desk, and rummaged through a pile of software until she found the disk she wanted. She carried this and the coffee across the hall to the computer terminals. When she fed the disk into the hard drive, the console buzzed softly then coughed up a riot of lime green figures that taunted her: "See what happens when you go away, what slaughter, what mayhem prevail? And these are only the cougar gall figures. Why don't you ask for the bear gall report? Or are you still avoiding that?"

The *latte* needed sweetening. Venus extracted a packet of sugar from her pocket, shook it, ripped it open, sprinkled it over the steaming liquid. A remarkable improvement. Another sip or two and she might feel starched enough to face the bear gall report. Nothing tops reading about slimy green gall bladders first thing in the morning. How the gall bladders are ripped out of half-dead bears by poachers so they can be sold fresh on the black market. Each case presented idiosyncratic clues to the poachers' identities, so you had to read it front to back. No skimming over the gruesome details. The hardest part was the politics of getting her hands on the bear gall report. Sparks wouldn't give it over without major melodramatics. Not to her, not to anyone. Except maybe Olson, because he was the boss. That might be the unpleasant route she'd have to take.

Olson, the regional chief of DOI's Fish and Wildlife Service, still hadn't come out of his office. From where she lounged at the computer terminals, Venus couldn't see inside Olson's office, but she knew he sat staring out the big windows at the socked-in harbor, trying to reconcile a nasty hangover with this wretched weather.

Oly Olson was egg-shaped, bald, and, when irritated, very hard boiled. Venus had noticed since her return to regional headquarters three days ago that Olson's dander seemed a little fluffed, that his silences fell too profound, that there lurked dark patches beneath his bloodshot eyes, hinting—no, shouting—of serious sleep deprivation and more. How could she forget? It was NBA season, the Sonics had made the playoffs, and Olson was a Sonics fan. They'd trounced the Lakers in the Kingdome last night. Afterward, Olson most certainly had binged. Now the residue of that bash threatened innocents such as herself. She could feel it coming as he communed with the gray pall, and then he barked suddenly, an ominous summons.

During three spectacular years in Asia, she'd almost forgotten Olson's bark. She stored the cougar gall report and approached Olson cautiously, with gentle steps, the way she might approach a sick rhino, minus the compassion.

His wide back greeted her. On his desk, an open carton of

Frango Mints had a come-hither quality. Smooth, rich, divine. Frango's deeply primal mint chocolate almond truffles. Oral ecstasy. He still hadn't turned around. She plucked a Frango, palmed it. Over his rumpled slumped shoulder Olson growled, "Pick up the letter on my desk and read it. Not out loud."

The white business envelope was addressed in bold type to the Commissioner of Fish and Wildlife, United States Department of the Interior, Washington, DC. The commissioner's name was Wexler, but it wasn't addressed to him personally, just to the "Commissioner." The postmark was January 1, this year, Ozone Beach, Washington. The letter inside was a computer printout that said:

> Wildlife Commissioner: Leroux Timber Corporation has already decimated the spotted owl population. Now they're after the brown pelicans down here. If you lazy sons-of-bitches at Fish and Wildlife won't police your own wildlife sanitary, we'll do it for you. Our operation may involve violence against humans. This is a wraning. The Pelican Petrol.

She held the paper out to light, then set it back down on Olson's desk. She said, "A wraning?"

"Typo. Like 'sanitary' and 'Petrol.' Literacy's gone to hell."

"I thought brown pelicans nested south of here. In balmier climes. By the way, happy first day of spring."

"Never mind spring."

Olson's swivel chair groaned beneath his bulk, rotating. When he faced her, she could see the dark patches under his eyes, deep in hue and sagging. His brow furrowed vertically, as if to ward off demons, or the urge to explode. Hoarsely, he said, "Their migration pattern's changing. You may recall that they usually fly up here during fall and winter, then head back south to reproduce. But lately some have been sighted along our coastline as early as April. So it appears their migration pattern's changing.

Maybe their roosting habits too. Something about DDE linked with the mating ritual. I don't know what.''

He fingered the mysterious letter and intoned, "Wexler received this in January. He's forwarded it to us because now he wants an investigation.''

Wexler was responsible for sending her to Asia, then yanking her back just days ago to this Godforsaken wringing wet handkerchief-knot corner of the world. At the moment, she was barely on speaking terms with him. To Olson, she said, "When did we receive it?''

"This morning, before you graced us with your presence. Wexler says he wants us to look at this Pelican Patrol, find out what they're doing down on our sanctuary.''

"If this letter was sent to Wexler in January,'' she said, "why didn't he worry about it before now? This is the end of March already.''

Olson shrugged tiredly. He didn't know. Didn't care. Venus's glance dropped to the cryptic letter. Olson's bloodshot eyes focused on the same place. She wondered what he would say next. She wondered if he was still awake or if he'd gone comatose on her, then he grunted.

"And then Wexler phoned this morning, after he saw the *Today* show. They reported Madge Leroux's big swim. He saw that on *Today,* and then he called me.''

"She was that important?''

"Since the spotted owl became a public issue, yes.''

"What does Madge Leroux have to do with pelicans?''

Olson snickered. "A lot has happened here during your absence. The world didn't exactly stop rotating when you left here. Things happened. One of those things is an extension of the biodiversity sanctuary down at Ozone Beach. We've tacked a brown pelican sanctuary onto the territory. The island that sits about a mile offshore at Point Danger. Where the old Point Danger lighthouse stands? Pelicans have discovered it. But you wouldn't know about all this, being gone in Asia.''

He was trying to tick her off. The Frango, wrapped in cellophane, tucked into her palm, was melting. She smiled tactfully.

Olson continued, "You remember that little island. Coast Guard abandoned it years ago. We inherited the land. So maybe two years ago, Interior's budget got decimated and regional was instructed to sell the lighthouse at public auction. Not the island, we still own that. Just the lighthouse. Guess who bought it, just for fun?"

She held up her free hand playfully. "Don't tell me," she said, trying to inject some humor into the pallid atmosphere. "Let me guess." She closed her eyes, squinted.

"Stop that," snapped Olson.

She said, "Madge Leroux?"

"Right. Never used it for anything, of course. It's inaccessible except by chopper, and then only in calm seas. No one from DOI has been out there yet, to my knowledge. Oh, I guess you could get out there in a skiff, if you knew the seas." He waved his hand tiredly. "She bought it for a toy, a lark. But then, I don't need to educate you about the whimsical rich."

He was goading. Trying to incite something. He needed a target, something to divert his mind from the dicey hangover. Her ancestry and her family's wealth were two of his favorite prods. But she wouldn't bite. The edges of her mouth curved up insincerely. Inside, her small, evenly spaced teeth had clenched, but Olson couldn't know this. He only saw her smiling in docile agreement. That frustrated him, but he wouldn't admit it. He continued.

"Last year, some brown pelicans were observed roosting in the lighthouse. Actually settling in there. So—remember, the federal government owns the island—we declared the island a sanctuary. In case you've forgotten, the brown pelican is an endangered species on the Northwest Coast."

Venus waited for the punch line. Intuitively, she felt Olson had an idea of connecting her and this frigid backwater called Ozone Beach. A repugnant thought. There must be more to life than the snarling, frigid Washington coast. There had been, before Wexler had jerked her back here to Puddle Town. Maybe it was the jet lag, or the malaria residue, or this leaky faucet in the local sky.

But something gnawed at her soul this morning. Venus clenched her fist. The Frango screamed, its wrapper crinkling loudly. Olson's ears perked up. She said, "I had a case like this in Burma last year. Turned out—"

"Can it, Venus."

"I was just—"

"I said, can it," Olson snapped. "We're sick and tired of hearing about your exotic, adventurous globe-trotting heroics. So just can it."

Over at the hot line switchboard outside Olson's open door, Dave, the duty officer, choked on hot coffee. Olson shot Dave an obnoxious glance that snared Venus in its wake. Mockingly he said, "Wexler wants you to handle this. He specifically said he wants you to go down there."

"I thought the Harbor County sheriff had it all wrapped up."

"Don't be snippy. We obviously have jurisdiction, since the body was found on our coastline."

"She might have been shot aboard a vessel, then deep-sixed, and washed in with the tide."

"Shut up, will you? Now, I spoke with Sheriff Ball this morning. He says there's some evidence of transients camping out on the sanctuary. That's grounds to arrest them right there. Probably she surprised them and they shot her. They were doing drugs or drinking or something down on the beach and she came along. I'm too tired to think about all this right now."

The Frango wanted to feel her tongue. She wanted it there. Olson began rubbing his eyes. Her big chance. She unwrapped the melting truffle, popped it. The Frango made love to her mouth. She swooned.

"Anyway," Olson droned on, "Wexler's more concerned about this pelican business. This should be your focus, your priority. I doubt there's much to uncover on the Leroux killing. But it's funny, I'll grant Wexler that, it is strange that this Pelican Patrol makes threats against the Leroux company and then she washes up on the beach down there."

Venus nodded. The swoon diminished in intensity, but a memory lingered.

Olson said, "So go down there, see what you can uncover in a tactful manner about this Pelican Patrol. Find out who they are, what they've been up to. They might be some new radical ecology group. Then find out if they had anything to do with Mrs. Leroux's murder. If not, find out what did happen to the woman. Is that clear?"

"Crystal." She smiled politely. No need to sass the regional dictator. In the few days she'd been back working, Olson remarked only yesterday, he'd observed a certain big-fish-in-small-pond aura around her. Olson said he'd already recorded three incidents of brazen insubordination. One more, Olson had warned, and he'd report her to Wexler. She needed a reprimand from Wexler like Seattle needed precipitation.

"Go down to Records," Olson said. "Read the brown pelican file. Every word. Learn something about pelicans. I bet you don't know a damn thing about pelicans. Then this afternoon I want you to scoot down to Ozone Beach. Ask around, see what cooks."

"I was planning to stick with the big-game-poaching investigation. The one we started over in Singapore? I'm halfway through the cougar gall report already. In fact, I was going to ask you to convince Sparks to give over the bear gall file. He's coded the disk and I can't get in.

"Besides," she added, "Ozone Beach National Park and the bio-diversity sanctuary are in Sparks's territory, not mine. My territory's the northern half of the Olympic Peninsula. Maybe you forgot that, in my long absence."

Olson growled, "I told you yesterday that I've got Sparks working on some poachers. Now pay attention. This is important: The natives down at Ozone Beach are a suspicious breed. They're not keen on outsiders."

"I thought Ozone Beach was a trendy resort town."

"Listen to me. Just listen, will you? Ozone Beach is a very upscale tourist resort. But the natives down there are peculiar. They don't trust anyone. They don't even like the tourists. What I'm trying to say, if you'd just give me the opportunity without interrupting, is that I want you in uniform down there so they know you're official."

"I'd learn more in street clothes."

"Don't contradict me."

"Why me?"

"Because Wexler said so. Is that clear?"

"Check." She started for the door. Olson raised a hand. She paused, fingers on the door knob.

Olson said, "They've got what they call a village council in Ozone Beach, with a mayor. Her name is Mercy, Mrs. Janice Mercy. Check with the mayor and council. They've been very supportive of the pelican sanctuary. They might know something."

"What about the local police chief? Shouldn't I check with the police chief too?"

"There is no police force in Ozone Beach. Only law is the sheriff's office at Oyster Bay. I'll have Sparks talk to Sheriff Ball. He knows Ball."

Venus remembered something. "Oh, and the autopsy...who did that? And why was it done before we got there?"

He sighed, a deep, dejected sigh. "Come back over here," he whispered hoarsely. "I'm not finished."

She went back over and stood near Olson's desk and watched his eyes. The storm brewing there wanted a vent. In measured tones he said, "When the remains were turned over to Ball, he contacted me. That was last night, just before half-time. In deference to the son's wishes, I granted permission to go ahead with the autopsy. The son had a local physician perform it. The physician is the official county coroner. It was all very legitimate. Of course, there are some test results that aren't yet in, but it's fairly obvious what caused death."

"Bullet?"

He spread his hands and smiled insincerely.

Venus said, "Okay, I think I've got the gist. I think I'm ready to cut out of here."

"Not so fast. Now listen here: This is not Burma. Not even close to it. You are not a guerrilla hero chasing big game poachers on the outposts of civilization. This is America. Ozone Beach may be remote and rural, and the natives may be peculiar, but it's also a politically sensitive place. Don't treat the villagers like rhino poachers."

She nodded. Maybe he was finished now. No, there was more.

"This situation demands tact and diplomacy."

"Yes, sir."

"Remember, we have more than a national park down there. That rock-island sanctuary is a political tinderbox. Do your research before you go off half-cocked. We can't afford to offend anyone in that town. And speaking of offending, try not to look so androgynous. It's disconcerting."

"God made me this way." For the hundredth time.

"Bull." For the hundredth time.

Over at the switchboard, Dave shook his head in despair, or weariness. Olson opened his desk drawer, rummaged, fished out a thin file folder labeled OZONE BEACH. He handed it to her. She was tucking it under her arm when Olson whined, "I miss the good old days when men were men and women showed off what they had."

"If I'm not mistaken, sir, the basic apparatus hasn't changed."

Olson's jaded eyes scrutinized Venus, this miniature person: flat, nonexistent chest, wispy adolescent boy's figure, hipless, a rebel's stance. Even with jaundice, she looked childlike, yet Olson knew she'd hit the big three-oh next week. He barked, "Don't go prancing around Ozone Beach like some hotshot future-heroine cartoon character just because you saved the entire rhino population of Southeast Asia. Which is really no big deal when you think about it. I mean, you didn't do it single-handed. Probably thousands of Karen gamekeepers armed to the teeth did the work and you copped the credit. I wouldn't put it past you."

He glowered. "Don't even mention it in Ozone Beach. Nobody likes a braggart."

The Frango's velvet edge had waned. A sourness formed on her palate, rage working to the surface. Over Olson's shoulder, she glimpsed Dave frantically signaling time out. Dave the Peace-maker. Dave, who one spring had single-handedly killed two big game poachers while defending a den of bear cubs, wanted none of this previolent foreplay in the office. She wanted to strangle

Olson. Dave didn't want her to, not here, not now. She caged the beastly urge, tried a softer approach.

"Olson," she said daringly, "I don't think this Ozone Beach is my cup of tea."

Olson rolled his red-rimmed eyes.

She explained, "I've been back in America less than a week. It's culture shock. I can barely adjust to the time zone, let alone some rural backwater. I just can't handle this rural aspect."

Sadistically he jeered, "What about Burma, or Myanmar, or whatever they call it now? You call the Chiang Mai urban?"

"That's Thailand." She let that sink in, then added, "Jungles are different."

Olson slammed a hard fist against his teakwood desk and yelled, "Stuff the bloody jungles! If Wexler hadn't been so naive as to buy your cockeyed fantasy about some mythical international poachers' fraternity, he'd never have loaned you to the Asian Wildlife Society and you wouldn't even know what a jungle looks like. And if you hadn't been so inept, you might still be over there instead of back here lipping off at me today. And I'll tell you something else. Only idiots get malaria. Haven't you ever heard of Off, for chrissake?"

He turned purple and shook a stiff finger at her.

"Now you listen to me, Venus. Wexler might have retired you. Instead, out of the sheer generosity of his heart, he brought you back here on payroll to recover from your illness. But Wexler did not grant you a paid leave of absence. He expects you to work like the rest of us. This piddly assignment down at Ozone Beach may not be your idea of exotic, but it's still the kind of work we do at Pacific Northwest. Is that clear?"

At the duty desk, Dave had buried his good looks in his strong hands. The phone was ringing but Dave wasn't answering. Venus felt sorry for him. She said to Olson: "This is my first bird case."

"Screw it up," the boss snapped tersely, "and it'll be your last."

THREE

Sparks

SHE was in the elevator, crushed behind a squad of Smokey hats, when she noticed the flyer. Some sort of public service announcement. It had been slipped into the Ozone Beach file, she thought, by mistake. It was a small poster, a glossy, four-color affair, an illustration of *Ursus arctos.* The text warned about poaching of *Ursus americanus,* the variety of bear that roams the Olympic Peninsula.

In the spring, black bears foraged in young timber stands, searching what used to be their lush native habitat for their first post-hibernation meals. Timber magnates and U.S. Forestry Service officials complained they couldn't control the damage to tree farms, so U.S. Fish and Wildlife joined with Washington State Fish and Game to sponsor bear hunts. To cut the foraging population. Control damage to the tree clone farms. So the timber could be harvested and shipped overseas, sold for titanic profits. For this, the native species were hunted and killed, and clone farms overtook old growth.

Hunters were chosen by lottery. There was a limit on the take, usually about twenty bears per authorized hunt on the Olympic Peninsula. According to this poster, some bears had been taken out of season. Poached. So what else was new? If you saw evidence of poaching, the poster asked you to contact federal or state authorities, it didn't matter which, by phoning a toll-free number, the Poacher Hotline. The poster wanted you to understand that wildlife was a two-billion-dollar industry in Washington State. It asked you to help save "product."

Sparks collided with her at the door to Records. He was on his way out, a fat file folder labeled BROWN PELICAN: HABITS AND

HABITAT clasped to his thin chest. At least she could say that about Sparks. That he was literate.

Tall, lanky, Sparks wore his uniform like a second skin. He'd been with Fish and Wildlife longer than Venus or Olson or anyone else now on regional payroll. Maybe twenty years. In all that time, he'd never been promoted above agent status. Sparks was possessive about his territory along the coast, but you got the impression he never burned with ambition. Life in the rain-soaked forest suited him fine.

Venus said to Sparks, "I need that file."

Sparks blinked, scowled. "Why, hon?" he drawled.

She told him. He listened, then said matter-of-factly, "That's my territory. Coastal range from Point Danger on south is mine. That includes Ozone Beach National Park, the adjacent sanctuary, and the pelican roost out there on the island. Which is officially a part of the sanctuary now."

Venus held up a small, delicate hand with short fingers, ringless. "Sparks, I'm not competition. Olson's just trying to mollify Wexler and keep me busy till the malaria fever wears off. Then they'll probably ship me back to Singapore."

Sparks guffawed. "Like hell they'll ship you back. You blew that one, hon. Like hell they'll ship you back."

"Anyway, I need that file."

Coolly, he handed it over. "It's a prank," he drawled. "That letter to Wexler was some prank. No such thing as the Pelican Patrol. Was, I'd know about it."

"What about the Leroux murder? Who did that?"

"I heard straight from Sheriff Ball that old lady Leroux got trussed up by some drug-crazed biker that was campin' on the beach down near Point Danger. You goin' down there?"

She said yes, then, "She wasn't just tied up. Somebody shot her in the back of the head."

"Think I don't know that? I knew that. Some biker did it. Ball's pretty sure of that. Anyway, it's my territory down there, I don't care what Wexler says. So you clear with me whatever you do down there, hear?"

"Olson tells me you're working on a poaching complaint."

He nodded.

Venus said, "Been a lot of poaching down there in recent years?"

He shrugged.

Venus said, "Any carcasses mutilated?"

He grimaced oddly, as if in pain, then slowly shook his head. "Naw."

"How about State Game? Have they tracked many poachers?"

Sparks shifted his weight. "You kidding? They're asleep. State Game is asleep. This whole damn state could be wall-to-wall big game carcasses and State Game wouldn't even notice."

"When can I see the bear gall file?"

"Whenever you want. Why?" Innocent. Like he hadn't been keeping it to himself.

"I need the code to get into that file. And the disk too. I need the disk."

Sparks's mouth puckered into a self-satisfied smile. "Ah, yes. The disk. And the code." He shifted again on his feet. He stooped down to Venus's height, knowing how she hated that, and patted her on the head, a gesture she'd always despised, a gesture scrupulously avoided in Asia. The head is the soul's temple. Sparks patted her soul and said, "Tell you what, sugarcake. You want the bear gall file? Okay. You behave yourself real good down there at Ozone, and then when you get back here to the office, I'll have that disk sitting on your desk. That's a promise."

"With the entry code."

He nodded. She watched him sidle nonchalantly out the door, disappear down the long corridor, his cowboy boots clicking machismo rhythms against the marble floor. In her time away, Venus had forgotten about the fierce rivalry between certain State Game and federal Fish and Wildlife agents. Sparks had avidly promoted the rivalry. He'd always held State Game in venomous contempt. They impinged on his turf.

She went into Records and spent the next hour in a hard chair reading about mammoth birds with seven-foot wingspans, these living remnants of prehistory, flying dinosaurs wiser than any human on the ways of the sea. After a couple hours more, she packed it in, convinced there was only so much you could learn about pelicans in one sitting. On the way out of the building, in the Bumbershoot's pink granite lobby, she went over to the public phones and fed one. She pressed some buttons. When Olson came on the line, she said, "There's a flyer in the Ozone Beach file. With a picture of *Ursus arctos* on it."

"Correct." He sounded shaky. Maybe the d.t.'s.

"Ah...what's it doing in here?"

"I put it there."

"Why, Olson?" She caught a glimpse of her image in a mirrored wall and at first didn't recognize herself. She didn't like what malaria had done to her looks. The jaundice tinted her skin saffron. The saffron clashed with her Key lime eyes.

Olson said brusquely, "It is a public service announcement. I want you to ask the Ozone Beach post office to tack it up on their bulletin board."

"The illustration on this flyer is *Ursus arctos,* sir."

"So?"

"That's a grizzly."

Silence.

She said, "All ten of them live in the Cascades. There aren't any grizzlies left on the Olympic Peninsula. The flyer's text accurately describes the black bear, but the picture's a grizzly. Somebody goofed."

Olson yelled, "Hey, Venus. Nobody's goddamn perfect. Except, of course, you. You know what? I feel sorry for your mother. I mean, with all Lady Bella's wealth and fame my heart still bleeds for her. I bet having you back home is sheer agony. I bet you drive poor Bella frigging bananas."

"I'm her favorite offspring," she lied.

"Bull," he said and hung up.

She plunged into the fog, back on the Blind Mice trail, located the parking spot where she'd left her Harley, and rode across the Pier 91 bridge to Lady Bella's castle on Magnolia Bluff. Bella wasn't up yet. Venus sat zazen for a while, then mooned over coffee and a toasted crumpet. Some days were grayer than others.

FOUR

Raffles

SHE'D COME INTO her tent one night in the Chiang Mai and crawled onto her cot to undress. It's not easy disrobing under a mosquito net. She was dozing off when a nasty tingle erupted down around the ankles. After the third or fourth bite, she flung off the net shroud, switched on the light, and peered through the mesh.

On the precise spot where she should have been dozing, a mosquito stood poised like a Stealth bomber on alert. *Inside* the net. Mosquitoes weren't supposed to know how to penetrate these nets. Evidently, one did.

After pensive reconnoiter, she tried shadowboxing around the bed. No results. Lifting an edge of the mesh, she mimicked the mosquito mating call. No takers. Then someone up at the lodge rang the poacher alert, so she dressed quickly and strapped on her pistol. On the way out, she drew the gun, aimed at the occupied bed, and fired once. Then she went into the jungle to track humans. They were easier.

Ten incubation days later, on one of those perfect Singapore evenings, a fragrant tropical breeze wafted abroad, and in the garden bar at Raffles, a Malay waiter in white mess jacket hovered discreetly at her elbow. They were languishing in lofty rattan on the grand lawn, sipping Slings, she and the man she'd pinned her dreams on, Reuben, the Singaporean Jew. There was a Finn drinking with them, a metafiction novelist named Anssii, who was tanked on Slings and waxing cynical. Reuben yawned widely, but Venus was entranced by Anssii's hypnotic slurred loquacity and by his paleness. Another part of her wanted to sidle over to the buffet when, without a speck of handwriting on the wall, the fever hit, peaking instantly. She dropped like a stunned fly on Raffles's manicured lawn.

Reuben bent down, felt her forehead, groped a pulse.

"Malaria," he whispered hoarsely to Anssii.

"Malaria," slurred the Finn enviously. "How exotic."

Blood from fruit. Asian mosquitoes got finicky feeding on the corpulent durian and other fleshy breadfruits. The next logical food source: succulent human flesh. Hers.

Reuben and a sloshed Anssii hauled her to the Tropical Medicine Infirmary on Old Bugis Street, where the resident Hindi physician pumped her full of mega-quinine and other potent substances. The diminutive Stealth bomber had dropped a load of drug-resistant *Plasmodium falciparum.* They call it cerebral malaria, because after feeding on your liver, these orgiastic parasites breed profusely and whole armies march to the brain for the final, fatal denouement. Very exotic.

The practical Hindi advised lighting a funeral pyre. Reuben had the gall to place a satellite call to Bella in America. Bella snared the next available first-class lounger on Singapore Airlines, and that was where the megillah unfolded. Mothers should not be gorgeous movie stars with British titles.

Venus never really knew what transpired during the following weeks. She spent them in coma, with brief sorties into consciousness to spew quinine and get popped with nonsterilized needles. Reuben later remarked that on the third day, Anssii came to commiserate and promptly fainted on the threshold, proving just what sort of mettle he was made of. Anssii left Singapore the following morning after instructing Reuben to mail him Venus's black leather jacket should the worst befall her. Expatriate friendships are like that.

Reuben also informed her, much later, that Bella had captured Singapore's heart. That didn't surprise her, what with Bella's finesse, but Venus felt slightly annoyed to learn that Reuben counted himself among the masses charmed by the enigmatic diva. Mothers should lose charming, especially when their stricken offspring lay clutched to the Grim Reaper's fevered bosom. Actress or not.

The quinine days stretched on. Once the Hindi physician stole into her room, shook her semiconscious to whisper that the enemy host now feasted upon her neocortex, but not to worry. Karmic death, assured the doc, is finally painless. Then he stole away, leaving her bedside poorly attended for the duration.

While fever demons haunted Venus, Reuben escorted Bella around Singapore like she was some sort of VIP. They dined nightly in Orchard Road's flashiest clubs, where Reuben deflowered Bella's Anglo-Saxon palate with biting *sataays,* the thick, divine flesh of durian, suspicious pâtés, and the wicked sting of Singapore Slings. Reuben flew Bella in his Skyhawk to Malaysia, sailed with her to Johore, lounged at her lithesome side on Sulawai's immaculate beaches, the king of Sulawai guarding Her Ladyship's other curvaceous side. All very straight-arrow and decorous, Reuben would later assert. But Venus would never know. She was in a coma.

She woke to a team of tropical disease doctors flanking her sickbed. What woke her was a comment by one of these hovering bug aficionados. To paraphrase: "Oh, I see. So you administered quinine, did you, even though it is a totally antiquated therapy?"

"Correct." The voice of the Hindi in charge. "We also pumped in mefloquine and even tried the Chinese herbal remedy, artesunate. But the patient was so far gone, and the disease so completely drug resistant, that in the end, we simply pumped in the whole kitchen sink and hoped for the best. It would appear that we have failed." As he lifted the bedsheet over the patient's pale, wan face, Venus's eyes slowly opened and her parched lips uttered, "Father."

The Hindi murmured vexedly about certain pea-in-the-shoe Westerners who insist on clinging to a semblance of life, thereby thwarting a Higher Plan and botching up the statistics. No one should survive this stuff. Adding insult to injury, she lay trespassing upon a sorely needed hospital bed. Would she kindly rise and take a telephone call?

It was America calling. Wexler, from Washington, DC. Wexler wanted to speak with the attending physician, so she handed the receiver over to the Hindi. In vain, she eavesdropped on his muffled murmuring. Presently he handed back the receiver. Wexler told her the doctor had recommended a recuperative period in malaria-free climes. She hadn't heard the doc mention this, but Wexler insisted. Furthermore, he knew just the place.

Wexler said three years in Asia had been ample time to uncover an international poaching conspiracy, if one actually existed, and that she had obviously failed miserably. The big game poachers remained active in America, but her harebrained theory of un-covering a link between them and Asian black marketeers had borne no viable fruit. Her Oriental junket had proved downright idiotic and the malaria only confirmed this. Wexler wanted her back at the Pacific Northwest office, to resume her old duties there. Was that clear?

None of this made a whit of sense to her, but nothing would have in her fragile condition. She argued with Wexler. She was on the brink of blowing wide open the world's most powerful poaching conspiracy, she was sure of it. More than a few illegal animal slaughters were involved. There was more to this than Wexler could possibly grasp at a distance. Her Asian adventures had indeed borne provocative fruit, and she would deliver the goods, given just a little more time.

Wexler balked. "You'll report to regional HQ in Seattle no later than Monday morning."

Her brain, a battlefield of maimed parasites, malfunctioned at this point. Wringing her flimsy hospital gown, she protested ve-hemently. No one should have to return to the womb, especially one where inclement weather reigns. Of course she wished to remain on payroll. But she could serve her own country better in these more exotic climes. Wexler shouted that her own country might be Cream of Wheat but it needed her now. She detected a hint of urgency in his voice. Placatingly, Wexler added, "Besides, a fresh perspective might untangle that ravaged brain. Now put the doc back on."

Having conferred again with Wexler, the Hindi touched the sleeve of her hospital gown. "May I have a word with you?"

She followed him behind a curtained screen. Furtively, he

placed a small cylindrical object in her hand. "A souvenir." He smiled broadly.

She regarded the object in her hand. She looked at the doctor. He seemed proud, as if he'd just handed her the Nobel prize.

"Nice bullet," she said.

He nodded. "Nine millimeter. I did not report it to the police."

"Where'd you get it?"

"Why, from your little rump. I removed it while you were in the fever." He studied her face quizzically. "Do you mean to say you didn't know it was there?"

She said no and felt the cheeky flesh in question. A hardened area, like tender scar tissue, met her sensitive digits. The Hindi smiled now. He'd figured it all out.

"It probably occurred just as you were stricken by the malaria fever. Someone tried to murder you, but the fever struck you down before the bullet that was aimed at your heart, or maybe your head, ended up in your fanny."

"But if that's true, there must have been blood..."

"Hmmm. I see what you mean. Ah, I've got it." He snapped his long fingers. "Your friends didn't notice the bleeding because they were very drunk. I recall that they reeked and staggered as they brought you into the emergency. Also, they had wrapped you up in blankets because you were chilled. Perhaps that explains it."

"Was I delirious?"

"Very much so. You uttered some quite peculiar phrases."

"Like what?"

"You thought you were a bear. Someone had chopped off your paws and was preparing a soup from them. You said the soup would be seasoned with bear gall, then served to a sacrificial victim. You were simply dotty, there is no other explanation. You had a very high fever."

He leaned in close and whispered, "I know who tried to murder you. It was Lok Toy's men. Lok Toy, the Chinese pirate who sells animal organs. I know because they tried to break into your hospital room one night, but I prevented them. You are very lucky. Everyone's trying to kill you. Even the mosquitoes tried.

Through all this, you did not succumb. Your karma is in excellent condition!''

He loaded her flight bag with anti-malarial medications, in case the purge had failed. She'd know by the high fever, a fever so distinct it could be mistaken for nothing else. Reuben finagled airline passage for her Harley. Bella, who had taken to wearing loud sarongs clasped at an ample bosom with her Diamond Crown of Britain, packed her portmanteau and steamer trunks, bid farewell to the king of Sulawai, sighed beneath the Manila palms, and accompanied her home. Over Hawaii, in the first-class lounge, Bella sipped from a fluted champagne glass and blithely dismissed her daughter's mutterings.

"Nonsense," snapped Lady Bella. "You are staying at home with me."

FIVE

Fog Signals

VENUS, WHAT IN God's name are you doing?"

"Eating a crumpet, Mother."

"You eat far too many crumpets. I'll have my coffee now, Stephen. That's a darling. Pass the sugar, Venus, if you please. What is this mask of gloom you are wearing?"

"It's the weather. Just the weather."

"This is Seattle, dear. Love it or leave it. I won't have wallowing depressions in my home, malaria or no. The eggs are lovely, Stephen, just lovely."

Lady Bella Winsome-Diamond was dangerous, as women with exquisite legs and strong wills are bound to be. Proximity to Bella was as tricky as a topiary maze. Vanity Fair at its zenith, Bella was a sleek, dense-boned sterling creature who could seduce or destroy with one swift arch of a magnificently curved brow. Venus had braved guerrillas in the Chiang Mai, poachers in Rangoon, pistol whippers in Malaysian jungles. Yet, returning home to dwell in the actress's aura, mother or not, had sent her reeling into a grim funk. She feared Bella's refined wrath, adored her divine whimsy, despised her snoopy fan clubs, and preferred to practice familial loyalty from great distances.

Five progeny had sprung from Bella, between stage and screen roles. Such was the fertile destiny of baby boom Mackerel Snatchers. Venus's four siblings had inherited variations on Bella's elegant limbs and regal greyhound carriage. But Bella must have stumbled in the third sequestering, for the middle child sprang forth on April Fool's Day, an iconoclastic infant who smiled constantly and refused to cry. In public, Bella referred to the grinning Venus as "God's Little April Fool." The joke was on Bella, though, for while the genetic roulette wheel had spun out an anatomically correct female with standard gear and inclinations, the adult Venus turned out no larger than Peter Pan, revealing a renegade gene in the otherwise pristine family soup. Her siblings sniggered at Venus's miniature stature, but she was left-handed and swift and they only dared guffaw behind her puny back. Bella, on the other hand, saw no humor in having borne forth such a curious twig, worried that any child who wouldn't cry must certainly be mentally challenged, or more British than Herself, and often remarked that when it came to certain offspring, Divine Providence had a distinctly warped sense of play. Venus soon learned to wince.

"VENUS, why don't we go shopping this morning? A Claude Montana might shoot civilization into you. That haircut is far too primitive, by the way."

"Sorry, Mother. I'm off to Ozone Beach today."

"Don't be silly. You can't drive to the beach in this fog. It's pea soup. You'll end up as one of those white crosses they plant on rural hairpin curves. Stephen will drive us downtown. Men know how to negotiate fog."

"Really, Mother, I can't make it today. I'm working."

"Nonsense. You don't work."

"Mother, for the last eight years I have been gainfully employed by the United States Department of the Interior, in the Fish and Wildlife division."

"That's recreation. What I mean is that you do not have to work. Never had to. You should try to kick back and enjoy your good fortune."

"Also, I'd like to point out that the malaria fever burned my hair to a frazzle and it had to be cut off."

"Why look, Venus. Out in the garden near the salmon camellia. There is a man with a gun. An Oriental. Is he a friend of yours?"

"Oh my God, duck, Mother. He's going to shoot."

"Don't be melodramatic. I should probably go out and see what he wants."

"Come under the table. He's one of Lok Toy's triggermen."

"What do you mean by triggermen? And who is this Lok Toy?"

"Please, Mother, just duck. He's going to shoot."

"See, now he's gone. He must have had the wrong address. I wonder if that was Sue Lane's new gardener..."

"That man had a gun drawn."

"Come out from under the table, Venus. The Oriental man has gone away. He was probably just chasing crows. They're taking over the world, you know. I mean the crows."

THE FAMILY ESTATE ON Magnolia Bluff functioned like a distant British colony, Bella at the helm. There, Venus's childhood had been supervised by sundry servants and nannies who came and went at the same ratio as Bella's sterling silver vanished. Venus knew that sister Dagny and brother Rex, the older sibs, were stashing the silverware in a compost heap behind the herb garden wall. She never snitched, just watched the servants come and go through Bella's furiously revolving door. Blood is thick.

No American flag waved over the Diamond children's youth. Bella's first loyalty embraced the British throne, understandably, since at birth she'd inherited the title and a Shetlands castle. Her golden voice and savvy élan had propelled the enchanting young Bella onto stage center at the Royal Shakespeare, and there American producers discovered Lady Bella Winsome at the tender age of fourteen. The rest was legend.

When she married Venus's father, an American spaceship designer, Bella moved to the United States but retained the Shetlands castle for impromptu clan gatherings. Lady Bella's star soared in America, but her front lawn remained a Victorian beachhead dedicated to defending monarchy's genes from New World dimestore pretenders. No child of Bella's would be seduced by a McDonald's fry cook or tempted by cheap nouveau sleaze. Like medieval princelings, Bella's children were required to commit to memory the family's royal lineage, drawn with scrupulous care on the age-worn leaves of a thin brown volume placed daily beside the nursery television set, presumably to achieve some osmotic saturational effect. The young brain is vulnerable. Thus,

Venus found youth fraught with coats of arms, family tartan wars, and volumes of genealogical propaganda, and she grew up knowing more about her royal ancestors than about herself. Bella ran a tight ship, then and now.

"VENUS, you aren't going to Ozone Beach wearing that black leather outfit."

"My uniforms are being dry-cleaned."

"I don't approve of one of my daughters dressing like a common Hell's Angel. Panache is one thing, weather-beaten quite another. Why don't you wear those new tweeds I brought you from Harrods? They make you seem taller. And more ladylike."

"More coffee, Mother?"

"Thank you. I wonder if that Oriental gardener knows anything about rhododendron bonsai—"

"That man was no gardener."

"—it's all the rage in England. And speaking of Oriental things, don't you feel any remorse at all, Venus?"

"Over what?"

"You know perfectly well what I mean. For having flubbed that Asian assignment."

"I didn't flub. Rounding up an international poaching ring takes time. I needed more time, that's all. Anyway, you didn't have to come to Singapore while I was in the hospital."

"Why, Venus, how ever can you say such a thing? Of course your mother should attend your sickbed. I don't care if you are twenty-odd years old. Besides, I quite enjoyed my stay in Upper Oceana."

"So I gathered."

"I still say that man in the camellias was Sue Lane's new gardener."

SHORTLY AFTER HER fifth birthday, Venus's father died suddenly. Heart attack. An astronaut who knew her father once told her that he had died from overachievement and said that was the price we paid for progress. She remembered him as very gentle, quiet,

actually shy, and she remembered that he wore wire-rim glasses
and that once he said her hair reminded him of an angel's wings.
She remembered other things too, but mostly that all the memories were good.

She'd dreamed of being an astronaut. After prep schooling,
Bella packed Venus off to Oxford, her alma mater, for Shakespeare and lepidoptera studies. At twenty-two, Venus returned to
America and immediately applied to NASA's astronaut training
program. Eight years later, she remained on the waiting list. While
waiting for NASA to discover her, Venus went to work for Interior because the position offered adventure and the opportunity
to observe several endangered butterfly species in federal wildlife
sanctuaries. Maybe because she'd always been perceived as a
fragile being, she'd developed a love for Nature's fragile creatures, an appreciation for the inherent strength hidden in delicate
beauty. Sooner or later, NASA would breed the nearly extinct
Oregon Silverspot butterfly in space, and surely then they'd come
knocking. (The malaria might change all that, though.)

Venus wasn't at all fragile, if anyone ever took the time to
notice. Wexler had noticed, and maybe Olson. They had sent her
to special agent training school, had placed the first gun in her
hand and taught her that protecting the environment isn't always
a pretty job. She hadn't yet taken a life, but a few big game
poachers had stared warily down the barrel of her small, efficient
Smith & Wesson.

The first time Venus recalled crying was after her father's funeral, and then she cried in the privacy of her bedroom, servants
listening through the door. Courtship came late, at twenty-one, a
brief passionate interlude in London that ended civilly one fog-
bound morning over tea and crumpets. No tears, just, "Pass the
marmalade, will you please, before you leave?" Meanwhile, the
deep spiritual abyss that had formed when her father died drove
a spike of cynicism into her psyche. It played out in a bleak,
world-weary sense of humor. She often thought she heard her
father's voice, calling to her on a crowded street, whispering her
name in the silence before sleep. She remembered the sound of
his voice and treasured it, and its memory crushed her.

"IF YOU'RE GOING TO Ozone Beach, though I can't imagine why anyone would be foolish enough to go there this time of year, you must have tea with Madge Leroux. I'll phone ahead and say you'll stop this afternoon."

"Have you seen the morning paper, Mother?"

"Of course not. I never read at the table."

"Madge Leroux is dead."

"Don't be silly. Woofy Benson saw Madge just last week. She was the picture of health."

"She was murdered. The story's in the morning paper. They haven't identified the killer. She was shot."

"Oh dear. Another funeral. I'd better phone Father Dylan."

"Did you know her well?"

"Heavens no. She was much older than I, by a long shot. But we saw each other socially. Madge was a patron of the arts, on the periphery of the film world, and once upon a time wielded considerable social influence."

"What happened?"

"Environmentalism became fashionable. You know that beastly man she was married to, the tree murderer? When the spotted owl became an issue, Madge was practically blackballed by these phony society mavens. As if she were responsible for her husband's corporate affairs. She was actually cast out. You know how fickle these yacht club people are. I wonder how young Parker is taking it—"

"The son?"

"You remember Parker, Junior. Dagny dated him before she abandoned her morals and slinked down to San Francisco. I'll never understand why Dagny snubbed Park, Junior. Woofy tells me he's never married, but there is no question he's straight as an arrow. Now, whom do you suppose would murder Madge?"

"The Harbor County sheriff calls it 'death by misadventure.'"

"Rubbish. These rural sheriffs haven't any imagination. So, what else will you be doing at Ozone Beach? Besides stopping by the Leroux's to offer our condolences to young Park."

"Madge's remains were found on the sanctuary. I'll be looking into that. Also, there's some problem with pelicans roosting in her lighthouse.''

"Pooh. The natives are making it up."

"What do you mean?"

"This pelican brouhaha. Woofy was down visiting Madge last week and heard all about it. Woofy told the whole disgusting story on the set yesterday."

"What set?"

"Leek Soup."

"Leek Soup, did you say?"

"It's a code name. We are sworn to secrecy over the film's actual title and subject matter. The director is a terribly bright Brazilian gentleman whom I shall not name."

"You're back at work, then?"

"I have never worked a day in my life. Making films is dabbling. You know that I love to dabble."

"What else did Woofy say?"

"About Madge? Oh yes, the pelican business. Stephen, bring me my little address book digital device, will you? You know, of course, that Madge's lighthouse was declared a part of the biodiversity sanctuary?"

"I'm aware of that."

"Madge signed an agreement to do nothing with the lighthouse which might disturb the birds and other creatures on that island. Honestly, if people would spend less time fussing over birds and more time cleaning out their closets, this world might have a wisp of hope. Thank you, Stephen, that's a darling."

"Stephen is thirty-five years old, Mother. Don't you think calling a servant 'darling' is deprecatory?"

There are no servants in my home. There are domestic staff. "Stephen is not a servant. He is my personal assistant. And Stephen adores whatever I call him. You are so out of touch with Western mores, Venus. The Orient has muddled your cultural heritage. Now tell me why you have taken this sudden large interest in poor Madge's lighthouse."

"Mother, your train of thought is mind-boggling."

"Never mind. Continue with the Madge business, if you please."

"Interior received a note postmarked at Ozone Beach. From a group calling itself the Pelican Patrol. They claimed the pelicans down there are in some sort of danger. They threatened violence if we didn't rectify the situation. They tended to place blame on the Leroux family."

"Absolute Siwash. The natives dreamed it all up. I don't know how Madge endured those pastoral minds. The truth is, the natives have always envied the Leroux because of their vast holdings, and their considerable influence. When Madge acquired the lighthouse, I recall, the natives were livid. They made a big stink in the news media. If the village couldn't own that old landmark, they didn't want anyone to own it. It was sour grapes. They cooked up this fiction about victim pelicans in order to discredit Madge in the public eye. As if Madge couldn't manage that herself."

"Was she using the lighthouse for anything?"

"Please. It is practically inaccessible. She bought it just for fun. Haven't you ever dreamed of owning a lighthouse?"

"It's all very fishy."

"Venus, you don't think this Pelican Patrol murdered Madge?"

"Maybe."

"But that is impossible."

"I don't follow you."

"You never could. I'd better phone Father Dylan. Dear Madge hadn't a friend in the world besides young Park. And he won't be in any condition to orchestrate a funeral."

"Duck, Mother."

"Venus, what on Earth...?"

"Get down! Here, I'll help you."

"Venus, I do not appreciate being shoved to the carpet in the midst of my breakfast. My goodness, what was that dreadful noise? Oh, hello, Stephen. Fancy meeting you under the breakfast."

"Madam, the person is wielding a weapon—"

"Mother, someone shot through the window. Look. He's running away. Did you see him, Stephen?"

"The Asian chap in the camellias? I thought he might be a cohort of yours. Until he fired the gun."

"You two are being alarmist. That was a sonic boom. And just look what it's done to the dining room window."

"That was your 'gardener,' Mother. You see? The bullet shattered the window. And here's the bloody slug, lodged in the table leg."

"Honestly, Venus, I wish you wouldn't employ vulgar pronouns. And please, in future, have more discretion choosing your friends."

SIX

Ozone Beach

THERE WERE TWO new tires on the Harley. Venus stowed her gear in the fender case, including the little Smith & Wesson. In one jacket pocket, in case the fever rose, she carried some exotic green pills, and tucked in a breast pocket she carried a letter. Not just any letter. The crisp sky blue envelope had arrived in the mail shortly after the window sharded. The sight of Reuben's spiky cursive on the pale blue cockle paper had instantly elevated Venus's mood. She'd open it later, in private, away from Bella's inquiring eyes.

Benny Goodman blew through her helmet headphones, and underneath, the new haircut felt mean, like the black leathers and the tinted Serengetis. She looked good on the Harley in spite of the malaria pall, indisputably the hottest item rolling down Highway 101 this misty March morning. And to beat it all, with Reuben's letter fairly singing at her breast, she felt spring fever coming on. She gave timber queens and pelican wingspans scant thought riding south toward Ozone Beach.

She felt good now, freed from the minimizing shadow of Bella's expansive persona, free from Olson's bald threats. On this open highway, far from Bella, far from Olson, here was Venus, here was Reuben, close to her heart. Drive it home, Benny.

By noon, the cloud bank cleared and whitelight sun bathed Highway 101. The Harley purred on a gentle curve, gliding past the turnoff to Humptulips and the ancient totem pole decorating the Quinault reservation's general store. Then the highway cut a curvaceous swath through dense coniferous forests. Sunlight filtered through towering Douglas firs and ancient cedar stands, where spotted owls hid. It hadn't all been clear-cut yet, but after a three-year absence, Venus noticed more thinning out.

Damp air mingled scents of moist black earth, moss, and musty fungi. *Genus amanita,* Death's Angel mushrooms, spored here beneath maidenhair ferns. Along the roadside, wild rhododendrons blazed Day-Glo pink, a brilliance inspired by all the rain. A stirring in her heart, like native pride, burst forth in scat song. Benny's "String of Pearls" echoed in the wind.

From Oyster Bay on the north, to the Hyak River on the southern edge, Ozone Beach National Park embraced thick, rolling Olympic foothill forests inhabited by families of black bear, deer, Roosevelt elk, spotted owls, endangered butterflies, ancient cedar groves, and other precious life-forms. On the southern end, the park's border followed the Hyak River until it spilled into a shallow tideland marsh. At the ocean's edge, between the Hyak and Point Danger jetty, stretched miles of arrow-straight silver-sand, swept-dune beach, the crown jewel of Ozone Beach National Park and Bio-Diversity Sanctuary. Along this stark sand bar, the geoduck, a clam with an obscenely long neck, oozed abundant in season. Black bears dwelling in the surrounding park forests lumbered down to the beach at night under moonlight to dig for geoducks. The Quinault and other coastal tribes considered geoducks sacred food, but uninitiated tourists reeled in repulsion on sighting the bizarre clam natives called "gooeyducks."

In summer, when the rains let up, the rich flocked to Ozone Beach, wealthy clam diggers and gilded old barnacles who in twilight years found verdant forests and raging seas the only safe thrills left. A youthful crowd came too, to decorate Ozone's fancy resorts and loll obsessively on canvas chairs at the sparkling politically correct tideline like so many trendy lemmings. Paradise. It was, if you were a fish, or a crustacean.

If you had old money, which meant before Microsoft, you knew of this place called Ozone Beach. If you studied Washington State road maps, you knew that this tiny village, completely surrounded by federal lands, could be reached only by helicopter via Oyster Bay, or by a single, narrow graveled national park road. However you got there, Ozone Beach in summer was the place to be seen in your best Patagonias, a place to observe orca pods by day and to network by night. But to visit during off-season, October through May, was tantamount to social suicide, unless, of course, you owned one of the private estates adjoining the beach sanctuary, or a high-rise condo with ocean view, or if you were taking a spa cure. Ozone's prolific seaweed reputedly possessed miraculous cell-rejuvenating properties. By all accounts, the village's humble origins as a camp for lighthouse construction crews had gone west on a tide.

Little was known about the natives, except that they all descended from the original lighthouse construction crews, and that some inhabited neat wood-frame cottages along the beach. Some farmed cranberries in the scarlet bogs adjoining the park grounds, others serviced the resort elite. No one really knew what the natives did during off-season, when the rains came and the tourists fled. The natives' mysterious, bucolic nature amused the seasonal lemming set, and by the same token, the natives barely tolerated the "influxers."

If you had ever visited Ozone Beach, as Venus had many times in childhood, with Father, Bella, and the sibs, you remembered it as a spot on Earth where things weren't quite on-center, where a million tangled vortexes sucked up negative ions bounding off phosphorescent surf, warping the rich, salty air. A queer outland inhabited by queer species, including the bipedal variety.

The Harley scooted around a hairpin curve, past the turnoff to Oyster Bay, through another perilous curve by a road sign that said OZONE BEACH NATIONAL PARK AND BIO-DIVERSITY SANCTUARY. Turning right off a tarry access road, Venus headed west as far as you can go without swimming. Around the last curve she heard the ocean's hypnotic roar. Seagulls glided across the horizon, screeching. Up ahead, the trendy village came into view.

Ozone Beach was twelve blocks long and three wide, its narrow lanes so clean your shadow sparkled. A discreet sign placed the population at 242, and a few of these statistics now meandered along the main drag, Lighthouse Lane. They all had that clam digger-protects-his-bucket look, a wary, sidelong manner of watching a stranger roll into town, especially one on a Harley.

Venus pulled up to a pristine curb and parked. She fished the *Ursus arctos horribilis* poster out of the fender case, then the handgun. She holstered the gun under her jacket and set out on foot.

The village wallowed in a marriage of architectural convenience. Swank modern high-rise condos soared above trim quaint-chic beach cottages, their walls whitewashed until they shrieked. Geranium window boxes winked at wee stone paths behind low picket fences. On Lighthouse Lane itself, a few à la mode specialty boutiques, a couple terribly British inns, a Japanese sushi bar ("Closed for the season"), and some tactful gift shops all catered to the flush summer clientele. A place called Trixie's Agate Shop had its show window crammed with mammoth geodes, thunder eggs halved and polished, clam shovels, and striped beach umbrellas for rent. A note on the door disclosed the phone number for Trixie's answering machine and underneath that a parenthetical statement warned that Trixie's prices held firm.

Directly across the street from Trixie's Agate Shop sat the Upper Crust Bakery, heavenly scents wafting, and next to that a real estate office, shades drawn, no sign of life. Then came a small public library, a volunteer fire department equipped for one-alarms only, a snakey lingerie boutique, Heard's Grocery, and beside that, the Ozone Beach post office. Venus went there first.

A poster on the door depicted brown pelicans diving for fish. The caption read: THE BROWN PELICAN NEEDS YOU. To find out why, you should contact the U.S. Department of the Interior's Fish and Wildlife Service. A picture of Olson formed in her mind, the former Olson, Olson the hero, whom she respected and admired. Then Olson's life took a tragic turn, then the weight gain, then the lethargy. His heroics now consisted of producing these kitschy posters and flyers. It was easier than leaving the office. Safer. He didn't even drive a car anymore. Not since the wreck. She shook off these thoughts and went inside the post office, walked up to the counter, and smiled at the clerk.

The postal clerk had pale freckled skin and teased auburn hair. On her blue uniform shirt a name tag said LOLA. When she saw Venus, she scowled. Her eyes danced over the black leathers. She glanced furtively at a bulletin board where the "Wanted" posters hung. Venus's mug wasn't there. She glanced back toward Venus but never got a fix on her eyes. Venus said, "I'm looking for the mayor of Ozone Beach."

Without moving her lips, the clerk murmured, "Janice Mercy operates the chowder bar on Beach Drive."

Venus said, "That's the last lane down here beside the beach, right?"

Lola nodded so imperceptibly that Venus wasn't sure if she agreed with her or had a muscle spasm in her neck. Venus said, "Does Beach Drive intersect Lighthouse Lane down by the beach?"

Muscle spasm.

"Would that be north or south of the intersection? I mean the chowder bar."

Lola pointed west toward the beach.

Patiently Venus said, "Now, at the intersection down here, where Lighthouse Lane meets Beach Drive, do I turn left or right?"

Immobile lips, but a thin word escaped: "Left."

"She there now?"

Lola shrugged.

Venus showed her the *Ursus* poster, explained its merits and deficiencies. Lola stared, tight-lipped, expressionless. Lola's earlobes had a strange translucent luster, as if made of some material other than skin. Pearlescent latex, or Corian, the stuff Bella's kitchen counters were made of. Venus didn't make an issue of this. Instead, she explained about the anti-poaching campaign, asked Lola if the Ozone Beach post office would display the *Ursus* poster.

Lola winced, confused, as if deep inside she wanted to believe that she and Venus represented the same species, and for a moment Venus thought she might defrost. Then she turned icy again and wagged her head. She pressed thin lips firmly together and murmured, "No."

"How come?"

Lola ignored this. She began sorting through a stamp drawer. Venus persisted. "How come you'll post the brown pelican propaganda but not the poacher warning?"

Lola opened her mouth about an inch, then snapped it shut. She squinted and spoke in that trick voice, lips sealed tight as a razor clam. "If you wish to discuss poachers," she said evenly, "you had better speak to the mayor."

"Oh? Can the mayor tell me something about poaching?"

Lola shrugged.

Venus said, "Another thing I wanted to ask you, Lola. You know this timber queen whose corpse was found up here at Point Danger? They pick up the killer yet?"

Another muscle spasm, then Lola walked away. She retreated to the mail room and watched Venus from that safe distance. Venus went over to the "Wanted" posters, studied them for a while. Then she left. She made a mental note to return later and ask Lola if she could throw her voice.

After Venus had gone, Lola picked up the telephone, punched in some numbers, and, keeping her eyes on the front door, spoke earnestly into the receiver.

THE PACIFIC ROLLED, foaming, cresting over a broad expanse of fine wind-dappled silver sand. Venus stood on Beach Drive above the grassy dunes, leaning against a low redwood bulkhead. On the beach, an ebb tide clawed dimple holes made by geoducks and razor clams. Huge logs lay helter-skelter along the high tideline, warrens of tangled driftwood, perfect for playing hide-and-seek.

She recalled a day at this beach with her father. He had taken her clam digging. It must have been midsummer, for he wore khaki shorts and no shirt. His hair, a mass of ash blond curls, billowed in the warm sea breeze. He was drinking Miller's from a bottle. He set the bottle down in the sand and with a long narrow shovel began digging at the tideline. Venus watched, fascinated, as he extracted the strange thing from the hole he'd dug. It had a rough gray shell and out of the shell oozed one long gray meaty finger. Her father held it high so Venus could see how long it was, how fabulous, how bizarre. He said she could touch it if she wanted to, and she did. It felt slimy, and alive. He dropped the clam in a bucket and they carried it back into the dunes where a family picnic was in progress. She remembered Dagny's and Rex's hooting laughter at the sight of the geoduck. The two-year-old twins, Bart and Echo, were too young to find humor in the clam, and wanted only to grab it, hold on. Bella refused to inspect the gross thing, but Venus had staunchly defended the homely bivalve against the family's jeering insults. After all, Father had dug it for her.

SPINDRIFT rose from the ocean waves, twisting, sparkling, carried on the wind. A salt tang energized the air, mingling with verdi-green perfumes floating off the evergreen forest. Near the horizon, shrimp boats bobbed. Beyond, a little to the north, a monolithic crag shot up out of the churning seas. Breakers crashed violently against the rock's sheer cliffs. From this distance, the structure perched on top resembled a rocket ship on its launchpad. Venus recognized it immediately, though she hadn't seen it in many years. The Point Danger lighthouse. Once a bright beacon guiding great vessels imperiled in mean Pacific storms, the lighthouse didn't blink now, or sound a sonorous horn. It just loomed there on the horizon, geriatric and lonely. A retired hero. The idea troubled her.

Reuben's letter had suffered minimal wrinkling on the trip. She felt the thin envelope. A page, maybe two inside. She glanced at her Swatch, then facing into the wind, toward Singapore, she opened the envelope and read Reuben's letter.

Dear Venus,

Aung Sung Khm gave a party at her club last night, and everyone there asked after you. I told them all, as you instructed, that you are in Rangoon tracking the poacher Praht Wasdee. Of course, they all believed the story as it's very credible, and it does sound more exciting than "in bed with malaria," so I didn't feel too bad lying for you. Khm says a party isn't the same without you here to regale us with fabulous tales of your adventures.

As you requested, I did some research on the vessel that the smuggler Lok Toy uses in his operations. The Stella Maris registry shows a vessel named *Barnacle Bill* is registered to Lok Toy Enterprises, Ltd., Singapore. Just as you had guessed. Also, according to the *Singapore Times'* maritime calendar, the *Barnacle Bill* sailed from Singapore Harbour one week ago last Sunday, its destination given as Seattle, USA. The cargo was listed as "tropical fruits."

Some disturbing news. Your two colleagues, Chandrak and Pornchen, the Thai Wildlife Commission undercover agents, have mysteriously disappeared as of last week. I hear this through the grapevine, but from a credible source. You might want to verify the story with your contacts in Bangkok.

I am guessing that you believe the *Barnacle Bill* isn't hauling exotic fruits and/or that it will return to Asia loaded with animal organs. I hope I am not breaking security by writing this! And I'll bet Chandrak and Pornchen are working with you on this business, and aren't totally disappeared but are in America with you. Oh, what a fine detective I would make!

By the way, Khm and I were married on Monday evening in a lovely little ceremony at Raffles, in the orchid garden. We had a sort of whirlwind romance after being just friends for four years. We're very happy and hope that you will come soon to our new residence in Singapore (address enclosed), bless it with your presence.

Please convey my warmest regards to Bella, and tell her that she is much missed in these islands. It was so gracious of her to come here while you were in hospital. And for your information, I didn't sleep with Bella. I barely touched her and then only with brotherly affection.

Fondly, Reuben.

Fondly. She crumpled her dashed dreams into a tight ball, shoved it into her pocket. A cold breeze came up out of the southwest. Something caught in her throat. She swallowed, shut her eyes. The air hinted trouble and menacing dark clouds loomed on the horizon.

SEVEN

Mrs. Mercy's Chowder

MRS. MERCY WAS TALL, top heavy, with a stance like an habitual swimmer or a fish with feet. She was guarding the cash register just inside the entrance to Mercy's Chowder Bar. One well-groomed hand rested on the till. She wore an expensive Donegal tweed suit, a cream silk blouse with a tasteful cameo brooch at the neck, Amalfis on fin-shaped feet. She fought fifty with luminized golden hair molded into a page boy. She had a competent jaw and moist copper penny eyes. Her thin lips were tinted Day-Glo pink, like the rhododendrons. She had a couple flashy rings on her fingers, a gold Rolex at the wrist. She wasn't Venus's idea of a Pacific Northwesterner of the rural variety. Maybe the natives had changed that much during Venus's years away. Or maybe the mayor was one of those smooth Californians come north. Certainly Ozone Beach had gone upscale. All Venus knew was Mrs. Mercy wasn't the kind of gal who wore clam diggers and baked Apple Bettys.

When she spotted Venus her brows shot up. The mustaline scanners dilated, blinked. Her Day-Glo lips compressed tightly, stifling a gasp, and her discriminating hand automatically clutched the cash register. Warily, she studied the sides of Venus's haircut, punked back with Wet the way a city slicker wears it, and just as warily she ran her peepers around Venus's outline, reading her aura. When she had partially recovered from the shock, she tried smiling, but the corners of her mouth were stuck.

Venus showed Mrs. Mercy her badge. When the mayor saw this, she nearly choked. Her hand on the till twitched. Her frigid voice said, "What do you want?"

"I understand you're the mayor of Ozone Beach, Mrs. Mercy."

A prim nod.

"How's business?"

"What do you mean?" Her voice was low, well modulated, very controlled.

"You sell much chowder off-season?"

"We manage."

"You and Mr. Mercy?"

"Mr. Mercy is deceased. I am a widow."

She wasn't sorry about it, either.

Her chowder bar reeked toney ambience. A few tables were now occupied by off-season polyester tourists gaping out enormous picture windows at the brawling ocean while lapping chowder from deep bowls. From Mrs. Mercy's Chowder Bar, they could glimpse whales, shrimp boats, even the breakers crashing against the rock island where Point Danger lighthouse no longer blinked. Picturesque, mused Venus, but there was a coldness about the atmosphere. No bona fide clam digger would feel at home in this trendy tourist trap. Venus said, "I guess you know something about brown pelicans." Mrs. Mercy nodded tersely. Venus explained why she had come to Ozone Beach. She didn't mention Madge Leroux right away, just the threatening note signed by the Pelican Patrol. Venus said, "Have you heard of the Pelican Patrol, Mrs. Mercy?"

A slow shake of the head, eyes averted.

Venus said, "Their message suggests that my agency isn't doing its job." Mrs. Mercy snickered slightly, but nothing else escaped the narrow lips. She shifted her weight on the Amalfis and focused on some ethers. Venus thought about going over to Trixie's Agate Shop, borrowing a clam shovel, and using it on Mrs. Mercy's mouth. She tried another angle. "Are you an environmentalist, Mrs. Mercy?"

This struck a chord. Huskily Mrs. Mercy intoned, "Every citizen of Ozone Beach is dedicated to the preservation of all endangered species. We are all environmentalists here."

"So Ozone Beach officially supports the sanctuary out at the lighthouse?"

"This village spearheaded the drive to have Point Danger light-house and the island on which it stands declared a sanctuary."

A waitress emerged from the kitchen, puffing beneath a tray of seafood. She was young, athletic, and loathed her job. She carried the tray over to a table and slung plates of clams at three men in Hawaiian shirts. The men had tucked paper napkins like bibs around their jowls. The waitress glanced up, noticed Venus, and visibly paled. Like she had seen a ghost. Then she turned and sprinted back into the kitchen. To Mrs. Mercy, Venus said, "I understand the lighthouse recently hosted some pelicans."

"I don't see what that has to do with the village of Ozone Beach."

Cold and huffy. Venus had never seen a live mackerel before, but she guessed it might be somewhat like Mrs. Mercy. She said, "This message we received about the pelicans being in some danger down here, with a threat of violence attached, was post-marked at Ozone Beach. As mayor, that makes it your business."

Mrs. Mercy blinked. Went into trance. Focused on the ethers again. Traveled in her mind. She was gone a long time, so Venus picked up a menu and read it. She charged an arm and a leg for a bowl of homemade chowder. The menu said Mrs. Mercy's chowder contained only the most succulent geoduck meat, fresh milk, Idaho spuds, and some organically grown (top secret) herbs. The menu was replete with testimonials from chowder fans all over the world, including one Lester Sleet of Midway, Kansas, who said: "Mrs. Mercy's geoduck chowder makes Dungeness crab and Chinook salmon obsolete." Presumably Sleet had never heard of overharvesting, the Grand Coulee Dam, and El Niño.

After a while, Mrs. Mercy's eyelids fluttered. Coming out of trance, she sighed impetuously. She rapped hard white knuckles against the cash drawer and declared bitterly: "Federal Fish and Wildlife agents do not wear black leather."

A man entered the chowder bar. He had on rugged work cloth-ing and heavy, waffle-soled boots. Maybe a logger, or a fisher-man. He had translucent skin, like the postal clerk, Lola. He had the wary Ozonian eye, the same tight lips. He had come to fetch a take-out order. Venus watched Mrs. Mercy ring up the sale.

Cartons of steaming chowder and cash bills exchanged hands deftly, in silence. No overt hostility but no neighborly gesture, either. The merchant and patron had probably made this exchange dozens of times. They functioned like separate units of the same well-oiled robot. So this was the body politic of Ozone Beach, Washington. The customer departed. Mrs. Mercy fished a tiny key from her jacket pocket, locked the cash drawer, then looked up in mock surprise.

"Why, I thought you'd gone."

Venus smiled impishly. Over at the Hawaiian shirt table, someone yelled, "We'll smoke wherever we damn well please!"

The harried waitress had come back out of the kitchen. Now she bent over the table, speaking softly, earnestly. One of the shirts blew smoke at the waitress's face. Flushing deep scarlet, she waved it away. Now everyone in the restaurant paid attention. Mortified, she fled, sprinting toward Mrs. Mercy. She braked hard and implored, "That table over there insists on smoking. I told them the rules, but they just yelled at me. Can you do something, Mrs. Mercy?"

Mrs. Mercy glared across the room. You bet she can.

"Never mind, Meredith. I'll handle this."

She checked the cash drawer to be sure it was locked, then brushed past Meredith and strode over to the Hawaiian shirt table, now enveloped in thick smoke.

Venus said to Meredith, "Maybe you could move them to the smoking section."

Meredith gaped, then laughed. "Ever been to Ozone before?"

"A few times, years ago. Probably before you were born."

"I'm older than I look. And it's against the law to smoke in Ozone. Didn't you read the sign at the airport?"

"I rode in. On the park trail."

She gave Venus the once-over. "Yeah," she said. "I guess you did."

She had long blond hair that had never touched a curling iron but had absorbed lots of sunshine. Blond eyebrows and thick blond lashes. Eyes the color of Santa Monica Bay. Her pert nose moved when she spoke and the freckles sprinkled across its bridge danced. Venus said, "Isn't a smoke-free environment a little extreme for a tourist resort? What if some tourist wants to light up?"

Meredith made a face. "They go bananas. Like these guys over here. But the village council, see, it passed this anti-smoking law a few years back. They're all nonsmokers. Jeannie Winters, she just got elected to the council. She's a reformed smoker. They made her quit before she could serve. That's how strict they are. But I happen to know that Jeannie smokes up a storm over at the Bell Buoy. That's hers, the Bell Buoy Lounge, her private turf. You can do it in private." She reached out, fingered the lapels on Venus's jacket. "Gad," she quipped airily, "these are awesome imitations."

"They're real leather."

She backed off, appalled, crestfallen. "How could you do that? How can you wear animals who've been slaughtered just for human decoration?"

Leather was hard to explain, even to herself. Meredith glared at her. Venus couldn't think of anything to say in her own defense. She was relieved to notice Mrs. Mercy striding toward them wearing a triumphant air.

She'd eighty-sixed the whole lot of Hawaiian shirts. When the dust cleared, she caressed the cash register tenderly, a sort of beatific expression lightening her brow. Meredith brushed past Mrs. Mercy and disappeared into the kitchen.

Venus scratched her head. The new haircut itched. She said, "I don't get it, Mrs. Mercy."

"Get what?" Janice Mercy sighed wearily. Apparently no simple cold shoulder would dispatch this miniature person, this busybody.

Venus said, "If Ozone Beach is such an environmentally correct town, why are you, as mayor, so reluctant to cooperate with an agent of the Fish and Wildlife Service?"

"Where did you get that accent?"

"I beg your pardon?"

"Your English isn't domestic. Where does that accent come from?"

Venus shrugged. "I was born in Seattle. I've been out of the country for several years. Maybe that's what you hear."

Mrs. Mercy studied her hand. The one guarding the till. She turned it over and read its palm. She inspected the fingernails, the moons. Her mind was full of sundry strategies. Life in Ozone Beach was complex enough without an interfering government agent, particularly one with a distinctly foreign lilt in her voice. But this person existed, this person was stubborn, and her credentials were in order. Try as she might, Mrs. Mercy could not ignore certain realities. She studied Venus the way she looked over village improvement plans. Resigned now, she sighed. In measured mayoral tones, she began her speech.

"Ozone Beach is not a town. It is a village. Furthermore, the village of Ozone Beach is a peaceful, private community. We cherish our privacy, our crime-free environment. We don't even have a police force—don't need one. This is a progressive, mannerly community of high consciousness, free of the environmental perversions which plague urban areas. We aim to keep the village energy pure and positive. And for your information, the citizens of Ozone Beach are far better qualified as guardians of these beaches and forests and the wildlife within than any outsider, government agent or not. We don't need your kind down here."

"This wouldn't be one of those cult towns, would it?"

Tersely she snapped, "We are not cultish. Clannish, perhaps. But there are no cults in Ozone Beach. Religion is an opiate I detest. Habits are terrible, nasty things."

"No crime, huh?"

Mrs. Mercy leaned forward and spoke earnestly in a hoarse whisper. "Do you know the history of Ozone Beach, Washington?"

Venus shrugged. She was no historian. Mrs. Mercy nodded, acknowledging the visitor's ignorance. "You should," she said. "Then perhaps you would comprehend just exactly why you are not welcome here."

Venus displayed mild interest.

"Some years ago," began the mayor, "this village was invaded by a gang of...outsiders. A motorcycle gang called Satan. Savages, doped up on drugs. They came in here and rioted on our beaches. The National Guard marched in and we had terrible battles right down here on the beach. When it was over, our citizens had been robbed and beaten, our homes set on fire. Ozone Beach was looted, burned to the ground. The National Guard went away and that was the last peep we heard from the government. We were left with nothing but ruins. Ashes and broken hearts.''

Venus faintly recalled the incident from a television broadcast she had seen years ago. She said, "What did Satan have against Ozone Beach?"

"Nothing. Absolutely nothing." Mrs. Mercy sniffed primly.

"You're kidding."

"I never joke about anything. Now where was I?"

"The part about the looting and burning."

"Ozone Beach was completely destroyed. For the next few years, this village was literally a tent city. We, the natives, resurrected Ozone Beach one building at a time. We had no help from outsiders or government agencies."

"Where'd you get the funds to rebuild?"

A pregnant pause. Then: "I am sure you've heard that necessity is the mother of invention. We created the new Ozone Beach and now we aim to protect it. We don't need anyone's help. Nobody comes in here without an invitation."

"What about the tourists?"

"Oh, the tourists." She waved a hand dismissively. "Of course we let them in. This beach and the forests surrounding our village are, as you know so well, all federal land. And since your agency has so inappropriately granted public access to the wildlife sanctuary, why, tourists just flock to our doorstep. We could hardly refuse to feed and lodge them, could we?"

"Is the Leroux family part of the local clan?"

Mrs. Mercy reached for a small object on the counter near the cash register. A sand dollar, dried and bleached bone white. She played with it, caressing the smooth ridges on the Star of Bethlehem. She shook the sand dollar and the Doves of Peace inside softly cooed. Very quietly, she said, "The Leroux estate survived

Satan. It stands in the foothills above the village. It isn't really a part of Ozone Beach. Neither is the Leroux family."

"Outlanders?"

"The Leroux are criminals," she said bitterly. "Everyone on the Olympic Peninsula despises them. They have ravaged our forests. They buy up timberland, take leaseholds in the national forest, clear-cut them to death, sell the prime timber to the Japanese, and then sell the land they've virtually stolen to these sleazy developers. Park, Junior is even more ruthless than his parents were. There'll be hell to pay around here now."

"Was Mrs. Leroux on the local blacklist?"

"Madge Leroux was a snooty old bird who whored off decent society and never contributed anything."

"That's a pretty judgmental statement."

"I know what I'm talking about. I don't care what you think." Leaning across the counter, she whispered hoarsely, "Listen…it took twelve years and countless millions to resurrect this village after Satan. And then what happens? This timber shrew scoops up our ancestral landmark at an illegal government auction and then has the impudence to pass a glossy brochure around town advertising her intentions to develop a business out there. A columbarium, of all things."

"She said that?"

A prim nod, then, "And then the Leroux corporation ran a sleazy ad campaign on television claiming that they'd bought the lighthouse to protect an endangered species, bragging that they were 'giving something back' to the environment. It makes me ill just to think of those deceitful lies. But that's how all these timber companies are. Deceitful. Like the government agencies that claim to preserve sacred lands for wildlife and then lease out parcels for clear-cuts. They're all deceivers."

Venus looked at Mrs. Mercy. She appeared to have aged rapidly in a matter of minutes. The corners of her mouth sagged and below the stubborn chin a crepey vertical jowl appeared. But the eyes, the penny-shaped orbs retained a glint of fighting spirit. She was a tough cookie. Had to be. She was mayor of the Village of Ozone Beach. A veteran of the Satan war.

Venus said, "Illegal government auction?"

"That's right. And eventually we'll prove it. We have filed a lawsuit. But that is our business, not yours."

"Why didn't the village, if it wanted the lighthouse, bid on it at the auction?"

"Because the federal government did not have the common courtesy to notify us of the event."

She might be paranoid. Venus said, "I guess now that's all moot. Now that Mrs. Leroux has passed on."

"What do you mean 'moot'? The lighthouse still belongs to her estate. Her son will inherit it."

"The island and the lighthouse are under federal jurisdiction now as a bird sanctuary. The Leroux estate may own the lighthouse, but they can't alter it in any way, or even use it for any purpose, without the express permission of Interior. Besides, you said her company intended to help the pelicans. I gather she opted to leave the landmark alone."

"All lies. I heard from a reliable source, which I am not about to divulge, that the Leroux were going ahead with the columbarium scheme. And now I absolutely shudder to think what the son might decide to do with our ancestral landmark."

Venus shook her head. "Interior won't permit any activity out there. I give you my word on that."

"Ha. No one ever turns down a Leroux. Money sings in Washington, DC. Park Leroux will buy off your agency."

"Returning to the pelican issue—"

"I have nothing to offer in that category. I have never heard of this group you are calling the Pelican Patrol. I am not aware of any people like that in my village. I haven't a clue who shot Mrs. Leroux and set her body adrift like that. I simply cannot solve your riddle for you."

"Set adrift?"

"Whatever." She sounded exasperated. "She washed ashore, didn't she? She was murdered, wasn't she? So she was probably set adrift, don't you think?"

Venus nodded. "Sounds plausible. By the way, the clerk over

at the post office said you could tell me something about poachers.''

"Lola said that?"

"Implied."

"People don't poach pelicans."

"I didn't mean pelicans."

"Oh.'' The mackerel chill revisited her voice. Her eyes glazed
over again. She said, "The Quinault do all the salmon poaching.
We have no Native Americans living in Ozone Beach. They all
live on the reservation up above the park."

"Not salmon poachers. Big game poachers. It's bear poaching
season."

"Well, I don't know anything about that sort of activity."

She was leaning against the cash register, glancing sideways at
her reflection in the shiny, mirrored surface. Her earlobes had the
same pearlescent latex look as Lola's. It must have to do with the
climate, the cold, clammy, saltwater climate. Or possibly Venus
had been too long removed from Anglo complexions to grasp the
nuances of texture and shade. She wanted to ask Mrs. Mercy
about Ozonian skin, but instead said, "Maybe you could rec-
ommend a motel?"

Mrs. Mercy frowned. "You're staying over?"

Venus nodded.

Janice Mercy formed a silent O with her lips, held it for a
moment, then said, "We have several exquisite resorts. And some
lovely little B-and-B's. They all require advance reservations, of
course."

"Any plain old motels?"

"There is one. The Driftwood Inn. One block north of here on
Beach Drive. But I should warn you: There is not a very warm
feeling for government agents in this village."

"Why's that, Mrs. Mercy?"

"Don't trifle with me. I've just told you why."

She fished the cash register key from her jacket pocket, fit the
key into the lock, turned it. Now Venus understood the signifi-
cance of this gesture. It meant Janice Mercy wanted to be left
alone.

EIGHT

Poachers

CROSSING BEACH DRIVE, Venus jumped to avoid a pushy black town car that slinked haughtily around the corner. Tinted windows obscured the car's interior. At the intersection where Beach Drive met Lighthouse Lane, the arrogant boat turned wide, straightened, then glided east toward the foothills. Someone tapped Venus on the shoulder. She turned around. The waitress Meredith, huffing, out of breath, said, "On my break. Walking up the beach. Come along?"

Venus said, "Whose barge?"

Meredith laughed. She had nice chimes, like Bella's, only less rehearsed. Meredith said, "That's Park Leroux, going home from his biweekly massage. My boyfriend's his masseuse. Actually he's a physician, but it's a small town, so his main business is his health spa. It caters to tourists. It's pretty famous for its seaweed body-renewal system. Divers' Spa, over at the golf course, across from the airfield? Oh, I keep forgetting, you didn't fly in. Anyway, his name is Chick. Boss name, huh? Chick Divers. I don't know what the 'Chick' stands for."

She talked a blue streak. Why? They walked down a flight of redwood stairs into the sand dunes. Meredith continued chattering.

"Park's mother was murdered a few days ago. Before that, she went to Chick, too. For the seaweed treatment. That was her car, the town car. Her driver, too. She had the windows tinted so the locals couldn't see her. My friend Richard says she was afraid someone might kill her. Maybe she was psychic."

Sandpipers skittered out of restless reeds to the tideline. The tide ebbed and the shore quivered like putty as Venus removed her boots and socks and sank bare feet into the damp sand. Overhead, gulls soared, screeching, winging out to deep water. The air hung heavy, ominous. Later, Venus would remember the intuitive warning signals she felt now, this deep dejection that weighed down her spirit. Right now, she blamed Reuben for ruining the first day of spring.

Meredith, in her waitress uniform and a new pair of K-Swiss, stretched and bent, as if warming up for a marathon. She had a lean, solid build. She probably worked out regularly, maybe swam a lot, most likely was a vegetarian. Not chowder bar material, Venus thought.

Walking north along the tideline toward Point Danger, they passed a string of sleek high-rise condos, several walled estates, and at the village edge a row of neat Victorian-style cottages. Soon the cottages lay behind them, and the dense national park forest dropped steeply down to meet the beach at a massive driftwood bulkhead.

Up ahead Point Danger's natural rock jetty jutted out into the water, a cemetery of boulders crowned with ancient barnacles that Venus knew from childhood forays bloodied bare feet. On the jetty, she found a smooth boulder, sat down. Meredith sat beside her, and for a few minutes neither woman spoke.

Near the Point Danger jetty lay a maze of twisted driftwood that fickle waves had tossed ashore. In a cluster of granite boulders, a family of gray seals splashed in a tide pool, honking. Otherwise the beach appeared deserted. Offshore, the ocean churned, a restless steel gray soup. On the horizon the old lighthouse loomed, grim and foreboding. Meredith pointed at the driftwood maze, wonder in her youthful voice.

"This is where they found her body. Mrs. Leroux."

Venus couldn't see her face, just a freckled profile, the thin lips parted slightly. When she next spoke, her eyes half shut, Meredith's tone of voice was deeper, matter-of-fact.

"Strangers aren't welcome here."

"I get that impression."

"It's true," said Meredith. "No one comes snooping around this village without the natives' blessings."

Venus said, "You a native?"

She shook her head. The blond hair flowed like silk. "California. La Jolla. You know where that is? Up above San Diego. I've been here a year now. It's okay, except for the damn rain."

"What about your boss? She a native?"

"Janice Mercy? She's mayor, isn't she? They wouldn't elect an outsider mayor. Sure, she's homegrown. They say she's a descendant of Ennis Ozone, the man who founded this village."

"What's it like working for her?"

"Like being an indentured servant. She's a slave driver and she watches you like a hawk. Always worried you're going to clean out the till when her back's turned. But it's a job."

"You don't go stir crazy here?"

She laughed, turned toward Venus. She had a pretty smile. "When I get too restless, I slip up to Seattle for some fun. Chick doesn't approve. My significant other, you know? The doctor."

"Park Leroux's masseuse."

"Mine too. I'm hooked on his treatments."

The wind blew a lock of California sunshine across her face. She reached up, brushed it back. Looking out across the waves, she said softly, "They'll be coming soon. Any day now."

"Pelicans?"

She nodded. "I heard you mention them to Mrs. Mercy. Down on the California coast, where I come from, their colonies are immense. But the ecology has been all messed up by pesticides and industrial chemicals. DDE's the worst. It thins their eggshells. They break before the chicks can fully develop. The population has dropped drastically over the past twenty years or so. They want to survive, though. They're scouting new nesting sites, flying up north here, checking out real estate. Like a lot of Californians. Ha ha." She shrugged. "Maybe they could adjust to this climate, breed here. It's their last chance, on this coast anyway."

"You sure know a lot about pelicans," Venus said.

"Ask me anything. My dad's an ornithologist at UCSD. He used to take me out to the islands to see the pelican colonies. I pretended I was one of them, learned their dances, their rituals. I really believed it for a while, that I was a brown pelican trapped in a human's body. That's how close I am to them. How close I feel."

"That why you migrated up here?"

"Maybe." She studied Venus through blond lashes. "Yeah, that's why. I met this fascinating lady, an ornithologist, down in San Diego. She got me interested in the migration pattern. She used to live here in Ozone, and she'd come down to UCSD to work with my dad on a research project. She talked me into moving to Ozone Beach, then by the time I got here, she'd gone, moved away. I heard she ran off with a cowboy from Montana. The unfunny part is that she used to be married to my present male friend."

"Richard?"

She smiled. "I mean Chick. Her name was Carolyn Divers. I loved that lady. She was my role model, my mentor."

Silence. Then Venus said, "According to the mayor, Ozone's loaded with pelican enthusiasts."

"Ha." Meredith laughed harshly. "Hardly. I mean, like hardly. These locals aren't interested in ecological issues. They might pretend to be, but they aren't really."

"They supported the bird sanctuary out there."

"They supported the sanctuary because they want the lighthouse protected from the public. They have a thing about that lighthouse, maybe it's a superstition, I don't know. For some reason, the lighthouse is sacred to the locals."

She flicked sand off her shoes and said casually, "Mrs. Mercy says you're some kind of government agent."

"Department of the Interior. Fish and Wildlife Service."

"You got ID?"

Venus showed it to her.

"Okay, now I believe you. I bet you carry a gun too."

"You bet right."

"Well, I don't like guns."

"Why the security check?"

"Just curious. Anyway, I'm not allowed to discuss the lighthouse controversy. It's taboo. And Chick is on the village council. He'd kill me if he caught me talking to an outsider about the lighthouse. They've got this big lawsuit in the works, you know, and they don't want anyone to mess it up for them. That's what Chick told me."

Venus rubbed her jaw. She could think better on her feet, pacing. She wanted to pace, but the jetty didn't have the right traction. She pulled her socks on, then her boots, stood up. She said, "You ever hear of a group called the Pelican Patrol?"

"I told you, I'm not supposed to discuss these things. I absolutely swore to Richard that I'd keep my mouth shut."

"I thought his name was Chick."

She blinked the periwinkle eyes. "Richard and Chick are two different dudes. Chick Divers is my lover. Richard Winters is my best friend. I hang with one, confide in the other. But I'm not going to cry on your shoulder about it." Meredith stood, brushed off her waitress uniform. She was still trying to decide if she could trust Venus. After a minute, she said, "Okay. I'm going to tell you something. But if anyone asks, I'll deny I told you. I need to tell someone. An outsider. The locals would never understand, and besides, as far as they're concerned, I'm a foreigner too. They don't trust me."

"Small towns are like that."

"Well, here goes. The United States Navy's using this lighthouse as a secret base."

"For what purpose?"

"I don't know. Whatever they're doing out there, it's top-secret stuff. And if they're not gone soon, they'll scare the pelicans away."

"The navy in Madge Leroux's lighthouse?"

"Madge never knew about it. Her son cut the deal with the navy. He leased them the lighthouse without telling his mother."

"How do you know that?"

"Carolyn told me about it. The ornithologist who disappeared? She told me before I ever moved up here. She knew a lot more about it, but that's all she ever told me. Then, Park, Madge's son, got drunk one night a few weeks ago and told my friend Richard that he'd leased it to the navy. Richard and Park are buddies.

Then Richard told me about it. But I wasn't supposed to tell anyone. I sure hope you're trustworthy."

"What would Navy want with the old lighthouse property?"

"I don't know." She seemed frustrated. "But anything the military does has *sinister* written all over it. Park told Richard the navy man called the operation 'Rain Dance.' Whatever that's supposed to mean. That's all I know."

Rain Dance. A nice sound, nice image.

"Mayor and council know about this?"

"I doubt it. I sure haven't told Chick."

Something below the jetty, on the beach at tideline, had attracted Meredith's attention. A man, wearing a yellow rain slicker and yellow sou'wester, stood at the water's edge. Meredith cursed. Venus said, "What's wrong?"

"What you told Mrs. Mercy. And the fake ID you carry around. You lied. You're no government agent."

"What? What do you think I am?"

Meredith did the thing with her lashes again, peering through the blond veil. She glanced at her wristwatch, her tone of voice expressing more disappointment than hostility now. She pressed her lips together, as if forcing them to stop chattering. They had chattered too much already. Still, some words came out.

"That dude down at tideline...he's Navy Intelligence. I've seen him around Ozone before. Richard told me he's a big-time secret agent. Well, he's obviously following you. He came into the chowder bar right after you left, asked Mrs. Mercy some questions. Now he's down here on the beach. He wouldn't spy on another government agent. So you must be lying about who you really are."

"Maybe he's following you, Meredith. Maybe you're hiding something."

Meredith turned pale again, like she had in the chowder bar, when she had first noticed Venus. Then she read her watch, her eyes avoiding Venus's. "I'm going to be late," she said brusquely.

"Anyway," said Venus, "it looks like rain."

As they stepped off the jetty, they did not see the young black bear lumber out of the park, over the driftwood logs. He paused, his moist black nose sniffing the air. Then he moved cautiously down to the tideline, and there began gorging on something he found edible. The women had rounded a bend now, and even if they turned around, they would not have seen the cub slow waltz into the surf. He rolled over in the water, slowly, as if in a semi-slumber. Then a loud sound pierced the air.

Venus stopped, listened. Gunfire, followed by a horrible baying sound. Another shot. She shoved Meredith behind some logs. Five shots altogether, then silence. Venus raced across the driftwood bulkhead, Meredith close behind. The gunfire had come from above the beach, somewhere inside the park. Venus drew her pistol and stepped into the dense forest.

Overgrown salal and wild huckleberries made a thick tangled carpet. Venus hadn't been here in many years; still, this forest held a womblike familiarity. No path here, but remnants of an old logging trail. She followed its steep climb uphill, deep into the forest, Meredith keeping pace behind. No more gunfire sounded, only the melancholy cries of gulls overhead, and receding into the distance, the ocean's fitful roar. When they reached the crest of the ridge, they stood in a pine needle-carpeted clearing facing a small wooden shack. A park ranger's outpost, in the heart of big game territory. Roosevelt elk, black bear, white-tailed deer. No rangers visited the shack during off-season; at least, they weren't required to check this outpost until May or June.

It might have been a hunter illegally out for venison, shooting the white-tailed deer, a protected species. Or a Roosevelt, for its splendid rack. That too was illegal. Sometimes a Roosevelt or a white-tail would wander off the park onto Highway 101 and get massacred by a swift-flying logging truck or a carload of tourists. When this happened, the law said that the vehicle's driver, if he or she survived the impact, was entitled to the venison and rack. It was illegal to hunt them, but you could play "Chicken," and if you survived, keep the corpse.

She'd heard another sound along with the gunfire, one too awful to mistake for a native species. The baying of hounds. Reaching the top of the ridge, she thought she might head them off.

She circled the ranger shack, studying the soft pine needle-covered ground, Meredith in tow, babbling again, giddy from the closeness to danger.

A padlock hung from a metal clasp on the shack's front door. The windows were shuttered and the rear door bolted from the inside. Venus noted this in passing as she stepped onto a narrow footpath behind the building. This path, she recalled from a park map, led back down to the beach just north of Point Danger jetty. Here on rich black soil she came upon two neat sets of human footprints and several sets of animal prints. Hounds. She went back to the shack, carefully inspected the ground again, found faint tire marks in the clearing. They must have driven into the clearing, dropped off the two hunters and the hounds, then an accomplice drove off to meet them at another designated spot. They wouldn't return to the clearing, in case the gunfire had attracted attention, in case a trap had been set for them. Anyway, such little time had passed, there might still be enough left to prevent a kill.

Brushing aside scrubby low bush and maidenhair ferns, she headed north along the ridge, then downhill toward the beach. She pushed deeper into the forest, where daylight barely penetrated a thick evergreen mantle. She could hear Meredith chattering behind her, had to stop, warn her to keep still. Very still. Now the forest floor grew damper, the footprints more pronounced. The tracks had been made by heavy, waffle-soled boots. Two pairs, one about a men's size ten, the other a men's size twelve or maybe thirteen. The small set led the larger set by half a pace. The tracks led northward a little farther, then west down a steep muddy slope. The ocean's roar grew loud again as they neared the beach. When they had walked nearly a mile, circling back toward Point Danger, she stopped.

She was standing on a mossy knoll at the forest's edge, where the forest met the ocean beach at the wild, topsy-turvy driftwood bulkhead. She was standing very near the boulders at the jetty, in sight of the tide pool where the seal family had rollicked. They'd abandoned their bath in the wake of gunfire. She was standing at the site where the footprints abruptly ended. Meredith stood behind her, peering over her shoulder. Venus was standing beside the fresh, bloody, mutilated carcass of a young bear.

He was about four years old, mating age, still thin from winter hibernation. He had come out on the cusp of spring to forage for food. His chest had been blasted open with a shotgun, his body hurriedly disemboweled. His paws and his genitals had been severed and stolen.

Meredith retched, then vomited.

NINE

The Lightkeeper

A CHILLY SOUTHWESTERLY hurled salt spray off the Pacific, whipping up the dunes. They walked south along the beach, over a high sand ridge. The ocean churned, an agitated green; the waves held restless wanderlust. The family of seals emerged from its hiding place behind some black boulders and headed out to sea, into the imminent storm.

Meredith, still retching, stumbled on a dune. When Venus helped her to her feet, she seemed embarrassed, jerked away from her, but she couldn't hide the fear and revulsion. Emotions, Bella always said, were impolite, impolitic, and dreadfully boring. The inability to conceal emotions was a trait of the ill-bred, in Bella's book. This rage that Venus now felt had escaped the family armor Bella so fastidiously forged around her offspring. She wouldn't bother shooting the poachers when she caught them. She'd chop off their hands and feet, gut them. They'd feel the mutilation. Like the bear felt before it died.

Meredith's complexion had turned a sickly green. She vomited intermittently on the dunes. Her teeth chattered, her body trembled violently, jerking. She turned, waited for Venus to catch up, and said, "You have to see this stuff all the time?"

Venus nodded.

"And you don't throw up?"

"Used to. Not so much anymore." Venus slipped an arm around the trembling woman. Meredith didn't resist.

Meredith said, "Even sometimes?"

"Sometimes, yes. I've puked up my share."

"I hope you catch the bastards."

She clutched Venus's arm, her tear-stained face twisted in pain, the Santa Monica eyes now full of fury. She shouted above the wind, "When you catch them, you let me know. I'll be a witness. I want to help."

"Okay."

Meredith said, "I have to hurry. She'll fire me for being this late. I have to run now."

"Sure. Run on ahead. And, hey..."

Already sprinting toward the village, Meredith looked over her shoulder. Venus called out, "Take care of the pelicans."

"I will. I promise." Shouted through the wind. Then she disappeared down the beach.

A small cottage, the first sign of civilization, marked the edge of the village. The board and batten wore a fresh coat of dove gray, the hurricane shutters had recently been painted charcoal. An ancient brass ship's bell hung on the front porch. Venus walked up the stone stairs to a whitewashed wood porch, crossed the porch, and rang the ship's bell. It clanged petulantly above the relentless ocean roar.

No response. She rang again, louder, harder. When the clanging ceased, she heard a gruff voice shout, "Portside!"

She turned left onto a narrow side porch where a weathered man sat on a wicker chair. Willow thin, he had grizzled white hair and a full, white captain's beard, craggy features, and sharp blue eyes. He wore a navy blue crew sweater and a pair of spotless white bell bottoms that stopped halfway up his calves in true sailor fashion. On his feet were white crew socks pulled taut above blue canvas deck shoes. A fat hand-rolled cigarette dangled from his lips. He half dozed in his chair. Opposite the whisperthin old man, in another wicker chair, sat an Asian boy.

He was about eight years old, small, delicate. He had the broad flat nose and the eyes of a Chinese, but with skin the color of café au lait, and his straight, silky hair was more chocolate than black. He might be part Malayan or Indonesian. He was definitely part Chinese. He wore a school uniform, short charcoal trousers, knee-high argyles, a white shirt with a red tie, and a navy blazer. A book in his lap lay open to a colorful chart depicting jellyfish varieties. The Asian boy glanced up from the jellyfish, studied

Venus, twitched his broad flat nose, and glanced back at the jellyfish. To the old man, the boy quipped, "There's a freak on your porch."

Venus showed the old man her badge, asked to use his telephone. He nodded silently, and after she explained about the dead bear, he rose arthritically from his chair and loped across the porch. She followed. He opened a door to the cottage, beckoned her inside. She could feel the Asian boy's hard stare on her back.

The cottage had one large room with picture windows facing the ocean. In the fireplace, embers glowed in the grate. On the mantel, a wood and brass clock resembled a ship's steering wheel. It said four-seventeen, same as her Swatch. Two tall bookcases flanked the fireplace, crammed with books, mostly dog-eared, leather-bound volumes ancient from use. Two Stewart plaid wing chairs basked in the fire's ember glow. A small footstool rested beside one chair, and under the footstool lay a pair of scuffed house slippers. The old man's chair. The other wing chair presumably hosted company. Across the room, in a small alcove, a wooden platform supported a thin mattress covered in tufted cotton ticking, the pillow, sheets and a handmade "wedding ring" quilt neatly folded and stowed on a low shelf. In the rear of the cottage, the small head's door stood slightly ajar. Near that door, another alcove opened into a tiny kitchenette, a stainless-steel dog dish marking the entrance. Empty. On the wall of the kitchenette hung a telephone.

The old man watched as she charged the long distance call to DOI, listened while she connected with the Seattle office. Then he went back outdoors, leaving her alone in the cottage. The telephone reception reminded her of sounds in a conch shell. When Olson came on the line, she told him about the killing.

Olson barked, "Don't jump to conclusions."

"What is that supposed to mean, Olson?"

"It means you're in Leroux territory. They've had a chronic problem with bears tearing up their young stands. Oftentimes when that happens we have to bend the rules for them. Like, if a stray happens onto their land and starts ripping bark off the young trees, and if one of Leroux's hunters happens to shoot it out of season. Oftentimes we bend the rules for Leroux Timber. It's no big thing.''

"How long has this been going on?"

"Oh, forty, maybe fifty years. I'm not saying it's legal. I'm saying it's tradition. Sometimes tradition is more sacred than the law."

"The bear was shot on our property, on the sanctuary, not on Leroux land."

"They lease some stands in the national forest up above the park."

"This was on the sanctuary. Not on a leasehold."

"Then it might merit investigating. But Leroux's stands border the park. My guess is we'll discover the bear was shot by one of Leroux's hunters after it damaged their stands, in which case, even if the kill happened on the sanctuary, we'll let it go."

"Olson, are you telling me that these kills have been going on for many years in Sparks's territory, and all this time you and Sparks haven't reported them?"

"We don't report kills made by Leroux's hunters. We never have. I don't plan to start now."

"Even out-of-season kills?"

"Yes. And don't get so puffed up about it. They only kill when the individual is threatening the young stands."

"This bear was disemboweled and its paws and genitals cut off."

A heavy sigh came over the conch. Olson said, "We'll look into it. If we find the individual was threatening Leroux's stands, mind you, we'll have to let it slide. Do you understand, or do I have to spell it out for you?"

"Spell it out."

Silence. Then, "Listen here, Venus. I sent you down there on this Leroux business. It's far more important than a bear kill, which is not your concern. I'll tell Sparks about it and we'll look into it. There are politics down there that you don't know about. And they don't concern you. Is that clear?"

"No. Who did you say autopsied Mrs. Leroux's remains?"

"I didn't say."

"Then who did?"

"I told you before, some local doc down there did it. I don't recall the name. Anyway, he'll be contacting me directly with the autopsy results. I arranged that. So you wouldn't have to worry about it. By the way," he sounded patronizing now, "is that malaria fever coming back?"

"How about Chick Divers? Does that ring a bell?"

"I really don't recall the name."

"I think you're lying, Olson."

Fury. Olson shouted, "Listen here, Venus. You just don't go around accusing people of lying. It isn't ethical. Just for that cocky remark, I'm faxing a memo to Wexler. Maybe he'll finally take my advice and can you."

"By the way, I think I met a member of the Pelican Patrol."

He hadn't heard that. He'd already hung up.

Olson might be right about one thing: The fever might be coming back. Now that unique headache, prelude to unspeakable hallucinations, teased her skull. She choked down one of the exotic little pills and went outside. On the porch, the old man waved a grizzled hand, indicating an empty chair. She sat down wearily. The Asian boy watched her through silky lashes. The old man said, "Name's Rutledge." A craggy name, like his features and his voice. He nodded toward the boy. "This here's Timmy Divers. Chick Divers's boy."

Rutledge offered her a navy-cut number rolled up in Zig-Zag paper. She took it, thinking a nicotine hit might ease the headache and her stomach's memory of the bear parts up on the beach. Had Meredith not been present, she would have vomited at the scene, but she had that much control over bodily functions, to not vomit in public. Not out of courtesy so much as from some ancient face-saving gene she'd caught from Bella. Now she felt grateful for that inheritance. She lit up with a Bic Rutledge handed her.

The Asian boy screwed up his little nose, waved a petite hand at the cigarette smoke, faked an elaborate hacking cough. To Rutledge she said, "Your grandson?"

The gravelly voice held a hint of irony. "Hell no. Ain't no grandkid o' mine. Timmy's in the private school here in the village. Teachers farm out the youngsters couple of times a month. Cheap trick t' give themselves days off. But I like Timmy, so I agreed to give him lessons. Generic maritime stuff. Sorta thing he'd never get from a classroom. Or television neither. A little marine biology, little navigation, hands-on stuff." He shook his head. "Not much of a student, though. Too nervous."

Timmy's cough had worsened. Rutledge frowned at the child and said gruffly, "Go on, boy, get outta here. That cough's gratin' on my nerves." He winked at Venus. "Go inside now, Tim, get you a glass of water. Do as I say."

Timmy made a rude face, but he went indoors, taking his lesson book and the hack along. Venus told Rutledge about the Pelican Patrol business and the reason she'd come to Ozone Beach, including the timber queen's murder. He listened intently, his bright blue eyes sparkling. He was an old geezer, she thought, but his brain had plenty of spunk. When she finished, Rutledge leaned over a porch railing and spit into a loamy garden bed.

"Landlubbers," he said.

Then he laughed.

Venus glanced up. Timmy Divers watched her through a window, his nose pressed against the glass. When she made eye contact, he screwed up his face and his mouth formed a snarling little curve, exuding a furtiveness that disquieted his prey. She was his prey.

Rutledge said, "You ever hear what happened out yonder at Point Danger lighthouse?"

"What happened?"

The nicotine from the fat cigarette had skimmed the edge off her headache and nausea. She relaxed for the first time in longer than she cared to remember. Rutledge continued.

"This was back years ago. Lightkeeper out there come over here to the mainland 'n' found himself a wife. Took that little bride out there to live in the lighthouse. Nothin' out on that rock but the lighthouse 'n' a patch o' grass you could make a puny garden on.

"Well then, after a year livin' out there all alone with the old man, little lady went stark ravin' mad. Threw herself into the breakers 'n' never did come up. Deep-sixed herself. A light-keeper's life isn't for everyone.''

He sucked air between his teeth, little corncob rows. He said, "Now, I'll tell you something else about this here light. It never failed. Never. In all the years that light fought the storms out yonder, it never went out. Till they turned it off.''

Venus was thinking about bear paws. Asians slice them and fry the meat with bok choy. Or boil the paws and make a broth of bear paw soup, an Asian delicacy. First they chop off the claws.

The other part of the bear that many Asians crave is the gall bladder—*xiong dan* in Chinese—the slimy green bag containing gall. *Xiong dan* is "cold" medicine, believed to ward off "hot" diseases, like fevers, or infections, and to increase the consumer's life span. Male bear genitals, like other big game genitals, are prized aphrodisiacs. Still, *xiong dan* rates as the caviar of traditional Asian pharmacopoeia. Not only in Asia, but in any country with an Asian population, *xiong dan* and big game genitalia, organs, and limbs, even hearts and brains, are served in certain Asian restaurants and can be bought dried and powdered, in herb balls, or, in season, absolutely fresh, usually under the counter in Asian apothecary shops. In much of Asia and most of the United States, killing bears to harvest organs is illegal, hence the stuff is sold on the black market. In New York's Asian district, Vancouver's and Seattle's International District, San Francisco's Chinatown—all over the world, but increasingly in the United States—for the right price you could have a fresh bear gall bladder delivered to your front door.

In spring and autumn, black bears are especially active, foraging for brambles and berries. They're fond of pink salmon berries and the wild cranberry. Rolling in scarlet cranberry bogs is one of a bear's favorite pastimes. They mark trees, mark off personal territory. They like to claw off the bark of young, tender trees, eat the meaty sapwood underneath. They like to rub up against tree bark because during spring molt, they itch. Because their activity threatens clone farms, state game and federal wildlife officials began experimenting with alternate feeding formulas, but the bears preferred fresh sapwood from young trees. So state game organized the hunting lottery "hot spot" bear kills. The hunters were allowed one bear each, and stringent documentation regulations applied to hot spots.

If you want to hunt bear in the Pacific Northwest, you're required to hunt with registered bear hounds. You can't bring unlicensed hunters along. When you've bagged a bear, you're required to skin the carcass, including the head, and turn the head and hide in to state game or federal wildlife officials, whichever had authority over the terrain. You must include the small premolar, first tooth behind the canine, upper or lower jaw. The premolar is used to determine the bear's age. Then you have to file a report detailing your kill. All this, if you're following the letter of the law.

Poachers come in a multitude of disguises, from all walks of life. They kill for profit; organs of rare species sell for more than heroin per powdered ounce. *Xiong dan* is a poacher's gold. Four-year-old bears, in their first springtime mating season, before they've mated, have the biggest galls.

Some poachers pose as guides, operating out of phony storefronts, selling "guided tours" of national parks to a wealthy international clientele willing to pay hugely for the thrill of taking rare species in native habitat. The phony guides guarantee kills and never possess proper permits.

All poachers are swift, quick to cover their tracks. Because poachers will kill their own family members to escape detection, the DOI doesn't depend on informants. Whoever buys from a poacher is usually too terrified to cooperate with DOI officials. Unless they leave behind a gut pile, poachers are almost impossible to trace. Because bullets can be traced, they use shotguns. The gut pile was all Venus had to go on.

RUTLEDGE lit up another homemade. He offered Venus one. She took it, stowed it in her pocket. For later, maybe. Behind Rutledge, Timmy Divers persisted, staring through the window, snarling. The kid jangled her nerves. Now Timmy tapped menacingly on the windowpane.

On the ocean, winds whipped up, blowing salt spray onto the

porch. The sky turned black, and thick thunderclouds rolled in off the horizon. Rutledge stood up, invited her indoors. She followed him, hoping he owned a teapot and some strong English tea. Timmy had curled up in the visitor's wing chair by the fireplace, pretending to read his lesson book. Rutledge went over and ruffled the boy's rich brown hair. Timmy glanced up. A cherub never smiled so sweetly.

Rutledge fetched a bottle of Four Roses bourbon, cheap, reliable. He motioned Venus into the kitchenette, where he poured two fingers into a juice glass and handed it to her. She bolted it. Rutledge poured himself an equal measure and bolted that. When they returned to the main room, Timmy was singing softly in a high sweet voice:

"Her body lies over the ocean,
    Her body lies over the sea..."

Rutledge said, "Put that book up, son. I'm gonna read to you now. And stand when grown-ups enter. Where's your manners?"

Timmy stifled a guffaw, stood, focused his eyes straight ahead at Venus's legs. Sullenly, he said, "Would you like to sit down?"

Very formal. Very polite. When she took the chair he reluctantly offered, a faint growl rose in his small throat. He marched over to the hearth, to a brass coal bin, lifted the lid, fished out some kindling wood, and handed it to Rutledge, who was poking embers in the fireplace. The whole time he was doing this, Timmy watched her like a hawk.

Rutledge lit the small bundle of twigs and set a cedar log on top. While he worked his cheeks like bellows, Timmy made demon faces at her. Like he could put a hex on her. On a small table near her elbow lay a box of stick matches. She took the fat hand-rolled cigarette from her pocket. Keeping her gaze fixed on Timmy, she struck a wooden match on the sole of her boot, held the flame to the cigarette, and inhaled. She didn't want to smoke, but she lit up anyway. Anything to annoy the brat. She exhaled. Timmy hacked broadly.

Rutledge got the fire going. It roared, the blazing glow turning Timmy's coffee-colored skin a deep golden shade. Rutledge searched the bookshelves. After a while, he plucked a thin green volume from a shelf, dusted it off, blew on it. He went over to the wing chair opposite her, snapped on a table lamp, sat down and opened the book. He motioned Timmy over to him. Timmy sat on the little footstool beside the wing chair, very near Rutledge's knee. He chewed his fingernails, and through veiled lashes he studied Venus's black leather.

Rutledge cleared his throat. "Time was," he said, "when I could recite all the sea lore by heart. All the shanties, 'n' most of Melville too. Nowadays, I need a prop." Reciting from the thin green volume, his gruff voice resonated over the crackling fire:

> *"'Twas a mean and dreadful night at sea,*
> *Windswells high as the mast,*
> *When Captain Danger summoned me;*
> *He cried, 'Lad, we're home at last!'*
> *'All due respect, O Captain Mine,'*
> *Me says in frightened voice,*
> *'Ye must be mad, or fever-blind*
> *T' call this your home of choice.'*
> *And sweepin' me hand across me brow,*
> *I added for good measure;*
> *'These seas are meaner than e'er I've seen;*
> *How can they bring ye pleasure?*
> *Or do you mean to tell your crew,*
> *O Captain, Dear and Brave,*
> *That home for we that's paid our due*
> *Lies here in a watery grave?'*
>
> *"Then Captain Danger pointed north*
> *Across the churning seas.*
> *'Land ho!' he cried, and, 'Sally forth!*
> *Forget your mutinies.*
> *For at portside I've seen a rock*
> *High as the cliffs of Dover,*

And starboard, lo, a looming knoll,
Dressed in thick green clover.'

"We the crew was startled then
To see what we did see.
For weeks on end in brawling seas
We'd planned a mutiny.
But now we follered the Captain's eyes
And saw this with our own;
A craggy island off portside,
Starboard, a mainland home.

"'O Captain Dear,' me says just then,
'You've saved us from our doom.
Then be it known for future kin
What hero brought us home.
T'won't be England, this queer new shore,
But the land becalms a stranger,
And here we'll carve your name in stone,
On the cliffs of the Isle of Danger.'"

Rutledge closed the book, lost in a reverie. One gnarled hand reached down absentmindedly and ruffled Timmy's hair. Timmy said, "Can I go home now? Before it rains?"

"Go on, son."

Timmy Divers ran outdoors, in a hurry to go somewhere. Venus noticed the boy had forgotten his lesson book. She noticed something else, too. Fear haunted the boy's eyes. Of what?

Rutledge went into the kitchenette, fetched the Four Roses. When they'd had their two fingers, he said, "Only, 'twasn't clover. 'Twas moss. They'd come upon the Pacific Northwest. Captain Vancouver came later 'n' took credit. But the Oxford gentleman, Captain Alfred Alan Danger, was the first white man on these shores, 'n' the old native legends bear that out."

Outside, the wind had gained velocity. It swooped, howling down the chimney, stirring the fire into a restless dance. A few fat raindrops splashed on the window glass. Rutledge eased back into the wing chair and added, "That's how Point Danger got its name. Lighthouse came later, after the Northwest coast had been surveyed by the white man, after they moved the Quinault and Hoh and Queets up onto the reservations. Government took over this land. Then in 1880, they started building the lighthouse. Too many ships goin' down out here.

"Roughest seas on the West Coast. Maybe in all the world. Took 'em over fifty years t' raise that light. Six men died out there buildin' it. High winds blew 'em off the rock. Their bodies were never found. Sank right t' the bottom, right down in Davy Jones's locker. That's deep ocean.

"See, there's a problem landin' tenders. No good mooring sites, not even for a skiff. 'N' there's a fissure on the south side. When a southwesterly blows, like this 'n' today, the seas come shootin' through that fissure 'n' make toothpicks outta ships."

"Did the Quinault ever go out there?" she asked him.

"Sure. Don't ask me how they managed that. There's evidence of a Quinault burial ground out there too."

"How do you know all that?"

He smiled triumphantly. "I was lightkeeper out there. First 'n' last 'n' only lightkeeper they ever had. 'Twas me who kept that light burnin' all those years."

"That was your wife?"

"Carrie Violet."

"Sorry."

"She done it to herself."

Silence. Then she said, "The Quinault went out there in canoes?"

"Sure. Me, now I've landed my skiff out there many a time. But I'm a trained sailor. I reckon the Quinault was sailors too. Sailor Indians. They used the rock as a ceremonial site, like I said. For burials. See, there's a coupla acres o' land out there around the lighthouse. They had their rituals there 'n' put 'em right in the ground."

"How did the Quinault feel about a lighthouse going up on their sacred ground?"

"Didn't like it. By then, they's all moved up here to the reservation up above Humptulips 'n' didn't have much voice in the matter. But they didn't like it.''

He took out his tobacco pouch, started rolling. Drum tobacco, gummed Zig Zags. His craggy facial features had softened as he spoke of the lighthouse, and his face glowed from the effects of the whiskey. A tenderness softened his voice that wasn't born of memories of Carrie Violet.

''Well then,'' he said nostalgically, puffing on the new cigarette, ''in 1913, the village was settled by families of the lighthouse construction crew. U.S. Lighthouse Service paid 'em fabulous wages to go t' work on the light. But so many men died out there on that crew, the villagers made a protest. They wanted the project abandoned. Too many kinfolk dyin'. Then old Ennis Ozone, he was crew foreman, he pulled a fast one on the villagers.

''What they did, see, the government claimed it had abandoned the project. Put all the crewmen back ashore. Then, in secret, they brung in Chinese crews from Asia. Shipped 'em right in here. Cheap labor. Called 'em 'coolies,' 'n' they was slaves, really. Slaves o' Ennis Ozone. He never allowed these Chinese t' set foot on the mainland, no. Old Ennis, he was the only villager to know what the government was doin' out there with them Chinese construction crews. Then, finally, in nineteen and thirty-six, the lighthouse was finished.

''They imported a Fresnel lamp from Paris. A beauty. The minute that Fresnel blinked on out there, 'twas love at first sight. The villagers, they set their clocks 'n' made their schedules by the lighthouse lamp, 'n' the sound o' the foghorn grew as natural to their ears as the roar o' the tides.''

He smiled and his navy blue eyes glistened. He was getting to the best part. He said, ''I was the first man to operate that lamp, 'n' the last. No other man was crazy enough to want the job. Ennis Ozone, he knew that. He brought me out there and he says to me, 'Rutledge, this here's your home. You keep this lamp burnin' 'n' you can stay here the rest of your natural life.' He said that to me. I lived out there forty years all by myself. And then, that one year with Carrie Violet, too. Heaven on Earth, it was. Heaven on Earth.''

"Why'd you leave?"

He shot her a hard glance. "Let me tell it my way."

"Suits me."

"That lamp," he continued, "was the finest first-order Fresnel you ever saw. Pure lead crystal, perfectly faceted. Never failed. Never. I should know." He ran a freckled hand across his beard. "'Course, it's true what they say about the fish."

"Fish?"

He nodded. "Gale force winds hit those breakers out there 'n' whipped 'em up. Breakers'd toss great fishes a hundred thirty feet into the air where the wind caught 'em. These flyin' fish sailed right into the lantern, knocked out some o' the crystals. Sure, it happened all the time. But the lamp, it never failed. 'N' those ships out there in the high seas, they depended on Point Danger light, on me.

"See, I worked for the old U.S. Lighthouse Service. Then when the coast guard took over all the lighthouses in the United States, they kept me on. No one else wanted my job. No one else knew how to keep that light runnin'. During World War Two, now that was a time no man can forget."

Rutledge stood, walked over to the picture window, looked out. As if to check if the lighthouse was still out there. It was. He came back over and sat down again. The bright navy eyes had become a young man's eyes.

He said, "When the Japs made their sneak attack on the Pacific Coast, all the lightkeepers from San Diego up to the Aleutian Islands was ordered to turn out their lamps. Government wanted a total blackout along the coastline. To confuse the Japs. To give our shore troops time to muster forces.

"'Twas the only time I ever defied my government. I kept my lamp burning. Yes, I did. Kept it burning straight through the blackout. You could see the Jap artillery boats and the subs out there on the horizon, and I guess the Japs could see my lamp all right. But, I ask you, what would you've done? A lightkeeper's job is to keep that lamp burning, to give guidance to the lost sailor. I didn't give a tinker's damn who it was out there. Japs or our boys. I wasn't goin' to turn out the light on 'em. If they'd ever gone down during the blackout, I'd be to blame. As light-keeper. So even during the blackout, I kept that lamp burning.''

He laughed. A small ironic laugh. "Then later, the government gave me a medal. Said my lamp had confused the Japs. Said the Japs thought it was an American booby trap, that it scared 'em off. I got that medal stowed here somewhere. Don't mean nothin', though. Just doin' my job."

He stood, walked to the fireplace, and stoked the fire. In the flame glow his face looked drawn, tired. She thought about leaving, it would be the gracious thing to offer. She was an uninvited guest, after all, and he had been generous and hospitable. But she felt comfortable in the wing chair by the fire, and the storm had moved in and was teasing the sand dunes. She stood. Rutledge kept on jabbing the fire with the iron poker. Over his shoulder, he said gruffly, "Sit down. I'm not finished."

She eased back into the wing chair.

"Well then," he said, settling once again into his chair, "it got so expensive replacing all that shattered crystal. So they shut her down. Said, 'We got a light up at Cape Flattery, we got one at Point No Point, and we got one down at Cape Disappointment. We don't need this one at Point Danger.' That's when they made a landlubber out of me. Since then, we've seen a lot of vessels go down out here. Since they turned out my light. Oh, the big ships, they sail further out now. Guided by buoys. Aero-beacons and -lasers. New-tech. But the smaller craft, the gillnetters and shrimpers and such that navigate closer to shore, they still depend on the light to guide 'em. Even the big vessels, when they're bound for the mouth of the Columbia, they look for Point Danger light. But it's out now. Has been for years."

"What happened to the Fresnel lamp?"

He shrugged. "Reckon she's still out there. Don't see why not."

"You ever go out there anymore?"

His gaze moved from the fire to the picture window. Steel black clouds billowed over the ocean. In a gentle voice he said, "Hell, you think I'm crazy?"

Yes, she thought silently. Yes, I do. Aloud she said, "Why

didn't you just stay out there after the coast guard abandoned the lighthouse? Live out your days on that rock?''

"That was my plan. But the government made me leave. I didn't fight it. What could I do? I just come off that old rock peacefully and settled into this landlubber's hovel. I'll tell you one thing, though.''

"What's that?''

"I still watch the place real close.''

The storm had rumbled over the beach and now was attacking the dunes. Rain fell in torrents. She faced a long wet trip back to the village. She stood again. This time he didn't object. He said, "I'll tell you somethin' else about this old lighthouse out here.''

"What's that?''

"She was murdered out there.''

"Mrs. Leroux?''

He nodded.

"Why do you say that?''

He grinned, stood up, stretched. He said, "Had to be. See, I was over on the point when they came to take her corpse away. I seen how she was bound up, hands 'n' feet. I seen what the killer had used to tie her up. Sailor's cord, it was. But not this new nylon cord, no. 'Twas the old hemp rope, kind you won't find in hardware stores these days. No sirree, the cord used to tie the old lady up come from the lighthouse. I know that for a fact. 'Cause it was my rope. I made it myself, and when I come off the rock, I left that rope behind in the light station.''

She said, "Maybe the rope was taken from there and brought to the mainland. Maybe that happened before Mrs. Leroux was murdered. Then the killer used the rope to tie her up, shot her. The murder could have taken place anywhere, and then her body dumped out here on the beach, to make it look like she'd washed ashore on the tide. And maybe the rope was used to make it appear that she was murdered out there.''

Rutledge chuckled knowingly. He didn't buy her logic. She said, "You're sure about the rope?''

"Made it with my own hands.''

He rolled another cigarette, gave it to her. "For a rainy day,'' he said, winking. He loaned her a plastic poncho, to keep dry on the trip back to the village. On the front porch, he stood near the ship's bell while she pulled the poncho over her head. She said, "Are there any Asians living in the village?"

"Only one. That's Timmy. But he wasn't born here."

"Where's he from?"

"Now that's a mystery. Just showed up with the Divers one day. Chick and Carolyn. Said they found him on the beach, abandoned. So they took him home. Carolyn, she's gone now. She and Chick split up a year ago last winter. But as to where the boy come from, no one knows. He don't remember himself. He's one hundred percent American now, though. Maybe you noticed that."

"What language did he speak when they found him?"

"Wasn't talkin' yet. Too young." Rutledge squinted suspiciously. "What makes you so curious about that boy?"

She explained about living in Asia. It was nostalgia, she guessed, that made her curious about Timmy Divers. She asked about the woods behind his house, the park forest. Had he seen any bears come around?

"I got bears in my woodpile all the time. Come down here along the beach from up in the park. There's somebody leaves 'em jelly rolls down here near these old picnic tables rangers built behind my place. There's one old bear, a big 'un; after he gets into them jelly rolls, he dances. Dances down to the tideline, 'n' dances right on into the waves. They almost killed him last week. Had him right where they wanted him. See, the jelly rolls is used as bait. But he got away. One of their bullets hit my border collie, killed him instead. That bear, he was lucky that time. My collie, Seltzer, he ran clean outta luck."

He waved as she headed into the storm. "Come back any time," he called out. "If you ring this bell and I don't answer, walk up to the point. I'll be there."

"Thanks," she shouted through the crashing thunder.

"And next time," he yelled, "bring some beef jerky and some grog."

Through the storm, she returned to the gut pile. Examining the bear's jaw, she found three premolar teeth left. One had been ripped out. Using her Swiss Army knife, she removed another premolar and pocketed it. She took off the poncho, made a bundle of the gut pile, and buried it in the sand. On top of the shallow, temporary grave, she placed a distinctive driftwood log, one she could describe to Dave and Claudia, DOI's forensics chief. She hoped the driftwood marker would stand up to the storm.

TEN

Popeye

EVERY ROOM an ocean view.

She went into the Driftwood Inn. There was a call bell on the reception desk. A digital clock on the wall said 6:05 p.m. From a back room drifted soft television static. Venus palmed the call bell. A woman appeared, clutching a coffee mug and a pair of reading glasses. Nordic blonde, very cool. She wore a chenille bathrobe, white with baby-blue ducklings on the pockets. She slid up to the reception desk, inspected the drenched stranger, handed Venus a ballpoint pen and registration card. Signing in, Venus remarked, "It's raining buckets out there."

The Nordic blonde stared. Raining buckets? So what's new? The drenched individual handed over a credit card. She studied it, nodded, her thin lips barely parting when she said, "One night?"

Years ago, thought Venus, some traveling carnival must have passed through Ozone Beach and the show's ventriloquist planted his prolific seed. She said, "Sure. One night."

The Nordic blonde handed her a key to Room 111. Then she went away. She went into the room with the television set. Venus could hear channels switch.

Room 111 had broad picture windows facing the beach. Venus parted the heavy curtains, looked out. A street lamp at the intersection of Beach Drive and Lighthouse Lane shone dimly through sheets of rain pounding against the black road. Behind the squall, beach and ocean had disappeared, but she could hear the breakers' driving, fitful roar.

Near the picture windows sat a small love seat covered in maroon chintz. In front of it, a knotty-pine coffee table with nothing on it besides a thick coat of polyurethane. From the low ceiling, a television set hung on a console. A sign on the set announced guests were entitled to complimentary HBO.

Beside a queen-sized bed, a small maple table supported a telephone and a ginger jar lamp that glowed soft yellow when she switched it on. The telephone had direct-dial buttons. The table had one drawer, containing a Gideon Bible and a thin telephone directory. She fished out the telephone directory. As she did this, something sparkled against the bed's snow-white pillows. She picked it up.

A foil-wrapped chocolate kiss. Underneath, a crisp white card bore the handwritten message: "Sweet Dreams, Your Innkeeper, Ingrid Hëll." Venus popped the chocolate kiss and leafed through the telephone directory. All this took approximately two minutes. In the bathroom, she peeled off her drenched clothing, the flooded boots. A fresh white terry robe hung from a hook on the bathroom door. Wrapping the soft robe around her, she stretched across the queen-sized bed and reached for the telephone.

Dave still had phone duty. Venus told him where the bear carcass was buried. He promised to fly down with Claudia, retrieve the remains so Claudia could autopsy. He had two messages for her. "You're supposed to call Agent O'Connor of U.S. Naval Intelligence," said Dave, sounding unimpressed.

"Who's he?"

"You never heard of Jack O'Connor?"

"Should I have?"

"Maybe not. Only the worldly-wise and well-informed know who Jack O'Connor is."

"I give up, Dave. Who's Jack O'Connor?"

"They call him 'Popeye.' He's top banana in the navy's Pacific Rim spy squad."

"What's that all about?"

While she listened to Dave, she massaged her frigid feet.

"Guardian angels of the Pacific Coast."

"I thought the Cold War had ended."

"Technically speaking, yes. But ever since they started building nuclear subs over here at Bangor, navy's put their guys out there too. It's become something of a tradition, I gather. They're aloof, don't mix with Coast Guard.''

"What do they do out there?"

Dave said, "They keep track of all those enemy spy boats disguised as innocent fishing vessels. And the subs. Don't forget the Russian subs. Vast fleets of them lurk in waters off our coast. Can't you see their periscopes from where you are?"

She peered out the window at the wicked black rain. "Sure, Dave," she said. "They're just swarming. What does O'Connor want?"

"He wanted to speak with Olson. But Olson had already left for the game. Play-offs tonight. Sonics and Lakers. Wish I had tickets."

"Uh-huh."

"O'Connor asked me why we'd sent an agent down to Ozone and I told him he should ask Olson that. Or talk to you directly. He didn't like that. After he swore at me, he left a number where he can be reached in Ozone Beach. He wants you to call him. By the way, it's the same number that you're calling from, just a different extension. One-sixteen."

Apparently O'Connor was her neighbor across the hall. She said, "Anything else?"

"Olson said to tell you Sparks is on his way down to check out the gut pile. He should be there any minute."

"And?"

"Olson said Sparks will be checking on your progress with the pelican business."

"Cute."

"Also, your mother called. She wants you to return her call immediately. Said it's important. That call came in half an hour ago. She has a gorgeous voice. Like chimes."

"Nothing from DC, from Wexler?"

"Nary a peep. Why?"

"He could at least have the decency to welcome me back."

"He will, all right, after that fax Olson sent this afternoon." She winced. "So he sent it?"

"Actually, he let Sparks feed it into the fax machine."

"Oh fine. Just fine."

Dave said, "How about dinner Friday night? Maybe Fuller's?"

Silence. Then, "I don't know, Dave... This jet lag—"

"Saturday then. Dancing afterward at Four Seasons."

"It's just that—"

"A night out will help you beat the jet lag. What's say eight o'clock, at your mother's house? I'll carry ID so you'll know me in a black tie."

"Why, Dave?"

"Because during the three years you've been away, I worked up the nerve to ask you. I got so brave that now I'm insisting. Eight o'clock, Saturday. Wear an evening gown."

"You've wanted to ask me out?"

"About five years ago, I drove by the Bensons' one afternoon when they were giving a garden party. You were there, standing at the bar. You had a dress on. Ever since I saw you in that dress, I've wanted to ask you for a date."

"I didn't think I was your type."

Dave laughed.

Maybe she'd put her foot in her mouth again. "I didn't mean to imply...I meant... It's just that you're so...with women...I never thought you were..."

"You can work out of this tangle Saturday night."

"Sure," she said, bewildered, and rang off.

A lot had changed in three years. Including Dave. Dave, her field partner, the pillar of virtue, sinfully handsome, a prince with perfect ears. This Dave had always been painfully shy around women. Not anymore.

O'CONNOR PICKED UP the phone on the first ring, like he'd been waiting. He was blunt. "This is Navy's investigation," he snarled.

"No way," she said. "Wildlife is Interior's bag. So's murder when the body's found on Interior property."

"I don't give a goddamn about Interior. The pelican protesters and this woman's drowning are Navy business."

"Since when was Navy in love with brown pelicans? Or timber

queens, for that matter? And anyway, who says the two are connected?"

"I want you out of Ozone, Diamond. Now."

"Tell you what, O'Connor. Soon as Olson gives the high-sign, I'll blow this clip joint. Ozone's not exactly my cup of tea. By the way, are you a Mercy's chowder fan?"

"Don't try clever with me."

"Who do you work for, O'Connor?"

"I've told you. Navy Intelligence."

"I'm with Interior. I take my orders from Interior."

"You're an idiot," he growled. "Don't you understand what's going down in Ozone Beach?"

"Frankly, no. Do you?"

He snarled, "Do you know who I am?"

"Sure. Popeye and Mata Hari rolled into one."

"You're a punk."

"Listen, Popeye, I've got to ring off now. Someone's knocking at my door. If you want to party some more, come on down to one eleven." She hung up. Cinching the terry robe tighter, she went to the door, asked who was there.

A tiny voice said, "Timmy."

She opened the door. The little snoop wore a green rain parka with a hood, and black rubber boots. They repelled water like a duck's back. She let him inside.

"Chick thinks I'm at the library," he said nervously. "He'll whip me if he finds out I lied."

"How'd you find me, Timmy?"

"I looked in all the hotel parking lots till I saw your Harley."

"How'd you know I drive a Harley?"

"Lola."

"Postal clerk?"

"Postmistress. She told me."

"How'd you get my room number?"

"There's a door on the beach side. I can pick the lock. We do it all the time. Me and some other kids. I picked the lock while Mrs. Hëll was watching TV. I came in and listened at all the doors. I heard your voice."

"Why do you pick locks, Timmy?"

He rubbed the raindrops on his nose. He said, "The village council pays us to spy on the tourists."

She couldn't think of anything to say to an eight-year-old intelligence agent. Finally, she joked, "You get minimum wage for that?"

"Five dollars if we find out information."

"Like what?"

He climbed onto the maroon love seat. His feet dangled, missing the floor by a mile. He said, "Like, if they're criminals. Who might make trouble in Ozone. Or if they talk with foreign accents. Like you. You've got a weird accent. This is a crime-free community. We don't want troublemakers coming in here."

"Besides mine, have you ever heard any foreign accents?"

"Yes."

He stared at his hands. The nails were bitten to the quick. He was too nervous for an eight-year-old. Very softly he said, "I heard the enemy."

"What does the enemy sound like, Tim?"

"Like Donald Duck. But sometimes they talk in English, only I can't understand them."

"Where were they?"

"Here in the Driftwood Inn. Last week. I reported it to Chick. He's on the village council. The village council gave me five dollars. The mayor said I had helped prevent an enemy plot. Mrs. Mercy—she's the mayor—said they were going to put fler...flerides... "

"Fluoride?"

"Uh-huh. She said the enemy was going to put fluoride in our drinking water. But the village council ran them out before they could do it. So they gave me a five-dollar reward for reporting them."

She looked at Timmy Divers. He seemed an exceptionally bright child, just nervous and misinformed. Still, she didn't trust him further than Lola could throw her voice. She said, "Why did you come here, Timmy?"

"Mr. Rutledge told me to. I forgot my lesson book. I went

back to his house to get it.'' He fished the book out of his rain parka and showed it to her, like proof. ''Mr. Rutledge said to find you and warn you. He said there's a man who came to his house after you left asking lots of questions about you. The man said he'd been following you around. He said he was a famous spy, but Mr. Rutledge didn't like him. He says the man is after you, and you should leave right away. He said it isn't safe for you in Ozone Beach.''

While she thought this over, Timmy bit his fingernails.

''Anyway,'' Timmy added, ''I know who it is. I know who's after you.''

''Someone's after me?''

''Uh-huh. I know who it is.''

''Who?''

''The manitou.''

''What's a manitou?''

''Spirits the Quinault left behind. Some are good and some are evil. This manitou's evil. It lives in the lighthouse. Chick says it rode Madge Leroux's body to the mainland. It came here to kill. It likes eating young kids. But if it can't find any young kids, then it will eat grown-ups, or even bears. You haven't heard about the manitou?'' She said no, she hadn't.

Timmy said, ''Everyone in Ozone knows about the manitou.''

''Where were you born, Tim?''

He stared at his dangling feet. Matter-of-factly, he said, ''I'm a boat person.''

''Do you remember where you were born?''

''Naw.''

''What about your parents? Do you remember them?''

His legs beat a slow hard rhythm against the couch. He said, ''I sort of remember my mom, but not too much. She was real pretty, though.'' He brightened. ''But I do remember my step-mother. Her name was Carolyn.''

''Where's Carolyn now?''

''Chick says she went to Montana. To live with a cowboy. I'm going to meet him someday.''

''Ever hear from her? From your stepmother?''

"No." Whispered.

"Ever write to her?"

"Chick says it's not a good idea to communicate with her. He says it will just make me more nervous."

"What do you think?"

"Chick says my stepmom's a very disturbed person. So I might be afraid."

"How long since you've seen her?"

"I don't know. Maybe last winter. She was really nice. She was a bird doctor. She took care of birds when they had broken wings and stuff."

Timmy gnawed at his fingernails. Venus sat down beside him. Gently she said, "You take medicine for your nervousness?"

"Phenobarb. It's great. It calms me down."

"What makes you nervous?"

"Lots of things. The manitou. School, sometimes. And our house. It's too big. I'm pretty sure it's haunted. Chick says the manitou ate the last family that lived there."

"You don't have to believe him."

"Buzz Barnes said it's true. He's on the village council with Chick."

Timmy looked up at her. His coffee-colored complexion had paled, the healthy glow had left his cheeks. His dark eyes had glazed over, the pupils pinpoints, as if he was trying to shut out the world. Softly he said, "I better go home now."

"It's pretty wet out there."

He nodded. "Dark too."

"Where do you live?"

"Over near the airfield. Chick runs the health spa at the golf course over there. We live in the spa."

"Ever rode a motorcycle?"

His eyes suddenly brightened. He smiled and said, "On your Harley?"

"Let's go."

On the way out, she stopped at the front desk, wrote a note to Thailand's wildlife commission, faxed it on Ingrid Hëll's phone. The Harley sailed smoothly through the hard, driving rain.

Timmy proved light cargo. He wore the helmet with Benny Goodman blasting in his ears. His thin arms circled her waist, gripping tight. Once he shouted, "This is cool." He seemed almost like a normal kid.

A marine architect's nightmare must have inspired Divers' Spa. Three faux poop decks jutted from the sides of a cruise ship façade, and above the shingled roof, a sort of crow's nest or widow's walk housed a soft green light that rotated. The structure didn't know if it should be a ship or a lighthouse or an ark. On the porch an engraved brass sign discreetly advertised SEAWEED THERAPY.

Chick Divers opened the front door. When he saw Timmy, he sighed tiredly and glared at the boy, who skulked past him and disappeared into the big house. Divers wore a white hospital coat, stethoscope dangling from his neck. One hand with piano fingers wore a surgical glove. He was about forty-five, fairly well preserved, with a broad Saint Bernard face, droopy eyes, thick lips, a face she wanted to like but couldn't. An agile face, she thought, one capable of many expressions, or façades, like the place he lived in.

Divers apologized for not inviting her in. He said, "Appreciate the trouble you took with the boy."

"No trouble." She smiled. "Timmy's a nice kid."

He nodded, tried to shut the door, but her shoulder got in the way. Venus said, "I understand you're a member of the village council, Dr. Divers."

"That's right." He scowled at her shoulder, ruining the Saint Bernard effect. Rain pelted the porch roof. She said, "I was wondering about something."

"What?" Impatiently.

"Did you know Mrs. Leroux?"

He nodded tersely.

She said, "Who autopsied her?"

He sneered and the Saint Bernard resemblance vanished. Coolly, he said, "I performed the autopsy. In fact, I am in the process of completing it at this very moment. So if you'll kindly remove your shoulder... "

Before he shut the door, she said, "Maybe you should stop scaring Timmy with ghost stories."

He shut the door quietly. She heard two bolts click into place, then silence.

ELEVEN

Scones

CLOAKED IN SYLVAN THICKETS, Madge Leroux's estate crowned a high plateau on the Olympic's western foothills. A steep winding drive snaked past haughty stone walls crowned with wrought-iron hooks poised to discourage riffraff. At the entrance, two elaborate, iron gates held the world at bay, and a conspicuous video monitor scanned the drive. There was an intercom to screen visitors. Venus pressed a button on the intercom, watched the camera swing around to view her, and imagined what sound it made inside while she waited for the signal to enter.

Burden, the Leroux family's houseman, was in the kitchen when the buzzer sounded. Aware that the security guard was on his break, Burden abandoned his station and went to check the monitor. Peering into the screen, Burden saw the howling wind blowing garden debris every which way, slick rain pounding the drive, and a small bedraggled person who put Burden in mind of a drowning Chihuahua he had once rescued on the Thames. Venus identified herself.

Burden pressed a button. Outside, the gates made a whirring sound and slowly swung open. He watched the small person mount what appeared to be a Harley Davidson, if he knew his motorcycles correctly, and scoot up to the Italianate manor's front door. With considerable curiosity, he went to meet the daughter of his favorite cinema queen.

Young Burden had been imported by Madge Leroux on one of her Christmas holiday shopping excursions to Harrods, where their fates crossed in Ladies' Gloves. Burden had served several prominent London households, had recently managed the affairs of a duchess, and confided that he was presently between posts.

Taken with Burden's brio and distinct air of competence, Madge
Leroux offered the handsome, young Englishman a post on the
spot. On the spot, Burden accepted. Fifteen years had passed since
that propitious collision in Harrods' gloves, during which Burden
had served the Leroux family faithfully and impeccably. Never
mind the houseman's distinct abhorrence of the young master,
Park Leroux, Jr. Burden had adored Madge and tolerated the Old
Man, and through the years had even come to accept, if not sanc-
tion, the son's outrageous behavior. Now, as Burden hurried down
the echoing hall to the front door, he felt relieved that this
drenched biker creature was not another one of Park, Jr.'s com-
patriots, but rather the very blood and flesh of that divine Lady
Bella Winsome-Diamond, whose personal autograph he'd had
framed and hung in his apartment.

Burden opened the door and clucked his tongue. The small
creature on the front porch stood shivering, dripping like a shower
curtain. He motioned Venus inside, divested her of a nasty,
soaked leather jacket, and disappeared down the colossal hall,
returning shortly with a fluffy white towel. When she had ceased
dripping, Burden led Venus through the cavernous house. Over
his shoulder, he quipped, "I remember your mother in *Fortune's
Mistress*. Her most magnificent role, I think, although she is always superb. How is Lady Bella?"

"Don't ask," Venus groaned. "I get tired just thinking about
it."

Amusement played across Burden's tight mouth, the first sign
of jollity since the morning he had entered Mrs. Leroux's bedroom with a breakfast tray, only to discover her bed unmade and
the lady herself missing. Just now, Burden thought smiling felt
rather good. His mood elevated, he said, "Is your mother working
on something now?"

"Dabbling in a new film."

"Splendid." Burden clapped his hands. "Of course, I've seen
all her films. What is the new work titled?"

"Er, *Leek Soup*. That's the working title. I don't know the plot.
It's one of these hush-hush productions."

Burden nodded knowingly. "I'll watch for it. Now, just make

yourself at home in here. Young Mr. Leroux is up in Seattle making the funeral arrangements, but I expect him home within the hour." He parked Venus in a rococo living room and bustled off to prepare tea.

Madge Leroux's tastes had definitely run to late Baroque. Inspired by eighteenth-century continental Europe, from the high ceiling's florid plaster scrollwork to the extravagant gold-leafed furnishings, the Roman columns and expansive mirrored walls, the timber queen's living room transported a visitor into another, more frivolous era. Venus was studying a gold filigree music stand when she glanced up and saw a vividly rendered family portrait, hung low for better examination, resplendent with color and nuance. As she walked over to it, Burden came in carrying a large tea tray. While he arranged the tea things, she studied the painting.

Madge Leroux sat perched on a thronelike chair, flanked by her late husband and their only child, Parker, Jr. Judging from clothing styles, the portrait had been executed about ten years ago, probably near the time Old Man Leroux met his demise. In this portrait, Parker, Sr.'s eyes looked haunted, as if he intuitively knew that shortly after this family image was created for posterity, he would encounter a dreadful surprise. And he did. The details of that ugly death came back to her in a rush.

Parker Leroux had built the family dynasty on an ego as inflated as his lumber prices. Nine or ten years ago, he had entered an early grave, dispatched there by a Native American radical whose tribe's land Leroux had clear-cut without permission. Without permission, the radical had buried a tomahawk in Leroux's skull and lashed his corpse to a tree stump. Tit for tat. The widow Madge had not mourned publicly, though privately she might have grieved the loss. Then, without a stumble, she slipped deftly into her husband's handmade shoes.

She stepped gingerly in them, with flair. In less than a year, Madge had gained renown as a sharp business executive, a demanding perfectionist. To be fair, Madge did not earn her reputation as ecology's Lizzie Borden, she inherited that title from her husband.

On the throne, Madge appeared fragile, birdlike, with a Dresden complexion that probably never needed cosmetics and feathered white hair forming a soft halo around fine eccentric features. She wore a mauve Chanel suit and a ton of gold. It might be the contrast of the chunky gold jewelry against the petite, wayward facial features. Something didn't mesh, Venus thought, with this portrait and the image of a ruthless timber queen.

Young Parker must have been about twenty-seven in the portrait. She guessed this based upon a jolting remembrance of Park Leroux dating her older sister, Dagny, back in prep school days. She hadn't seen Park Leroux since, but now she recognized the cocky posture, the oblong shape of a skull inherited from his father, tailor-made for tomahawks. Park stood beside his mother's throne, one perfectly groomed hand resting delicately on her shoulder. Clean-shaven, polished, suave, a natural blond, he dressed impeccably, and he knew it.

Venus remembered a masquerade ball, Park escorting Dagny. Dagny had invested two weeks and a small fortune in her seagull costume. When Park arrived at the house on Magnolia Bluff, he wasn't wearing a costume. He wore a dark tuxedo with a pale rosebud in the lapel. She remembered thinking Park Leroux was too cool to wear costumes. Dagny burst into tears. Venus had been mortified to see this seagull, who was related to her, bawling. Park daubed at Dagny's tears with a silk handkerchief and escorted the seagull to the ball. Dagny returned in the wee hours, her feathers in disarray, and whispered that she'd lost her virginity in the backseat of the Leroux limousine. Bella never learned how that night ended for Dagny. Dag financed her abortion selling hashish to Sister Mary Mahoney, who taught French at Dagny's convent school.

Burden handed Venus a Wedgwood cup brimming with hot black tea. He knew about tea, how to brew it black as night and how to pull the leaves before the tannins set in. He took pride in his tea, and he took pride in his scones. From a plate on the coffee table, the scones' sweet aroma seduced Venus into a soft couch.

"Fresh from the oven." Burden indicated the scones. "My dear Scots aunt's recipe." The trick with scones, Burden said, was to keep the dough light, the oven hot. The aunt hailed from Dundee, where not surprisingly, she'd been in marmalades. Burden thought he'd inherited his aunt's culinary skills. Steam rose from the scone Venus buttered. Spreading marmalade on a bite-sized chunk, she said, "Did you enjoy working for Mrs. Leroux?"

Burden considered the question. He shrugged slightly. "We had," he said tactfully, "a sort of cat-on-a-hot-tin-roof relationship. I was the cat. But yes, I was very fond of Mrs. Leroux."

He emphasized the "Mrs.," as if singling Madge out from the rest of the clan. Venus said, "I imagined this place overrun with mourners."

A tiny smile played on his lips. "Hardly. Not many of that crowd are willing to fly down to Ozone Beach this time of year. The Leroux have a home in Seattle, very near your family home, I believe, where Mrs. Leroux spent most of her time...in the earlier days."

"Earlier days?" Venus spoke between bites.

Burden continued, "Before Mr. Leroux passed. Since then, Mrs. Leroux had spent considerable time and effort looking after family business interests here on the peninsula. She frequently traveled between this home and the Seattle residence. In fact, the family keeps a small Cessna at Oyster Bay just for that purpose. But as I was saying, Seattle was Mrs. Leroux's true home, and that is where she will be properly mourned. Oh yes, definitely. She had a jillion friends. I predict a packed house at the services."

He heard himself say that, and under his breath uttered a prayer that it would be so. The old lady had declined in popularity in recent years. Just to cover himself, Burden added, "Of course, when one reaches the age of Mrs. Leroux, many of one's friends have already passed away. Some of these seniors' funerals are absolutely deserted, if you get my point."

She nodded. Burden added quickly, as if to change the subject, "Mrs. Leroux much preferred Seattle's cosmopolitan climate. This, ah, village didn't suit her."

"You like it here?"

He pursed his lips. "Let's just say the weather doesn't agree with my arthritis."

"Okay." Venus buttered another scone. "Let's just say that."

Fussing over the tea things, Burden said, "More Keemum?" and poured it for her.

Watching his deft hand, Venus said, "What do you think happened?"

The hand didn't flinch as he replied, "I haven't yet formed an opinion. Not a firm one, anyway. She had some enemies. That was no secret. But there is no telling which one of them is actually capable—I mean in the clinical sense—of committing murder."

"What about her son, Park? What does he think?"

Burden made a sour face. "Mr. Leroux," he intoned disdainfully, "subscribes to the 'death by misadventure' theory." In the distance a bell sounded. Burden excused himself and hurried away.

Alone again in the *outré* living room, Venus rose, walked over to a bank of windows, and peered out. The windows faced south and west. In daylight, they would afford spectacular views of the Olympics' southern foothill ranges, of the village below, and of the beaches and the Pacific Ocean beyond. Sunsets from this vista must be magnificent. But after dark, like now, there was nothing to see through these windows besides the moon and the stars, which tonight were obscured by the storm, and the pinpoint lights of the village, flickering restlessly beneath rainfall. The village lights proved less interesting than the animated reflection she now observed in the window glass. Someone, in the room, moving behind her. She turned.

He had plucked a scone from the plate, was blowing capriciously at the steam rising from it. He was tall, with piercing blue eyes and a thick crop of jet black hair bound back in a ponytail. He wore Patagonias and expensive hiking boots. He appeared to enjoy excellent physical health, but was about to jeopardize this with the mountain of butter he lathered over the scone. He plopped a spoonful of marmalade on top of the butter, made a fat sandwich, and devoured the scone in two swift bites. Then he glanced at Venus and said, "Oh, hi. I'm Richard Winters."

He walked over to the window, stood dangerously close to her. He gestured, tapping the windowpane. He said, "If you look very closely, there against the sky, when the clouds break you can see the outline of the lighthouse. Watch now. See it?"

"Uh-huh."

"When the moon's out, it lights up the old lighthouse clear as day. Used to be, no matter what weather, you could always find the lighthouse. Bathed in its own searchlight. I guess I'm senti-mental. I miss that light. Miss the foghorn even more. Foghorn's the greatest musical instrument ever invented."

He turned to face her. They stood about three inches apart, and she felt trapped in his energy field. He said, "Your name's Venus. Ha. Guess how I knew that?"

"I'll bet a waitress named Meredith told you."

He grinned, went back over to the scones, plucked another from the plate, slathered butter on. While he had been standing close to her, she had noticed three things. First, his eyes were not so much blue as aquamarine. Second, he radiated a polarized energy field that attracted and repelled at the same time. A dangerous energy, like Reuben's. You should never get close to people with this potent energy field. They can suck you in and you might get stuck. Venus lingered near the window, maintaining a distance from Richard Winters. The third thing she had noticed was the ring finger of his left hand, with the gold wedding band.

Halfway into another scone, he said, "There's a Quinault leg-end about a tunnel. Legend says a tunnel runs from here on the mainland out to the lighthouse. Beneath the ocean, from Point Danger all the way out to the lighthouse. The tunnel is inhabited by spirit men. See, the rock where they built the lighthouse was the Quinault's sacred ceremonial ground. Till the white man des-ecrated it. Till the lighthouse went up. So when the lighthouse was built, spirits haunted it. That's why, according to Quinault legend, the old lighthouse service lost so many men trying to build it."

He munched on the scone, studying her the way Reuben used

to study her, with a thoughtful, penetrating gaze. He said, "Meredith says you're with Fish and Wildlife. I think it's great that you've come down here to help save the pelicans. You folks don't really deserve the rotten rep you've got."

She leaned against the windowsill and said cautiously, "Meredith didn't believe me."

He had made himself at home on one of two facing tapestry couches, in arm's reach of the tea tray. From his nest, he smiled, and even at this distance, she felt the radiation, his magnetic draw. He laughed. "I'm sure Meredith believes you're with Fish and Wildlife. She's just got this fantastic imagination and sometimes she gets paranoid. She's a sweet kid, though. Very genuine."

Venus approached the scones, careful not to step too close to Winters. In Asia, she'd learned how to skirt energy fields. Some magnetic fields produce a sort of human *feng shui* that could affect your ability to think rationally, or even cause misfortune, or worse. He sprang up and with elaborate, exaggerated gestures poured her another cup of tea and motioned to her to sit beside him on the couch.

All this folderol about energy fields might be pure nonsense. It might feel rather pleasant inside Richard Winters's aura, but to be safe, she sat opposite him, on the other tapestry couch, facing him across the wide gulf, defended by a coffee table, a tea service, a half-empty plate of scones. His facial expression indicated surprise at her skittishness. He couldn't read her mind, though. He couldn't know that for a few seconds she had waffled. He could not possibly guess that she now experienced some painfully familiar form of anxiety.

Winters poured himself a cup of tea. "Mer says you asked her about an environmentalist group. The Pelican Patrol. I never heard of it. But Mrs. Leroux was not murdered by pelican lovers, I can assure you of that. I can probably prove it too."

"How?"

He grinned. "Ask me in a few days." He glanced around the elaborate living room and added, "Who do you think will inherit all this?"

"The son?"

He shrugged. "Maybe."

Winters leaned back, raised the impeccably clean hiking boots onto the coffee table, as if he were at home. He'd visited the Leroux home before, many times, he told her. Their families were old friends, he said, though he was raised in California. He'd visited the Leroux home in Ozone Beach many times in his childhood. Then he and Park, Jr. had been classmates, and pals, at Stanford. Pals ever since, too. MBAs in hand, Park Leroux convinced Winters to move to Ozone Beach, go to work for the Leroux family business.

He was about her age, maybe closer to Dagny's. He must have been playing on the same beach as the Diamond children back in childhood. She might even have seen his sand castles, and he might have seen hers.

Winters continued, "I stand out like a sore thumb in this burg, but I've developed a passion for the Washington coast. I especially like the wintertime here, the storms on the ocean. And too," he added, "being a fairly recent convert to conservationism, I hope to contribute something to the Olympic Peninsula.

"When I came to the peninsula," Winters confessed, "I had no respect for nature, for these beaches out here, and the forests. In fact, as a timber executive, I despised the spotted owl protesters and their ilk. This is all history, though, from wa-a-ay back, when I was engaged to Lola."

Venus said, "You were engaged to someone named Lola?"

Winters grinned. "That really is her name. She was Park's secretary. Back in my early timber exec days, we were planning to be married. Until Jeannie came along. I dropped Lola and married Jeannie. Lola never forgave me."

Venus said, "Lola, from the post office?"

"That's Lola. Whenever I go in there to buy stamps from her, she stabs me with her eyes. She probably reads my mail, too. I didn't mean to hurt Lola, but you know how it is when Heaven walks right up to you and offers you the key to her heart?"

"No," said Venus. "I don't know about that."

Winter's mouth formed an ironic grin. "Jeannie was like that. Heaven. That was back in her natural period."

Venus stared. Winters explained, "Before the acrylic nails, the big hair, Jeannie made a great Earth mother. That's how she was when I married her. Turned out the Earth mother crap was just a phase, a trendy look she wanted to try on. When acrylic nails came out, Jeannie blossomed into her true self. You've got to meet her, really, to understand."

Venus was absorbing all this biographical data when Burden entered. "Mr. Leroux just telephoned. He has been tied up in Seattle with funeral arrangements." To Winters, Burden added, "Mr. Leroux wonders if you are available to fly the village helicopter to Seattle tomorrow. To deliver the remains to the Interior Department, so that they might then release Madam's remains to the funeral home."

Winters said, "Tell Park that, weather permitting, I'll deliver Madge."

Burden nodded gravely and went away.

Winters buttered another scone and quipped, "That's the only problem with living on the Washington coast. Every move you make depends on weather."

ON THE WAY BACK to the Driftwood Inn, Venus rode by Mercy's Chowder Bar. It had closed for the evening; and the proprietor herself stood bent over the cash register, counting the day's take. Venus could see Mrs. Mercy's muscular back through the window. A strong, broad swimmer's back.

The squall had gained force; winds roaring off the ocean rocked the bike as she swerved around a corner onto Beach Drive. She smiled to herself. She'd escaped Richard Winters's tricky aura, and she thought she'd learned something in the process. And too, she smiled because the Harley loved weather. She stopped at a gas station to quench the bike's thirst. Pumping gas, she saw Mrs. Mercy drive by in a black sedan. The mayor ran a stop sign.

BELLA came on the line. "Where have you been?" she said. "I have been trying to locate you for hours. Honestly, Venus, you're as shifty as a snake."

"Thanks. What's up, Mother?"

"This funeral business. Woofy and I had tea with Father Dylan. He saw Park earlier in the day and apparently the poor chap is in no condition to be handling this affair."

"Coked out?"

"That's not funny, dear. Park has received a severe shock. Father Dylan advised him to go back home and get some sleep. The boy hasn't slept in days, Venus, and he's absolutely exhausted. Father has sent Park home, and now Woofy and I in concert with Father will manage the funeral."

"You're pure gold, Mother. Where do I fit in?"

"I want you to leave this murder investigation business alone. Until after the funeral. Park told Father Dylan that the strain of everything is absolutely tearing his heart out. It's too much for anyone to handle all at once. After all, we have a coddled child here, who is unaccustomed to life's darker side. Can you do that?"

"No."

"Of course you can. If you want to, you can."

"Mother, I cannot suspend this investigation in deference to a suspect's emotional state."

"Suspect? What do you mean, 'suspect'?"

"Park is a suspect. Certain evidence points to him."

"Venus! This is your mother speaking. Do you hear me? You are not to unnecessarily upset that young man until his poor mother has been properly eulogized and placed in the ground. Can you promise me that much?"

"If you put it that way, yes. I don't intend to upset Park unnecessarily."

Bella eased off, murmured a few endearing words and hung up. Venus placed a call to Forensics and caught Claudia on her way out the door. When they had finished talking, she put down the receiver and lay back on the queen-sized bed. A twenty-minute snooze, she told herself, and then it's out again into that blasted rain.

TWELVE

Dreamboat

DIM LIGHTS. JUKEBOX BLARE. The Bell Buoy Lounge was hot tonight, small, cozy, and packed to the gills. Venus walked up to the bar and tried to catch the bartender's eye. He was preoccupied, and so was the dreamboat down near the crème de menthe.

She had raven hair. She wore it long with a lot of wing on the waves. She had deep hazel eyes, heavily made up. They were riveted on two men who leered at her from barstools. They were drunk and in love with her. She was on the service side of the counter, pumping draught Oly. She knew how to pump. She could blow a head like Baby Doe. She could probably do a lot of things. She was tall, perilously curvaceous, a theatre of self-confidence. She wore a skintight silver lamé leotard and black fishnet stockings with spike-heeled pumps. Her fingernails were acrylic, about ten inches long and curved. Her full lips were tinted blood crimson, as if she had just devoured one of her prey. She had fairly good peripheral vision. She noticed Venus. She made a sour face and said something to her two admirers. They guffawed. They adored her.

Venus's brother Rex had taught her to lip read. She'd practiced at Sunday Mass, her ears plugged with swimmer's wax. Before long, she could make out the entire homily. But Ozone's dreamboat could not have known this, could not have realized that Venus read lips.

"Check it out, boys," the dreamboat quipped. "The halfpint blond in black leather. Male or female? Woman or boy? Free beer for the winning answer."

"Gal," said one.

"Boy," said the other.

She sidled over, hands caressing her hips.

"Drink?" she said.

Venus said, "I'll take a near-beer."

"Oh yeah?" She made a face.

She slinked over to the cooler, pulled out a bottle, and slinked back to where Venus stood leaning against the bar. She put the bottle and a glass in front of Venus. She could pour it herself.

Venus placed some dollars on the counter. The dreamboat snatched them up and made change. Then she went back to where her fan club waited with bated breath. She crooked a finger under the winner's chin. She said, "You win, lover boy. At least, I think so."

While she pumped his freebie, the winner yelled, "Hey, Jeannie darlin', blow the head for me."

She wanted to do that. The way she did it reduced grown men to jellyfish. She seemed to like men that way. But she was a lousy bartender. She liked to talk while the barflies listened. Venus eavesdropped as Jeannie Winters's drawling oratory described her personal woes.

Jeannie Winters was the independent type who liked men to know she was kitten soft, squeezable, but hell on wheels in bed. She was thirty-one years old, give or take a decade, had two ex-husbands and one present spouse, whom she was preparing to discard momentarily. She got her BA and her first husband down in Eugene, and she inherited the Bell Buoy in that divorce settlement. No kids. Are you kidding? They ruin you.

Her second old man was an aspiring painter who mainlined China White and never sold anything besides watercolored cocaine mirrors. She'd had it with artists. The bastard.

The third and present husband, he was no better. After putting in fifteen loyal years with the Leroux Timber Corporation, the dolt screwed up and got canned. I don't care if you are Parker Leroux's best buddy, you don't tell off the old lady. Just exactly what he'd said to Old Lady Leroux to ruffle her feathers, well, Jeannie didn't remember. But it was something about the Point Danger lighthouse, about the birds that roosted out there. Some kind of pelican. Or was it flamingos? What Richard—that's the third hubby's name—did was this: He went off at the mouth to Old Lady Leroux about how her family's greed was destroying the Olympic Peninsula. He called her a timber whore, and he said some other things, too. She fired him on the spot. Who wouldn't, after all? And then he had the *cojónes* to come over to Mercy's Chowder Bar, interrupt a village council meeting, and break the news to little Jeannie in the presence of her fellow council members. Yeah, right in front of the OB village council. That's Janice Mercy, the mayor, Chick Divers, Ted Tennant, and Buzz Barnes. Well, Buzz was in Hawaii, thank God for little favors. Jeannie would have been mortified if Buzz had heard Richard brag about his big split with Madge Leroux.

So, yeah. Down the tubes went the fat salary and the pension plan, not to mention the employee shareholder stock. That was last December. He hasn't worked since then, except once a day he flies the Ozone Beach helicopter up to Oyster Bay and back. Mail run. Tourist run. But that's no big strain, and the village council pays him peanuts for that small job. She was getting sick and tired of Richard mooning around the condo, behaving very suspiciously, very secretive, as if he were planning some grisly deed, like murdering his own wife. So you can imagine how Jeannie felt when Madge Leroux washed up on the tide with a .38 bullet hole decorating her brain. Yeah, Jeannie seemed to recall Richard owned a .38, but she wouldn't go so far as to swear that in a courtroom. I mean, Dreamboat's not that suicidal.

Anyhow, living with Richard was just plain mortifying. She'd told him a dozen times if she'd told him once that he was a classic case of paranoid schizophrenia—I mean, why else would he have so viciously attacked the hand that fed him and Jeannie?—that he'd ruined his life and hers by blowing the Leroux Timber security blanket, that he was a total failure, and that she was getting sick and tired of him riding her sweet shirttail while he bottomed out from stress syndrome. No, he never took a dime from her, but that's not what she meant by riding her shirttail. She meant something else.

According to Jeannie Winters, Richard was a louse, a creep, shiftless, gutless; in short, a real shell of humanity. She had al-

ready filed for divorce and—need she mention?—Richard would
be heartbroken when she dropped that bombshell next week. Life
without her would be death itself. Well, Jeannie didn't give a
tick's ear. She had enough problems of her own, what with man-
aging the Bell Buoy, keeping wax on the Mercedes, and then too,
serving on the village council. She had responsibilities, damn it,
and no time to coddle a man who couldn't get it up more than
once a week with luck. Besides, Richard had tried to domesticate
her. Can you imagine that in this day and age? Well, Jeannie was
a free spirit, and if Richard couldn't take that, he could go screw
himself once a week. But not before Jeannie got the condo and
the car and the balance of their joint savings account. He owed
her that much, my gawd, after what he'd put her through. Do you
have any idea what it's like being screwed by a failed timber
executive? Anyway, he was obviously going impotent on her.
That, or he was giving it away to that Blake bitch. You know.
Meredith Blake, the blond bimbo who slings chowder over at
Janice Mercy's chowder bar? California broad. Jeannie had noticed lately that Richard and Meredith were spending a lot of time
together. Richard claimed it was all very innocent. Going out at
dawn together to see if they could spot the first flamingos—or
was it pelicans?—arriving. Bull. Richard never got up early for
anything besides nooky. Pelicans, my ass. Well, okay, I'll admit
it's possible. Even Janice Mercy claims she saw some strange
birds watering in a tide pool over by Point Danger. Speaking of
Janice Mercy, did you ever hear what happened to her old man?
This was ten, maybe twelve years ago. It's high. Really high.

He was madly in love with her, see. One day Janice and Mike
Mercy went for a drive up along the Northern Cascades Highway.
It was a beautiful day, one of those perfect autumn afternoons,
crisp and clear, the leaves all crimson and gold. Mike and Janice
were in peak spirits, in the rapture of love. They came to a lookout
point up there at timberline, at the edge of a high cliff. Mike was
driving. Suddenly, Mike hit the accelerator, headed straight for
the cliff, and shouted to Janice, who was in the passenger seat:
"This is as good as it gets, baby!" Then he drove over the cliff.

Janice rolled out just in time. God, can you imagine how warped that psychopath was? No, Janice wasn't wearing her seat belt.

Jeannie didn't tolerate warped personalities. Lately, Richard had evidenced signs of a bent psyche. Any man who'd stoop to sleep with that little slut of a waitress, well, he'd have to be whore-hopping mad. Yeah, he's slipping around all right. She was sure of it. It's been like that since December. Since Madge Leroux—may she rest in pieces—fired him. But things were looking up. She had a damn good divorce attorney who would screw Richard six ways from Sunday if he tried to fight the divorce settlement. Jeannie was going to have a ball taking Richard to the cleaners.

VENUS SWALLOWED the dregs of near-beer and watched Jeannie Winters weave her tangled web around the two drunks. In a few minutes, she came back over to Venus and said, "Another Shirley Temple?"

Venus said, "Why the heck did you marry him?"

Jeannie blinked once, twitched her nose, and snarled, "I don't like you."

"What in the world would you like?"

Jeannie Winters said, "I'd like you to beat it."

She was seriously considering Jeannie's suggestion when Sparks sidled up beside her at the bar and threw a damper on her fun evening.

Sparks crooked his finger at Jeannie. She scowled furiously at him but came over and said, "Same old thing?"

"Yeah." His eyes were riveted on her breasts. "And blow the head real good for me."

The draught delivered, Sparks swilled lustily, then smacked his lips. Watching her through half-shut eyes, he said to Venus, "Heard you been doin' my job."

She didn't say anything.

Sparks continued. "Heard you been trackin' poachers in my forest."

"I was up on Point Danger, on the beach near the jetty. Gunfire came from the woods. From the direction of the ranger shack.

There were footprints. I followed them to where the carcass lay. So yeah, Sparks, I tracked. And I found the bear on the beach near the forest edge.''

He'd been listening half-heartedly. His eyes and the majority of his awareness focused on Jeannie Winters's perilous curves. He definitely belonged to her fan club. Venus said, "I buried the carcass.''

"Hmmm?''

"The bear. I buried it in the sand and put a marker on the grave. We can go back up there now and dig it up.'' Testing his reaction.

Sparks drew back and gawked. "What the hell are you," he said, "a necrophiliac?''

"How long since you've seen a mutilated bear carcass, Sparks?''

But he hadn't heard her. As long as he was within sight of Jeannie, his attention span lasted only a few seconds. Venus waited until he had ordered another draught, then coaxed him away from the bar to a small table that had just been vacated. There was an ashtray on the table, with cigarette butts and ashes in it. She said, "I thought it was illegal to smoke in this burg.''

Sparks folded into the chair opposite her. He drawled, "This is Jeannie Winters's joint.''

"So?''

"So Jeannie's a village council member. She can do a lot of things other folks can't.''

"To shift subjects, what are you going to do about the gut pile?''

Sparks guzzled his draught. Without the visual stimulation of Jeannie, he was rapidly fading. Now his eyelids drooped. He was half asleep. He mumbled, "Gonna investigate.''

Then he guffawed.

She said, "The carcass needs to be autopsied. Sent down to the lab in Ashland.''

"Why?''

"This isn't your everyday poach, Sparks. This bear had its paws chopped off, and its guts ripped out.''

He drawled, "So?"

She stared at him. "You mean, this sort of mutilation has occurred down here before?"

"Sure. All the time."

"What have you done about that, Sparks?"

"What the hell do you want me to do?"

"Report it, for one thing. There's nothing in our files that mentions mutilation of bears in your jurisdiction. Or is that why you won't show me the bear gall file? Because I'd figure out what's going on down here? Is that it?"

Sparks smirked at her over his beer stein. Menacingly he drawled, "Don't tell me how to do my job." With his small chin, he gestured at the door. "If it isn't the Bobbsey twins."

Richard Winters stood at the bar's entrance. It wasn't Jeannie's soon-to-be-ex-husband who caused a stir now, but the man accompanying him, the tall, handsome, cocky-postured Park Leroux. You could hear the silence fall when Park Leroux walked in.

His thick yellow hair, prematurely gray at the temples, fell too youthful over the oblong skull. He had a Frenchman's nose but otherwise reflected the picture of Anglo-Saxon genetic pools. His hands seemed small for his build, the nails manicured and buffed. He had on an elegant black suit. His shirt had French cuffs with topaz studs. Studiously groomed, he had a roving eye, and right now it roved all over Jeannie. When he spoke, Park Leroux's voice thundered through the barroom.

"Richie, babe," he bellowed at Winters, "what did I tell you? The pretty little lady's right here waiting for her husband. Faithful as a nun, aren't you, sweetheart?"

Jeannie cozied up to Park. Park slid an agile, well-practiced arm around Jeannie's waist. Apparently unstartled by their familiarity, Richard watched silently as Park and Jeannie exchanged a long, fairly passionate kiss. He didn't interfere when Park's hands explored Jeannie. Now Park wrapped himself around Jeannie, whispering something into her ear. She giggled. Across the room, Sparks said in awe, "Would you look at that? Her ass fits right in the palm of his hand."

"Isn't that Richard Winters's wife?" Venus asked Sparks.

"Uh-huh."

"Then how come Park is fondling her right in front of her husband?"

Sparks shrugged. "Men like that sorta stuff."

"You think Winters is enjoying this?"

Sparks glanced at Venus. "Whatsa matter, honeybunch? You jealous?"

Jeannie peeled herself off Park, pulled two draughts, and blew the head off one. She handed the bald one to Park, the one with the head to Richard. She reached up, crooked her index finger under Park's chin, and said, "I threw the changes today."

Park smirked. "Oh yeah? What happened?"

Jeannie murmured seductively, "Everything's going topsy-turvy. There will be chaos. But I will be rescued by a sexy hero wearing a boss black suit." She placed a covetous hand on Leroux's derrière, in the vicinity of his wallet pocket.

Leroux played some more with Jeannie. Richard Winters leaned against the bar, watching them, appearing more miserable by the minute. Or was he just disgusted? Venus couldn't read his expression.

Sparks glanced at his watch, said, "Uh-oh," and mumbled some apologies. He had to meet somebody. He's late. He'll see her later. Then maybe they could discuss this poaching fable. Weaving through the barroom crowd, Sparks flicked some change onto the bar. Venus was watching Sparks's back as he exited the bar when Richard Winters appeared beside her. He indicated the chair Sparks had just vacated. "Do you mind?"

She shrugged. No skin off her back. Just don't sit too close.

Richard sighed wearily. "I need to divert my violent thoughts."

They talked about weather, the size of geoducks, anything but Jeannie and Park, anything but painful realities. Once, when he spoke animatedly, she thought he'd touch her hand, but he pulled back just short of it. Time passed and Venus felt a yawn well up in her throat.

"I know," said Richard, reading her mind. "I'm not great company. Have you ever felt humiliated in public?"

She avoided a direct answer. She said, "People can be very cruel." Her words drowned beneath a louder, more bellicose voice. Park Leroux's tongue had finished playing with Jeannie's roving shoulder. Now Leroux's wagger addressed some bar flies who'd heard it before. Natives, with pallid, waxen complexions, that cautious demeanor. Park swayed, his speech slurred, his voice loud, arrogant.

"Oh, I'll get the license all right. Never mind the frigging government. Then I'm going to open a casino out there. A very special casino."

Jeannie piped up, "Hey, that's nifty. A casino in the old lighthouse. That's really high." Her bewitching eyes smoldered. She purred, "Let's be partners, Park. I know the pleasure business."

Park winked at Jeannie, spread his arms generously, full of dreams and insincerity. Could this be a man in mourning?

"Why not?" he roared. "Now here's what I plan to do." He had everyone's attention now. In the far reaches of the bar, die-hard Sonics fans unglued from the NBA playoff on the big television screen to hear what Park Leroux had planned.

Park knew how important he was, how much authority his words carried in this village. He said, "It's your classic phallus, right? I'll have the lighthouse painted flesh tone and I'll do some things in neon that'll scare the pants off every goddamned frigid broad on the Washington coast. Yes sirree, you pissers are gonna wake up out here one morning and you won't believe your frigging eyes. God, what brilliance! I'm a goddamned genius. Bring me another drink, Jeannie doll."

Jeannie placed her hand on Park's arm, then slinked off to draw the beer. Park looked around. The barroom crowd had suddenly backed off. He might have offended them. Across the room someone shouted, "Leroux, your idea of a joke isn't funny."

Park was insulted. "The hell I'm joking," he bellowed. "You just watch, good buddy. You're gonna see what a Stanford education can do. When I get through with that old lighthouse, you'll understand the meaning of the word *genius*. Ha-ha. Neptune's prick.'' Then, tauntingly, ''You bastards gonna go impo...''

Jeannie kissed the word away, slipped the mug of beer into his hand. Swilling lustily, he surveyed the barroom. In the past ten minutes, he'd given these rural bogtrotters enough excitement to last them a lifetime. Park smiled to himself. He'd let them off easy tonight. Except for Richie. He blustered over toward Winters, Jeannie in tow. When he got up close to Richard, he slurred, ''What's the matter, Richie? Cat got your tongue?''

Richard stood up. Quietly, he said, ''I'm going home, Jeannie.''

Through narrowed eyelids, Park studied Richard. He sneered, ''No wonder Jeannie's horny.''

''If you weren't drunk,'' said Richard evenly, ''I'd beat the phony swagger out of you.'' He walked away.

Park bawled, ''Aw, c'mon Richie, babe. Don't be sore. Sure, I'm shitfaced, good buddy. Fella's got a right to get stoned when his mother kicks the bucket.''

Jeannie murmured, ''Let him go. He makes me feel tired.''

From the door, Richard called to Jeannie, ''You coming?''

''Can't.''

Richard said, ''Jim can lock up.''

''Still can't.''

''I think you should come home now, Jeannie.''

''Think whatever you want. I'm not ready to go home.''

He turned and walked out the door. Alone. When he was gone, Jeannie sniggered, ''He's going to Meredith. He's going to cry on her shoulder.''

Park said, ''Meredith's a sweet kid.''

Jeannie snorted. ''Men get tired of that.'' She massaged Park's leg.

Venus was thinking about going back to the Driftwood, soaking in a hot, detoxifying bath, when the yellow slicker walked in.

Tall, broad shouldered, musclebound, he swaggered like a man with a mission. Under the wide-brimmed yellow sou'wester, the navy officer's features were barely discernible, but Venus could make out a thick red mustache, a strong chin. So this must be

Popeye O'Connor. He walked up to the bar, ordered something in a low voice. The bartender poured two fingers of Gilbey's, handed this to the navy man. Popeye tossed some bills on the counter, raised the shot glass, bolted the gin. Turning, he surveyed the crowd. Scoping. Like looking for someone. She couldn't see his eyes, but she thought they focused on her. Then he set down the glass and left. She waited a minute, then followed him out.

Outside, rain fell in heavy sheets. Lighthouse Lane was deserted except for Venus and, farther up the street, the navy man. He moved quickly, walking west toward the beach, the ocean. She followed about half a block behind him. The slicker sped up his pace. She increased hers. He turned left onto Beach Drive, moving faster now, jogging. She broke into a sprint. She was about five yards behind him, beneath a streetlight, when he turned to face her. She was close enough to see the flashing white teeth below the red mustache when he laughed. Apparently something was funny.

She heard the screeching tires, but too late. The sleek midnight black car had spun out of hiding and raced at her full speed. For a split second, muscle paralysis set in, then she threw her body sideways, but not fast enough. The steel monster caught her shoulder. The impact tossed her over the redwood seawall into rain-drenched dunes. Through howling winds, she heard the car's tires scream, speeding away, then nothing but the driving rain.

"WEXLER here."

"Ever been to Ozone Beach, chief?"

"Ah...welcome home, Venus."

"We have a bad connection. Can you hear me?"

"Well enough. Why are you calling at this hour of the... morning?"

"A car just ran me down. I think the driver wanted to kill me."

"Oh? I'm sorry. Look, why don't you phone me in the morning? I mean, you must be all right now, because you're calling me..."

Perspiration dripped down her forehead. Her fever had risen

out there on the beach in the hard, cold sand. The hallucinations hadn't started yet, but yellow darkness visited her brain, her liver ached, and her shoulder throbbed in pain. She rubbed it. No broken bones, just bruises. And the damn malaria fever. She had dragged herself off the sand dunes, through the howling storm, limping, barely able to walk back to the motel before collapsing on the bed. To Wexler, she said, "Olson has me down here at Ozone Beach. Working on a murder, and some pelican harrassment."

"I know. I told him to send you there."

"My expertise isn't pelicans. So why me?"

A heavy sigh. Then Wexler said, "Your expertise is murder. That is why you were sent."

She said, "I track poachers who murder big game."

"Humans are big game, too."

"Apparently." She rotated her shoulder, wincing at the pain.

Wexler said, "Just let me sit up and put the light on."

In the background, she could hear Wexler speaking to someone. Maybe his wife. No, Wexler was a widower. All the same, she heard a female voice, someone in close proximity to the chief. Wexler rustled around, then came back on the line.

"Okay. I'm back."

"Any idea who tried to run over me tonight?"

"Not a clue. Is this some kind of new humor?"

Peeved, she said, "You sent me down here to this burg. Now I need some information no one else seems willing to supply."

"It's the middle of the night out there—"

"Just a couple questions. Then you can go back to whatever you were doing."

"Hold on."

Muffled voices. She tried imagining what sort of woman would share Wexler's bed. She was acutely aware of some infantile emotions, as if Wexler were her father.

Wexler came back and said, "All right. Go on."

"Why wasn't the lighthouse auction publicly announced?"

"What in God's name—"

"When this lighthouse out here was auctioned off by Interior, why didn't notices appear in the newspapers?"

"I thought they had appeared."

"Maybe Olson forgot to place the notices."

Again, Wexler sighed. "Olson is your superior. I don't want to hear this."

"Ever hear of the navy using the lighthouse?"

"How's that fever, Venus? Malaria's bad stuff."

"Does that mean 'negative'?"

Silence. Then, "That all?"

"Did you ever meet Chandrak and Pornchen, the Thai wildlife agents?"

"No. No, I never met them, why?"

"Chandrak and Pornchen and I worked together in Asia. We shared information. I have an idea that while I was out of commission in the hospital in Singapore, maybe Chandrak and Pornchen came to America. Following a lead. I have an idea Chandrak and Pornchen knew more than they shared with me." She shifted on the bed, trying to find a comfortable position for her shoulder. "Also, I was wondering why, just when I'm on the brink of a big score in Asia, you yanked me back to the Pacific Northwest."

"We've already talked about that. You are an employee of the United States government. Not a freelance adventurer."

"This is Sparks's territory down here. Did you know that? Maybe Olson forgot to mention how we divide things up at Pacific Northwest."

"I know how things work out there."

"You ever hear of a military operation called 'Rain Dance'?"

"Say it again?"

"Rain Dance."

"Listen here, Venus. I am in no position to discuss business, or anything, at this hour." He cleared his throat. "Furthermore, if you have questions about your duties and responsibilities, you should be taking them to Olson, who will, I am absolutely certain, convey them to me. We have a chain of command at DOI. Do you understand?"

"Yes, sir."

"Now that I've got you on the line, I should mention that Olson faxed a memo yesterday afternoon. About you. It wasn't complimentary. Do me a favor: Just do what Olson tells you, and try not to ruffle any feathers. I'm not in a position to say anything else right now, but I am asking you to trust me. Can you do that?"

"Yes, sir."

"Oh, I almost forgot. A letter arrived by diplomatic pouch from Singapore. For you. We expressed it out last night. It should be in Seattle before noon today."

"Did you open it?"

"It was addressed to you personally. I do not open other people's private mail."

"Thanks, chief."

"Now will you kindly permit me to go back to sleep?"

She wanted to tell him about the young bear. She had some fantasy that Wexler, being commissioner of Fish and Wildlife, being a fairly compassionate individual, would commiserate, get mad as hell, give her full reign to go after the poachers. But why bother? He obviously wasn't in the mood to handle a mutilated bear.

She rang off.

Ingrid Hëll had visited the room. Venus knew this because fresh chocolate kisses rested on the bed pillows. She popped another malaria pill, wondering briefly if the Hindi physician had slipped her placebos, washed it down with the kisses and sour, lukewarm tap water. She switched out the light. Hallucinations crept up and grabbed her.

THIRTEEN

Point No Point

BELLA SENT the news in with Stephen, who deftly placed a break-fast tray across Venus's lap, careful not to disturb the coverlet, or her bruises. The *Seattle Star* morning edition sat positioned prominently on the tray, and Bella had ticked off in her own broad stroke a small item on the third page of the Metro section. Venus pushed the newspaper aside, fumbled with a cup of hot tea. She vaguely recalled waking at dawn, drenched in a cold sweat, her body bruised and aching, and by sheer determination making the trip back from Ozone Beach. That was all she recalled. After Stephen went away, she swallowed some pills, washed them down with orange juice, and read Bella's ticked-off article about the Asian man with a gun. Her fever lingered around 103. She was laconic but lucid.

There wasn't much to say. Police had responded to a complaint that a man with a handgun was terrorizing placid gardens on Magnolia Bluff's west bank. Upon investigating, police apprehended the culprit in the Magnolia Village Starbucks, and after deft interrogation identified him as a citizen of Singapore. On holiday, he said. The gun business? He'd been shooting crows, he claimed, just for sport. Police gave his name as Lok Pan. They turned Lok Pan over to immigration authorities, and that was the end of that.

Lok Pan. Wasn't that the pirate Lok Toy's brother? Now it all made sense. Except the part about the black car in Ozone Beach. Who else, besides Lok Toy's gang, wanted her iced?

In the margin beside the article, Bella had scrawled, "What did I tell you? He was shooting crows."

Venus stared at Bella's strident cursive, then leafed through the mail piled on the bedside table. She uncovered the letter Wexler had forwarded, the one from Singapore via diplomatic pouch. On the blue onionskin envelope, Reuben's handwriting. She held the thin letter limply, let the pain subside, the anger quell. For three years she'd fantasized their friendship as a prelude to steamy romance. Khm, the beautiful Singaporean, could have any man in the world. Why Reuben? Venus knew why. Glumly, she ripped open the envelope.

Venus,

A quick note to inform you that Lok Toy's brother, Lok Pan, has gone to America. He might be looking for you. I know Lok Toy was behind that incident at Raffles, and his brother Pan could have been the gunman—I've heard Lok Pan's the family's assassin, and that he's something of a sharpshooter. Being a mere businessman I may not fully grasp the importance of Lok Toy in relation to your work. But I thought you needed to know about the brother.

Still no news of Chandrak and Pornchen, nothing has appeared in the newspapers here. Probably the Thai government wants to find them, so if they are with you, please tell them to contact their Bangkok office and so put a stop to all this speculation.

Khm and I are being honored at a reception on 15 May. We hope you will attend. Three in the afternoon, at Raffles, in the garden. Please join us, Venus.

All our affection, Reuben.

All our affection. Twisting the dagger in her heart.

Stephen swooped in as she buttered the last crumpet. "Your mother," he chirped brightly, "asked me to inform you that she has gone to the hairdresser."

"I thought today was tennis."

Stephen shook his head solemnly. "That was yesterday. Today is the quick comb-out."

"Stephen, what day is this?"

"Wednesday. You've been very ill."

She grabbed the newspaper. Stephen had it right. More than twenty-four hours had passed since the night at the Driftwood Inn. Tuesday had been totally lost and, according to the clock at her bedside, Wednesday morning had almost disappeared. Stephen said, "Time for a temp, miss."

She placed a thermometer strip in her mouth and thought about a few things. A minute later, she removed the strip, read it. Holding at 103. She dragged out of bed, shivered under a hot shower, dressed, and rode the Harley downtown.

In the forensic annex lab, Claudia hunched over a microscope. Dark stains, like old blood, streaked her lab coat. Her thick bobbed hair veiled her face as her deft hands smeared green slime on a glass slide. She placed the slide under a microscope, peered at her work. Venus stood beside Claudia, waiting until she had finished. When Claudia saw her, she jumped skittishly. "I didn't hear you come in."

Venus said, "I thought you were in Ashland."

Claudia smiled. "We got back early this morning. I brought the critical stuff back with me. Wait till you see this." She pointed at the microscope.

Venus peered through the lens. "It's pretty," she said. "But I don't get it."

"Well then, listen to this," said Claudia. She held up a sheet of paper like the Magna Carta. Knowing Venus would not comprehend lab jargon, she paraphrased.

"*U. americanus,*" she read, "identification number UA-100298, expired approximately eighteen hours before remains were analyzed. Examination of the cementum annuli on the remaining premolars indicate a male individual about four years old, in excellent health, disease free, thin from winter hibernation. Condition of the carcass indicates death due to shotgun wound to the heart. Coincidental with death, the individual was disemboweled, its gall bladder torn out and sex organs severed. Following expiration, all paws were severed. Two premolar teeth were missing from the jaws." Claudia paused to brush her gray-streaked blond hair from her face. She was a tall woman, big-boned Norwegian, with a little Italian husband for whom she'd changed her name from Olofson to Paganelli. Claudia said, "Now here comes the interesting part. Contents of the stomach," she recited, "included a half liter of sapwood, salal bark and leaves, and one liter of refined sugar in a doughy base."

Venus said, "Jelly rolls."

Claudia looked up. "Oh dear," she remarked brusquely, then continued. "We analyzed the doughy contents, which had been consumed shortly before death. Our analysis revealed traces of heroin."

Claudia folded the paper in half, handed it to Venus. "This creature was drugged," she said emphatically. "I later confirmed this with a test we do on the eyeballs. Heroin had been cooked into the doughy base. Somehow the bear happened across this spiked confection."

"Definitely jelly rolls."

"Sure," she said, "that makes sense."

Venus nodded. "A poacher's favorite bait. Only, this time laced with heroin. How would heroin affect a bear?"

Claudia shrugged. "Same as humans, I guess. Mind-altering. Hypnotic. Now remember, Venus, as far as I'm concerned, I've never seen this report. I understand you want this information kept between us for now, but sooner or later, it'll have to come out. You're responsible for that part."

"I understand. Thanks for going down there, Claudia."

Claudia waved a hand in the air, dismissing gratitude. "Don't even thank me. I wanted nothing to do with this subterfuge. I only did it because I trust your judgment. Anyway, you should thank Dave. He flew the chopper, and he's the one who found the gut pile. That was one helluva storm down there. We took Marla along too. She almost popped her kid over Point No Point."

"Marla's preggo?"

"Eight months gone. Actually on maternity leave, which is why you don't see her around lately. But we took her along. We needed one more person we could really depend on, and she wanted to go. By the way, we couldn't keep our trip from Olson and Sparks, obviously. But neither of them have seen these results. They haven't even asked me for the results. I think they're oblivious. So now the ball's in your park. Far as I'm concerned, this jelly roll analysis doesn't exist. Oh, and by the way, those two bullets you sent me for analysis—they're identical. They were fired from the same gun. So whoever shot at you over in Singapore apparently also shot up your mother's dining room window. Poor Lady Bella. That dining room must be a mess.'' She walked away.

Olson and Sparks were sprawled in chairs near the coffee station. Sparks sipped from a thick mug and Olson scanned the *Seattle Star's* sports section. The Sonics had won the NBA title. Olson would be unbearable. When he saw Venus, he put down the newspaper, folded his arms across his wide chest. He watched her pour coffee, stir in the sweetener. Sarcastically, he said, ''Nice work, Venus.''

She stared at him.

He growled, ''You frigging blew it down there.''

Sparks gloated. When he smiled, a tic went haywire near his mouth. He wiped his face and the tic and the smile disappeared. To Olson she said, ''Happy third day of spring.''

''Go to hell.''

Sparks could hardly contain his delight. Unfolding, he went over to the window and smirked out at Elliott Bay. You could actually see the harbor and the ships this morning. No fog, only some thin drizzle.

''Olson,'' she said carefully, ''the poaching situation down there is serious. We need to send in the team. Sparks and myself, Dottie, Eric, and Dave. We need to sniff out the hounds, the firearms, find the headquarters. We'll have to move soon, there's no time to be covert about this. They already know we're on to them. And too, someone needs to uncover their fence. My bet is Liu's Apothecary over on Maynard Avenue. Then we'll have to pull a raid down there. Let them think it's just a few of us, but we'll bring in the whole squad for this one. We'll score this time.

We'll crack the big network. I can feel it in my bones."

Olson stared at her. Sparks turned from the window and gaped. Olson said, "How's the fever?" Gently.

"Not bad. Why?"

"Why didn't you just stay in bed a few more days?"

"Why haven't you and Sparks reported the poaches down there?"

"We talked about that before." His eyes darted toward Sparks, then back to her. "It's a closed subject."

"Hey, guess what? Someone tried to run over me down in Sogtown. Maybe trying to kill me. Doesn't that bother you guys?"

Olson rose slowly from the chair. Because of his extra weight, he required more time to balance himself. He lumbered toward her. His hand reached out, felt her forehead. "Go on, honey," he whispered softly. "Go home to bed. You have one heck of a fever."

He turned then and rumbled down the corridor toward his office. She followed him, feeling Sparks's hostile glare on her back. Olson eased down into his chair, stared out the big windows. She leaned against the door frame. On his desk, the box of Frangos stood empty. After a while Olson said: "Wexler called. He wants the cougar gall report on his desk tomorrow. That means you wrap it up today and fax it. That is, if you're not going to follow my advice about going home to bed. I can always finish up that report for you."

"Give me one good reason why we're covering up this poaching incident."

"I don't know what you're talking about."

"Maybe you're afraid someone will find out you've been hiding years of illegal activity down there."

"I'm not afraid of anything."

"Then what's gotten into you?"

He stewed. Finally he said, "I've decided to take you off the investigation down there. I want Sparks to cover it from here on.

And maybe you should stop confusing innocent kills with illegal activity."

"I thought I knew you pretty well, Olson. Maybe I was wrong."

"Maybe. Now go on. I have some things to do."

She reached into her pocket, felt the forensic report. She almost took it out then to show Olson. Drops of sweat formed on her brow. She wiped them off. Her judgment suffered from the fever. Too hasty. She wouldn't show him the report just yet. She wouldn't mention the Thai agents yet. Be cautious. Or was that paranoid? She went over to the big picture windows, blocked Olson's harbor view. His eyes looked fairly clear this morning, as if he'd passed a sober night. But the pupils were very small. Maybe the light from the windows, or maybe he was on some drug. She didn't like the way his eyes looked at her. She said, "Spell it out for me. The part about Ozone Beach politics that I'm supposed to not understand."

"I told you, that subject is closed. So is the subject of Mrs. Leroux. So is the subject of pelicans. Your investigation is closed. Now, you are practically incoherent this morning. And I have things to do. Go home."

She went out, leaving him with his things to do. At the computer terminals, she pulled up the cougar gall report, finished it. Half an hour later, she faxed it to Wexler's office. She went out for a *latte*, brought it back, drank it. She paced a little. She saw Sparks sidle out of Olson's office, carrying a file folder under his arm. She went back to Olson's office. The door was shut. She knocked first, then opened the door, walked in, and said to the boss, "I'd like to go back down there."

"Negative." He shuffled some papers.

"It's important."

"Sparks is on top of things."

"The hell he is."

"Anyway, it is, as you pointed out in the first place, his territory." He glanced up at her, grinned thinly.

She said, "I'm going back down there."

As she turned to go, he said quietly, "Either you go home and sweat out that fever, or you stay here in the office and earn your salary. If you go back to Ozone Beach, you will find a severance check in your mother's mailbox."

Dottie had desk duty. On her desk lay a romance novel splayed open facedown. Beside that, for effect, a wildlife newsletter. Dottie once said that her romance novels worked as meditations. She read them like litanies or repetitive prayers to achieve a state of relaxation. As she passed Dottie's desk, Venus said, "Where's Dave today?"

"Didn't you hear? He landed a supporting-actor gig in some big-budget environmentally correct film. He's on the set today, don't you know."

Dottie stared at Venus. "You don't look so healthy."

The elevator door opened. Venus stepped inside. The doors closed. Suddenly she changed her mind. She wasn't ready to give up on Olson. The elevator had started its downward journey. She'd have to ride it out.

Olson had a passive-aggressive personality. He knew that by doing absolutely nothing he could drive people mad. He'd been practicing this strategy for several years now. He was very good at it.

Olson's roots were Scandinavian, ya sure, you betcha. The angst and the barriers were born the day his wife and daughter got wiped out in a head-on collision on one of those reversible Interstate 5 lanes. Two Ballard women driving to a Bellevue garage sale. Olson had never fully recovered. It colored his whole personality and added eighty pounds to his frame. He went around with this barrier up and this large chip on his shoulder.

When the elevator returned to the forty-third floor, she stepped out into the reception room. Dottie looked up from the romance novel and made a face. Venus didn't bother knocking on Olson's door. Turning the knob, she walked in. He looked up suddenly, startled, one of his fat hands half-immersed in a fresh carton of Frango Mints. Behind a sheepish smile, he swallowed something.

Venus said, "Call Wexler."

"I told you, I have already spoken with him."

"Did you tell him about the gut pile?"

Olson sighed tiredly. "No, I did not. Wexler doesn't want to hear every detail. We can't waste his time like that."

She faced him. "Did you read my report?"

"I did. All one and a half pages."

"The part about Jack O'Connor?"

"I did."

"What do you think about that, Olson?"

"I think it is totally irrelevant."

"O'Connor left a message here for you to phone him. Did you do that?"

Silence. Then, "I spoke with O'Connor, yes."

"What did he want?"

"He wanted us to stay out of Navy business."

"Were we in it?"

"O'Connor thought so. I didn't press the matter. By the time I spoke with him, you were already out of Ozone Beach. So I didn't press O'Connor."

She said, "Maybe you already knew what he's doing down there."

Olson opened his mouth but no words came out. She hazarded, "Maybe Wexler told you what the navy's doing in Ozone Beach."

Olson said, "No. No, he didn't."

She pressed on. Sooner or later she might strike the right chord. "Maybe the navy has pulled some strings in Washington, DC. Cutting Interior out of the picture. Because our investigation into the pelican sanctuary and Mrs. Leroux's murder might be interfering with some secret military project. A project called Rain Dance."

Olson seemed interested now. He said, "Go on."

"Maybe," she continued, "Mrs. Leroux discovered what is going on out at the lighthouse. She might have learned about this secret project called Rain Dance. Since she owned the lighthouse,

she might have been slightly ticked off that Navy was using it
without her permission. And maybe she complained about that to
someone. Maybe that's why she was murdered. She was interfering with a secret military project. And too, maybe there is no
such group as the Pelican Patrol. That could have been invented
to shift blame for her murder, to make it look like an environmentalist group killed her.''

Olson rubbed his jaw as if someone had just cracked him hard
there. He thought over what she had just said. After a while, he
replied, ''That's got to be fiction.''

''If it's fiction,'' she challenged him, ''then call Wexler. Tell
him what I just said. Ask him to refute it. Ask Wexler to say that
he's never been contacted by Navy, that he's never heard of a
project called Rain Dance. Ask Wexler to tell me it's fiction.''

Olson shook his head. ''You know I can't do that.''

She shrugged. ''Then I'm going back down there.''

Olson barked, ''Either you go home—''

''I know.'' The door shut smoothly behind her, on air springs.

Sparks had left a present at her desk. She carried the disk to
the computer terminals, read the note Sparks had scribbled:
''Here's your precious bear gall report. Put in 'gut pile' and it'll
come heavin' up. Ha-ha.''

Sparks wasn't always so hostile. But now she had invaded his
private domain. He seemed determined to drive her out.

The bear gall report came up immediately. But something was
dreadfully wrong. She stared. It couldn't be true. The report, au-
thored by Sparks, checked by Olson, indicated that during the
past three years, poaching *U. americanus* in Sparks's territory had
virtually ceased. Outdated statistical data, data she recognized
from six or seven years ago, purported to support the claim. She
stored the useless, fraudulent material. An eerie sense of aban-
donment gnawed at her. Where was Dave when she needed him?

Dottie came over with a fax. She read it in the elevator, on the way down, her worst fears now confirmed. Thailand's commissioner of Wildlife regretted to inform Venus that her colleagues, Chandrak and Pornchen, had disappeared while on assignment in the United States, where they had been tracking leads in the Lok Toy case. They were last heard from in a place called Ozone Beach, Washington. Bangkok suspected foul play.

FOURTEEN

Zen

THE OLD CHINESE MAN who owned Liu's Apothecary in Seattle's Chinatown was as coy as they come. Liu Ping had a bald pate, a long white goatee, and wore small round spectacles tinted dark green. He came from Chengdu on the last wave before Deng's final purge. In Chengdu, Liu had proled in a sweatshop. Now, in America, Liu owned his own small shop, and he prospered trading in Asian pharmaceuticals.

In Asian immigrant communities like Seattle's International District, gall from a four-year-old bear brought around fourteen hundred dollars per powdered ounce, twelve thousand dollars per kilo for fresh gall. More bears are slaughtered for their galls than for their hides, but paws and sex organs are valuable too. Still, gall is the poacher's gold, and because a poacher will take four-year-olds before they've had a chance to mate, bear populations have dropped drastically. Often a poacher secretly substitutes cow or sheep gall, tries to pawn it off as bear gall. But brokers who buy gall know their product, and as a double check, they usually require the poacher to produce another part of the bear, like a tooth, along with the gall, as proof the gall is genuine bear. Selling fake bear gall can get a poacher killed, if a fence catches him in the act. Rumor was that Liu Ping, the smartest gall broker around, had caught a couple poachers trying to sell him sheep gall. The poachers were never heard from again, but reliable sources told how their private organs had been displayed in Liu's back room. Liu Ping had a reputation for swift and horrible revenge.

The shop felt close, crowded, and smelled of eucalyptus and pungent lotus incense. One corner housed a small Buddhist shrine. Below the shrine, a jade green silk pillow supported a very small mongrel dog, hairless, bone white, with a wrinkled face and huge round black eyes. The dog was called Zen, and Liu Ping always told people that Zen was over two hundred years old. They didn't know if he meant human years or dog years, and he never offered to clarify that statistic. He might have stretched the truth, the way people do with thousand-year-old eggs. On this particular afternoon, when Venus entered Liu's Apothecary, Zen sat upright on the jade pillow, an ancient Chinese manuscript propped up before him, his muzzle in it like he was studying the text.

Liu Ping stood behind the counter, waiting on customers, wearing his usual pasted-on smile. He saw Venus enter the shop. He knew most of the Fish and Wildlife agents by sight, if not by name. He hadn't seen this one in a few years now. It must have been three years since she'd darkened his door. It was her, all right. She hadn't changed. Venus Diamond was her name. She always brought trouble. He pretended not to notice her.

Venus waited for the last customer to leave, then went up, took an object from her pocket, placed it on the counter. Liu Ping glanced down at the bear's premolar tooth. With that same pasty smile, he looked at Venus, then glanced over at the dog. Zen watched him now, waiting to see what would happen next. Venus said, "Have you seen one of these lately, Liu Ping?"

He shook his head slowly.

Zen growled. The old man hissed at the dog. Zen stuck his nose back in the manuscript.

"Liu Ping," Venus said, "according to Fish and Wildlife records, this is the third time this year one of our agents has come in here and politely asked you a question. And this is the third time you have lied. Now, I happen to know that you have sold *xiong dan* and paws from this shop. We have evidence to prove that. Do you recall the conditions of your probation?"

He nodded once.

"Then please be more cooperative."

An insincere bow. Zen growled, stood up, stretched, and came over to the counter. He barked sharply at his master, communicating in their secret lingo.

Venus said, "What if I can prove you had a woman killed?"

Liu Ping said, "Why would I kill a woman?"

"Maybe she was innocently trespassing on your trade. On your sources. So you had her killed."

While he thought this over, Venus leaned down to pet the dog. Zen growled low in his throat. Liu Ping said, "He does not like to be touched. It offends him."

She withdrew her hand and Zen relaxed. By then, Liu Ping had finished thinking things over. He leaned across the counter and whispered, "Listen. I didn't kill her. I know she got killed. But I didn't kill her. She was in the wrong place, see? She didn't belong out there. That's dangerous, see? I heard she was rich lady, huh? That doesn't stop her being stupid. She was in the wrong place. But I didn't kill her."

He grasped the counter and leaned back, wearing a satisfied smile.

"Who killed the old lady, Liu Ping?"

He shrugged. He didn't know.

"Come on, Liu Ping. I don't want to arrest you today. But I will unless you help me out."

"What charge?" Liu Ping frowned suspiciously.

"I'll think of one, believe me. Unless you help me."

"Like how?"

"Name your source."

"I already told you. Three years ago I told you."

"You lied that time. This time I want the truth."

"I don't trade in *xiong dan* anymore."

"You're a lousy liar, Liu Ping," she growled. Zen barked sharply and nipped at her ankles. She wanted to shake the old man but he was frail, he might break, and he possessed a wealth of information. She needed him and he knew it.

After a while, Liu Ping said, "You meet me later on. Not here in Chinatown, see? You meet me somewhere else. Maybe then I can help you."

"Where?"

"Say we meet at Pike Place Market. Under the neon clock. No, let's say the fish. Under the neon fish. Tonight. Nine o'clock."

He sounded almost sincere. "Okay," she said finally. "You better be there, Liu Ping."

"Don't worry."

"And don't bring any of Lok Toy's friends along."

Liu Ping opened his mouth slightly, then a small grin curved over his broad teeth. "Who is...Lok Toy?" he asked demurely.

She sighed. "Forget it. I'm so sick of coy, Liu Ping."

Zen licked her ankle. She winked at him. This time he didn't growl. To Liu Ping, she said, "Slick dog."

Then she left.

FIFTEEN

By-The-Wind-Sailors

RICHARD WINTERS deftly steered the Bell Jet Ranger above the coastline. In the passenger seat, Venus listened to his voice through a headset. Delayed one day because of foul weather, Winters had delivered Madge Leroux's remains to Interior this afternoon, landing the Jet Ranger on the roof pad of the Bumbershoot. Interior would release the remains to the funeral home. Venus had brought the Harley to the roof in the freight elevator, hitched a ride back down the coast with Winters. Now as she sat beside him, she wondered at the wisdom of this timesaving measure. In the chopper's cabin, Winters's human *feng shui* sizzled.

"All this shoreline," said Winters, "was fouled ten years ago when oil spilled from a sinking vessel. Literally thousands of sea birds, otters, and other marine life died. The populations and the beaches are slowly recovering, but it used to be twice as beautiful out here, if you can believe that."

She nodded, spoke into the headset, "I remember. Still, it's magnificent."

"The other day," said Winters, "a huge log rolled up on this shore, covered with By-the-Wind-Sailors. They're electric blue coelenterates, sticky jellyfish with clear, gelatinous sail flaps they use for tacking in the wind. They occasionally wash up along the coast attached to driftwood. They beach and die—the opposite of drowning."

He glanced over at her, noted her reaction to his commentary. She appeared bemused, nothing more. Winters went on.

"By-the-Winds have gradually migrated up the West Coast. Like the brown pelican. To escape pollution. Indian legend says By-the-Wind-Sailors are sacred messengers of Tyee Sahalee, the

Great Chief Up Above. You mustn't eat them till after they've died. Then they transform into sacred food. It's said that when you consume the blue medusa, in that communion, Tyee Sahalee enters your soul. Black bears are particularly drawn to By-the-Wind-Sailors." He pointed down at the beach and swung the chopper slowly through a wide arc. "Look."

On the shoreline, a family of black bears had surrounded a great log that had washed ashore. With typical curiosity, they pawed at the log, plucking off something, tasting it. Winters said, "Holy communion."

Winters kept the chopper high, to spare the bears the startling noise of whirring blades. Now finished dining, the bears moved single file along the tideline. A pair of twin cubs splashed in the surf, delirious with joy. The tide ebbed and flowed. The mother bear kept close watch on her offspring. An older sibling, about three or four years old, instructed the cubs by example on the ways of the tide. Then gently, he nudged one cub farther out into the surf. Froth rolled over the cub's back and it lurched in surprise. Another nudge, now the cub fell fully prone into the waves. Soon it would learn to swim, and swat salmon.

Winters said, "It's sort of a tradition with the bears around here to bring their newborn to this beach for swimming lessons. But this family, I know it from last year. And now I see they're missing a member. Might have been the four-year-old you and Meredith found."

Venus nodded. The headset bothered her. She pulled it off. The chopper blades nearly drowned Winters's voice, she could barely hear him, had to lip read. Richard veered the chopper to the right, headed north over the coastline, then slightly inland. They hovered above the national park now, on its border, above a body of deep scarlet water.

"Mrs. Bobbs's cranberry bog," Winters shouted. "Another favorite hangout for bears. They love her cranberries. Mrs. Bobbs hates the bears. She yells at them."

Minutes later, the Jet Ranger drifted smoothly onto the pad at Ozone Beach airfield. Winters brought it down with precision on the eastern edge of the field. Nearby, through a thin fog mist, the rotating light atop Divers' Spa blinked. Venus could barely discern the nautical outlines of the spa's decks. A fog had risen in the last half hour, a fickle mist renowned along this beach; it might grow thicker, settle in for days, or it might burn off by mid-afternoon. It all depended on the winds from the sea. It was just eleven A.M., too early to pass judgment on the fog.

She followed Winters into the hangar, a corrugated-steel Quonset hut. Maybe war surplus. Maybe from the Satan war. Winters's office occupied a small space in the front. It felt cold and damp in here, like outside. She could see her breath.

There was a desk with a laptop computer on it. Beside that, a telephone and chaotic piles of paperwork. There was a chair that swiveled, a coffee brewer, a couple overstuffed file cabinets, and a small window with an ocean view. Below the window ledge, a low table supported a small Buddhist shrine, a lacquered redwood frame holding a white porcelain Buddha. The figurine depicted the Indian Buddha, a youthful Siddartha Gautama. Seated in lotus position, Siddartha's hands rested in his lap holding a small spherical object representing fruit, or the pit of fruit, or the kernel of Enlightenment. She touched the figurine, felt the contours. An antique, judging from the finely cracked finish. Foshan clay, apparently a Chinese rendition of the Indian Buddha. The figurine's body had been glazed but the hands, the feet, and the head left as natural clay, a T'ang Dynasty.

Before the Buddha stood a dish containing a fresh-fruit offering. Japanese mandarin oranges, the thin tissue paper wrappings still on.

The only other thing in the hangar building was a tandem ultralight with a thirty-foot wingspan and bright green dragonfly wings. Venus walked around it. She said, "Nice rig."

"I'll take you up sometime."

He seemed preoccupied, anxious. He sat on the desktop making phone calls. She went over and pretended to study the ultralight, its open framework fuselage. Ultralights don't have cockpits, just seats, little engines for take off, and steering gear. This clever rendition had two seats. An ultralight built for two. And it had pontoons.

She heard Winters leave a message for Jeannie on a tape machine. He wanted to meet with her as soon as possible. He phoned someone else, she couldn't tell who, to report that he had returned from Seattle via Oyster Bay carrying the daily mail and one passenger with her Harley. He put the phone down, brewed some java, strong and thick, like boat coffee, where you boil the grounds. Not for sissies. While they drank it, he leaned against the desk, half sitting, and blew the steam off his coffee mug toward her. Bluntly, she said, "You think Park murdered his mother?"

He laughed. "Park? Naw. He was afraid of her. He adored Madge, but she terrified him."

She said, "Some mothers are like that."

"Madge was not your typical mother."

"What's a typical mother like?"

"Motherly. You know."

She said no, she didn't, and the subject was dropped.

Venus said, "What about the Pelican Patrol?"

Winters shook his head. "No such group. Doesn't exist." He grinned jovially. "Except in somebody's fertile imagination."

"Why do you say that?"

Winters shrugged. "It's a well-known fact that I'm the most vocal environmentalist in Ozone Beach, particularly when it comes to the pelican sanctuary. I was behind the drive to have the lighthouse declared a wildlife sanctuary, so if there were such a group as the Pelican Patrol, I imagine they would have made contact with me. And there has been no such contact, so I can only presume they don't exist."

"That when you converted?"

"When the pelicans showed up?" He smiled sheepishly. "Yeah, that's right. Before that, like I told you, I was your typical anti-environmentalist timber exec. A real ass, too. By the age of twenty-five, I'd turned into a blustery old man with no greater goal in life than to sell the most timber to the highest bidder for the greatest profit and drink myself under the dinner table every night. But that's another story.... You wouldn't believe how much of these forests out here I've personally shipped over to Japan.

And all the time, I considered these environmentalists a bunch of ex-hippie radicals who'd failed to adapt to mainstream America, who were stuck in an era. My knowledge of conservation practices, I figured, had to be superior to theirs. I had a Stanford education, I worked for Leroux, and I knew it all.''

''Who turned you around?''

He smiled grimly. ''A lady who used to live here. She took off to Montana, I heard, with a cowboy from back there. She was a great lady, and I wish we were still in touch. Her name's Carolyn Divers. She was the first environmentalist I could get close to. She was bright, professional, very intellectual, and she had a heart of gold. She opened my eyes. She got me interested in brown pelicans. That led to understanding air pollution, which led to clear-cutting and the lumber mills and how they contribute to the general imbalance. And here I was, near the top of the chain, six months away from being named to Leroux's board of directors. I had a lot of power over these forests out here. Then Carolyn got to me, and my whole life went topsy-turvy.''

He sipped coffee. She wondered if Jeannie had heard this speech before. She wondered if the speech was sincere. She was wondering what Richard and Jeannie saw in each other when he said, ''There's something you ought to know. It's been on my mind the past few days, since we met up at the Leroux house. I'm physically very attracted to you, and in other ways, too. It bothers me. I can't recall feeling like this before. About anyone, not even Jeannie. That's the truth. And you're totally different than Jeannie. But I feel a chemistry. I don't know why. You're not my type, and I'm probably not your type. And legally I'm still married. But I wanted you to know.''

''Why?''

''So you won't misunderstand or misinterpret my coolness toward you, my attempt to honor your personal space.''

She said, ''You know, Richard, you're one heck of a nice guy.''

''Thanks. I try.'' He grinned uncomfortably.

''I mean, too nice. People who are too nice are usually trying to hide something.''

He shrugged and showed her an empty palm. He couldn't help being a Goody Two-shoes when it came to lust. She said, "Let's drop the mannerisms and talk business instead."

"What business?"

"I want you to fly me out to the sanctuary on the island."

He seemed amazed. "To the lighthouse?"

She nodded.

He shook his head. "No way."

She said, "Afraid of a manitou?"

"Forget manitous. It's the weather. Too dangerous. You can't take an ultralight out with these winds. Maybe in a few weeks, when the winds die down. Not before."

"I mean in the chopper."

"Chopper's not for hire. It belongs to the Village of Ozone Beach. The village council only permits its use as a transport between here and Oyster Bay. For mail. Oh, and emergencies, like today. And tourists. They'd croak if I hired out with it."

"So we'll wait till after dark. When they won't notice. Go then."

"Are you crazy? Do you realize what would happen if a storm hit and we took a dive? We'd go down out there in the pitch dark. Forget rescue. We'd go down in that ocean and if the impact didn't kill us, within twenty minutes we'd be Eskimo Pies. I don't take risks like that. If I did, I wouldn't be alive today. Anyway, why do you want to go out there?"

"I'd like to see the sanctuary."

"Really?" He didn't believe her. "At night?"

She shrugged.

Winters eyed her suspiciously. "Wildlife has a chopper. Why don't you take Wildlife's chopper?"

She explained about her rift with Olson. Olson would never authorize her use of Wildlife's chopper. That's why she hadn't even bothered to ask. Winters said, "Sounds like your days at DOI are numbered." He added, "Olson reminds me of Madge Leroux. She had that hard-boiled edge to her, too. But underneath, she was a very nice lady."

He walked over to where she leaned against the windowsill.

He plucked a mandarin from the Buddha fruit offering, removed the thin tissue wrap. He turned it over in his hand, his fingers exploring the skin's bright puckered texture. She wondered how it felt to be touched by his fingers. He half sat on the edge of the desk, peeled the mandarin and handed her some thin sections. He said, "Why did you hitch a ride back here with me? You could have come back by the highway."

"I was in a hurry. When I heard you'd brought Mrs. Leroux's body to DOI, I jumped at the chance. I heard you'd landed on our roof pad, so I just hustled up there in the freight elevator. I was in a hurry."

"In a hurry to come back here? Why, for God's sake?"

"Because of a hunch."

"Oh yeah? About what?"

"Her murder."

He nodded thoughtfully. He walked over to the Buddha shrine, stood staring at Siddartha Gautama. She said, "Nice Buddha."

"Burmese."

"I'd say it's Chinese. Where'd you find it?"

"Gift."

"Oh yeah? From Jeannie?"

"No. Not Jeannie."

"I think it's Chinese. It's Foshan clay."

"No, I'm positive it's Burmese. Fourteenth-century Burmese."

"I think you're off by several centuries and several thousand miles. It was made in southern China, in a town called Foshan."

He shook his head firmly. "It's Burmese."

Silence. Light from the window revealed deep lines across Winters's forehead that she hadn't noticed before. When he was tired, mentally tired like now, his eyes lost their mischievous glint. He seemed emotionally exhausted.

She said, "I'm sorry."

He shrugged. "For what? Difference of opinion, that's all."

"I mean, about Jeannie."

"I don't want to talk about her."

"Suits me." Venus bit her lip. She said, "You a hunter?"

He shook his head. "Used to hunt, years ago. I gave it up. Too primitive for my tastes, killing animals. Like I said, I've changed.''

"Ever hunt bear? I mean, back when you hunted."

"Never killed one, if that's what you mean."

"The bear Meredith and I found was killed up near the ranger station in the park."

"Where exactly?"

"About half a mile downhill from the shack. Where the beach meets the forest at the driftwood line. The way you spoke about the bear family, about missing a member, I figured you must be interested in bears."

Winters nodded. "Sure, like everyone else around here, I keep my eye on them, I know their family groups. It's a part of life along this coast. They're our neighbors."

Venus said, "Ever hear of *xiong dan?*"

He nodded. "Sure, I know about bear gall, bear paw soup and all that. I'm a guy, remember?"

She said, "Does Park hunt bear?"

Winters laughed. "Park maybe has to shoot some bear when they get into his timber stands. But he'd never mutilate them. Hasn't got the stomach for it, or the motivation, for that matter. He doesn't exactly need the money. And by the way, Park did not kill his mother, if that's what you're thinking."

"How sure are you?"

"Let's say ninety-five percent. That good enough?"

"No."

"Ninety-seven, then."

"Why the confidence?"

"Because I know Park pretty well. And because I know where Park was on the night Mrs. Leroux disappeared."

"Where?"

"At my place," he said bitterly. "In my bed, with Jeannie."

After a while, she said, "Were you home?"

He shook his head. "I'm too nice a guy. I knew they had a thing for each other. I've seen it coming over the past few months, maybe longer. Park always made light of it, claimed it was an innocent flirtation. Jeannie flat out denied it. But I knew. On some level, I knew. Then the night Park's mother took that walk in the storm, I came home, drove up to my house and there was Park's town car in my driveway. The driver sitting inside the car, waiting, watching some tabloid TV show. Can you imagine how blatant that was? That was Jeannie's way of saying it's over between us. I did the decent thing. Drove away. I didn't go home that night.''

"Where'd you go?"

He looked miserable now. "Came here. I brought Meredith with me. Got pretty drunk, blissed out. Mer put up with my obnoxious behavior and then had the grace to cover me up with her raincoat before she left." He shook his head as if trying to fix a loose connection. "Park says it's all over with Jeannie. He's promised to lay off at least until Jeannie and I resolve things."

"Think you will?"

"What?"

"Work out your problems with Jeannie."

He stared at the ultralight. "That's not what I meant by resolve," he said finally. "I'm happy to say that Jeannie and I are history."

INGRID HËLL didn't flinch when Venus registered the second time. The Nordic blonde handed over the key to Room 111, as if Venus had never checked out. Venus went into her room, picked up the telephone, put a call through to Bella. Stephen answered. Bella was at Woofy Benson's for tea. Venus left a message, then put the receiver down. She paced for about ten minutes before the phone rang. These little rural information networks were amazing. It was Jeannie Winters.

"I want to see you," she snapped.

"What's the matter? Sink your claws into something you can't handle?"

"Shut up. I'm at the Bell Buoy. Be here in fifteen minutes. And if you're smart, you'll bring your piece."

Jeannie hung up. It was 4:06 p.m.

Venus waited five minutes, staring out the big picture windows. The fog had lifted, and beyond the ocean a horizon was visible.

Some thunderheads had formed in the long black clouds above the lighthouse. Another storm moving in. She loaded her gun and went out. She walked into the Bell Buoy at 4:20 p.m., one minute early.

Jeannie stood behind the bar, brushing a beehive hairdo, studying herself in the mirrored wall. Her lowcut black spandex bodysuit hugged its terrain like a Porsche. When she saw Venus's reflection she whirled around and said:

"I want you to help my husband."

"Help him what? Escape from you?"

Jeannie flung the hairbrush into a drawer, slammed it shut. She glared at Venus and spit, "This is no time for sarcasm. You need to prove Richard did not murder Mrs. Leroux."

"Who accused him?"

She consulted a flashy pendant watch hanging from a hefty gold chain that nestled between her half-exposed breasts. She snapped, "Forty minutes ago, Sheriff Ball did. He was here, wanting Richard. He had an arrest warrant with Richard's name on it."

"Where's the proof?"

Jeannie laughed shrilly. "Ball doesn't need proof. Anything he says is gospel in this country. Now, listen. The day before Mrs. Leroux disappeared, she filed a complaint with the sheriff's office. She accused Richard of threatening to kill her."

"Why would he do that?"

"Oh honestly." Testy. "Everyone knows that Richard and that little grope Meredith Blake are pelican lovers. Or is it cranes?"

"Pelicans."

"They're pelican lovers. Besides, that wasn't all Ball had to go on."

"What else?"

"Last year, my husband and Mrs. Leroux had a pretty swell tiff. Richard said some harsh things he didn't really mean. Among them, the idiot told Mrs. Leroux that she deserved to be shot for what she'd done to the ecology of the Olympic Peninsula. It was euphemism, nothing more. Then there's the antique Buddha. The one Richard stole from the Leroux house."

"Says who?"

"Sheriff says he's got proof. I don't know what. He didn't share that information with me. But I know Richard didn't kill her. He hasn't got the guts to kill a flea. I can vouch for that. He's totally harmless. And I seriously doubt he stole anything."

"Where'd the sheriff go from here?"

She shrugged. "I imagine over to the hangar. I just phoned there and there's no answer. Richard's not there, thank God."

"Why don't you ask Lover Boy to smooth things over with the sheriff?"

"If you're referring to Park, you're dumber than I thought. Right now, Park couldn't help a pigeon out of a birdbath. He's all worked up over his mom's death. He's over his head in business affairs, trying to sort out all the stupid deals his mother made. And anyway, he's up in Seattle for the funeral. Now, I need your help."

"You sure Richard didn't kill her?"

"I told you already. I am positive."

"Who do you think did?"

"I don't know. I only know Richard didn't. I want to help him."

"Why?"

She didn't like the question, but she had an answer ready. "Look," she said, "I'm poison. I know it, and you know it. But men don't catch on till it's too late. Till I'm in their blood. Then they'll die for me, or from me."

She reminded Venus of cerebral malaria.

Jeannie said, "Understand, this is between you and me. I don't care to have my low self-esteem broadcast all over town." She sighed, made a futile gesture. "Okay, so I made a stupid mistake. I should never have married Richard. I thought I loved him. But it was just playtime, you know? I think I've always been in love with Park. And I hooked him fast. Men are like that with me. But I am fond of Richard, and I want to help him out of this jam."

Venus said, "Where do I fit into your benevolence?"

Jeannie scowled fiercely and snapped, "I told you once, I don't like you. You are an embarrassment to the female gender. But

I'm setting aside personal prejudice for Richard's sake. I think you can help him. For one thing, you're an outsider here. You've got the kind of mind that thrives on trouble. Well, there's trouble right here in Ozone Beach, and the natives aren't doing splat about it. Everyone here is afraid of stepping on certain toes. Believe me, I don't relish turning to you, but I can't think of anyone else. I'll pay you. I'll be your client. I'll pay you cash.''

She produced a wad of fresh currency. Crisp hundred-dollar bills. She counted out ten and laid them neatly on the bar. She was all business now. "This is an advance," she said. "For expenses. I want you to start today. Right now. We'll discuss your fee later.''

Venus looked at the bills. She looked at Jeannie Winters. Jeannie watched her reaction intently, her iridescent dragon claws clicking against the bar surface near the stack of bills. Venus said, "I'm already employed.''

In singsong, Jeannie piped, "A little bird told me you're about to get canned.''

Venus let that slide and said, "Why'd you tell me to bring a gun?''

Jeannie fingered the pendant watch. She said, "Sheriff's office had a report that bikers are moving up the coast. Maybe Satan's gang again. Rumor is they're heading for Ozone Beach. Few years back, they destroyed our village. Rumor says they want to hurt us again. It's only rumor, but we should all be prepared. Everyone's arming themselves. Maybe today, maybe not for a week. They like to surprise. At least this time, we have some warning.''

"What does Satan have against Ozone Beach?''

"Beats me.''

"Does Richard owe Park money?''

She squinted. "No,'' she said firmly. "Richard would never borrow from anyone. Especially not from Park.''

"How about drugs?''

"Maybe a little pot now and then, back in the high-stress era. He's been pristine for years. Park's the crackhead, though.''

"Richard doesn't deal?''

She seemed appalled at the suggestion. "My husband may be a lot of things," she declared defiantly, "but he's never dealt drugs. This is a respectable, law-abiding community, in case you haven't noticed. Things like that don't happen here."

Venus said, "Does Ozone Beach have any Asian residents?"

Jeannie made a face. The question didn't make sense to her. She said, "The Sushi place is faux-sushi. Buzz Barnes owns it. Only Asian I ever recall is the Divers boy. He's this orphan they adopted. Other than him, this burg is lily white. Not that I'm prejudiced or anything. But as for Asian tourists, well, sure, they come here all the time. Usually in tour groups, busloads of them. Except those two guys from Thailand. Or is it Burma? Two guys about your size. They came into the bar last week. I heard they were lighthouse buffs. I think they belong to some international lighthouse buff's club."

Chandrak and Pornchen. Venus said, "What night was that?"

"Gawd, I don't remember exactly. It was a week ago. They came in here one night, and I think they took out a six-pack of Blue Heron. That kitschy ale? Anyway, I gather they're especially fascinated by the age of this old light. And probably because it's built out on such a treacherous spot. Oh yes, I remember something else. They didn't stay long, just overnight. I don't know why they left so soon. Seems like an awful waste of airfare, don't you think? Anyway, what does that have to do with the price of rotten eggs?"

Venus said, "I was wondering about a bear that was killed out here on the sanctuary, near the national park. The way the bears are mutilated suggests Asians are involved, or that at least they might be buying from the hunters. Do you remember what night you saw the two men from Thailand?"

She shook her head. She said, "Ingrid Hëll might know. They stayed at the Driftwood Inn. They left in a hurry, too. Went back to Thailand, or wherever they came from." She checked the pendant watch, pushed the hundred-dollar bills at Venus. "Take these, and then get out of here. In five minutes, I'm leaving for a village council meeting. We've got these bikers to manage, on top of everything else."

"Where's the council meeting?"

"Mercy's Chowder Bar. It's always there. Why?"

Venus was wondering what Asian boat people would think of America if they accidentally washed ashore at Ozone Beach, Washington. To Jeannie, she said, "You ever see a By-the-Wind-Sailor?"

Jeannie sniffed. "I've seen plenty of sailors. No Bedouins, to my knowledge."

Venus said, "Stash the bills. I'll be back later."

Then she left.

SIXTEEN

Whizz

LOLA WAS POLISHING the "Wanted" posters when Venus walked into the post office. Lola glanced over her shoulder, and her heart leapt to her throat. Something made her skittish, maybe black leather in the face of Satan rumors. She slid back around the counter and stood near the stamp drawer, defending it against assault. She was post mistress, wasn't she? Chin up. She eyed Venus warily.

Venus said, "Do you folks carry wildlife stamps?"

Lola shook her head.

"How about birds? Got any birds?"

Lola opened the stamp drawer, keeping one eye on the suspect, and fished out a colorful page of "Birds of North America." She placed it on the counter. Her fingers wore little rubber digitals, like miniature safe-sex devices. With the prophylactics, she pushed the stamps toward Venus.

Venus studied the stamps for a few minutes. There were cardinals, bluejays, robins, thrushes, crows, and a few other domestic species. Lola couldn't remember all of them. She had hundreds of stamps to memorize. Venus said, "What about exotics? Got any exotics?"

Lola shook her head. Venus paid for the page of domestics and a few blank postcards. Lola watched as Venus scribbled on the postcards, then licked stamps and stuck them on. Lola said: "You don't need that much on postcards."

Venus smiled. "That's okay," she said. "They snazz up the cards." She handed the postcards to Lola and added casually, "I remember years ago, the post office did a New Year's special. Even though January first is a national holiday and post offices are closed, some of them would give you a special January first postmark if you brought your letters in on New Year's Eve.''

Lola grimaced and her stomach churned.

Venus said, ''This was up in Seattle.''

Lola relaxed. Now it all made sense, and wasn't at all what she had imagined. She said, ''We don't do that here.''

''Not even this past New Year's Eve? On a letter to my chief in DC?''

Lola's eyes darted. Her heart jumped into her throat again. She shook her head firmly and scurried off to the back room with the postcards, to read them and cancel the bird stamps.

A sign on the door of Mercy's Chowder Bar said CLOSED. Venus gave the locked door a futile nudge. Through the glass, she saw people seated around a dining table. Mrs. Mercy sat among them, holding court, her Day-Glo lips hard at work.

There was Chick Divers. He sat on Mrs. Mercy's left. He had on a powder blue sweater with matching trousers and bone leather topsiders, and had exchanged the stethoscope for a flat gold chain. Beside Chick Divers sat a bald-headed man, middle-aged, with a florid face. He wore a red flannel shirt and had five o'clock shadow. His brow was furrowed, his eyes riveted on Mrs. Mercy. He must be Buzz Barnes. Beside him sat Jeannie, legs demurely crossed, writing on a legal pad. Maybe taking minutes. Beside Jeannie, going around the circle, sat Meredith Blake. She wore the waitress uniform, and the K-Swiss. There were dark rings around her eyes. Her face appeared drawn, and she scowled at Mrs. Mercy. She seemed to be the object of Mrs. Mercy's apparent excitement. Venus gleaned this from the way Mrs. Mercy jabbed her finger in the air about three inches from Meredith's nose, and from the way Meredith's chin jutted out defiantly. On Meredith's right sat a sober-looking thin man twiddling his thumbs. Maybe Ted Tennant.

Venus tapped on the glass door. Mrs. Mercy whirled around, scowled at her. She said something to the florid-faced man. From the way the mayor moved her lips, Venus gathered she wasn't welcome inside. The florid-faced man got up, came over, unlocked the door. He opened it about an inch.

"What do you want?"

Accusatory.

"How about a bowl of chowder?"

"She's closed." He pointed to the sign. "Village council meeting."

"Are you Buzz Barnes?"

"What's it to you?" He shut the door, locked it. He went back over, straddled his chair, said something to Jeannie that made her titter.

Overhead, the sky rumbled ominously. Dampness permeated the air, as if the clouds were perspiring. On the street corner, an elderly couple stood holding hands, frowning at the entrance to Mercy's Chowder Bar. As Venus passed them, the man said, "We're tourists here. You too?"

Venus said, "I'm no native." Fairly defensive.

Plaintively, the man said, "Why's she closed?"

"Some sort of village council meeting."

"Oh, that explains it," chirped his companion. "See, Henry, I told you there had to be a good reason."

Henry said, "We're pretty ticked off. Come all this way from Missoula just to try some of that famous Mercy's chowder and the dang place is closed."

The woman said, "They must be meeting about that genius they're going to lynch." She elaborated. "We're staying at a little B-and-B run by that man in there. That one, twiddling his thumbs? Mr. Tennant. This morning we heard Mr. and Mrs. Tennant talking in the kitchen. I'm almost positive they said something about lynching a genius."

Henry said, "Mrs. Tennant didn't say 'lynch,' honey. She said, 'run out of town.' And it wasn't 'genius.' It was someone by the name of Rhemus." He winked conspiratorially. "They're fixin' to run somebody out of town. We heard the same talk over at the Bell Buoy Lounge last night. Heard that lady bartender say the natives could lynch this Rhemus, and the local law and the United States Navy would stand behind the natives. Hell, it was some kind of metaphor, that's all."

Triumphantly, the woman said, "I knew I heard the word 'lynch' come up. And it wasn't Rhemus. It was Venus."

Down the street was Heard's grocery store. She went in there and picked up a six-pack of Rainier beer and asked the clerk about beef jerky. The clerk seemed horrified, as if she had just asked for smack, or human flesh. His expression told her that Heard's market was way too upstanding to stock beef jerky. She wondered where Old Man Rutledge shopped.

Her fever had started rising again.

The grocery clerk was about nineteen years old, with adolescent acne, and the word "man" didn't fit, but might in a few months. He was that close. He had auburn hair and a riot of freckles. He bore a striking resemblance to Lola over at the post office. He had the same mute clamshell lips. If a clam walked up to her right now and shouted in her ear, she would understand it better than this clerk muttering at her now. Something about money. She fished out some dollar bills. He palmed a few of them, and she stuffed the remainder back in her pocket. The shop felt close, confining. She felt dampness under her shirt. Sweat. Staring at the clerk, she had a vivid mental image of Mrs. Mercy in a laboratory, cloning all the citizens of Ozone Beach, Washington. The kid with the clamshell lips had a ruthless, hard glint in his eye. She left the shop, wiping perspiration off her brow, and started walking.

A bullet whizzed past her ear, ricocheted off a lampost, went astray.

She ducked through the nearest door, the door next to the grocery entrance. She thought the gunfire came from the west, near the intersection of Beach Drive and Lighthouse Lane. A memory picture of Popeye O'Connor, in his yellow slicker and sou'wester, visited her mind. Now she believed with all her heart that she had seen him in peripheral vision as she had exited the grocery shop. He'd been standing at the intersection, near the door to Mercy's, between Mercy's door and the street corner. She peered out the bay window toward Mrs. Mercy's Chowder Bar. No more elderly tourists. No more Popeye. The street was deserted.

The village council had also heard the gunfire. From where she

stood, she could see Chick Divers rush to the window of the
chowder bar, look out. No more shots were fired. Chick disappeared from the window. She looked around, realized she was
standing in the bay window of the snakey lingerie boutique. Turning, she saw the shop's sole occupant, a man of about seventy-
five years. He wore gray underwear and used a wheelchair to get
around. He had no teeth, and when he hissed at her it sounded
almost as resonant as the noise his shotgun made when he fired
it into the air. She fell outdoors, rolled, recovered balance, and
sprinted down the street. Passing Mercy's, she caught sight of
Chick Divers on his way back to the window. It was a council
meeting they'd remember for a long time.

At the corner of Beach Drive, she was surprised to find the bag
of Rainier beer still under her arm. Her gun was out. She'd drawn
it in the roll at the old man's boutique and somehow managed to
hang on to the beer. Now at the intersection of Beach Drive and
Lighthouse Lane, she leaned against a lamppost. From here, she
could watch both streets. They were deserted. Everyone had run
for cover. No automobile, no bicycle, nothing moved along these
streets. Everyone was hiding. Maybe from Satan. The only sign
of life wafted from the Upper Crust Bakery, the scent of fresh-
baked goods.

Over her shoulder, the thunderheads had raced past the lighthouse and now approached the beach. These rain clouds were
precursors, a dense gray mist that shepherded the big buffalo
clouds across the sky. Raindrops began falling.

The rain fell sparsely, but the drops were large, heavy, as from
a faucet. Just two drops formed a puddle. Puddles formed, and
more fat raindrops splashed down and made the puddles grow.
Now the drenched streets flowed, gutters gurgling, drinking down
the rain.

She stood for fifteen, maybe twenty minutes in the rain, her
senses keenly attuned to danger. She had been trained to face
danger square on, never to turn her back on danger and run. That
was suicide. She stood beneath the dripping faucet in the sky,
waiting. Waiting for Popeye, or whoever the gunman was, chal-
lenging him—or her—to face her out in the open, square on.

While she stood in the rain, she thought about the words "Rain Dance."

What did it mean? Rain Dance. Sounded like a Native American name. Rain Dance. That's what the rain was doing now. Dancing. A slow, heavy dance. A prelude to the thundering buffaloes. Rain Dance.

No more shots were fired. The streets were still deserted. She stood a few more minutes in the rain. Then she crossed Beach Drive, took the redwood steps to the beach, turned right. The pounding surf roared in with a vengeance. Shivering from the cold, she headed north on the damp, rain-dimpled sand.

Rutledge wasn't home. She clanged the bell several times. No response. She left the six-pack of Rainier on the porch. The rain had subsided temporarily, but more black thunderclouds rolled in herds toward the shore. This reprieve was a slick joke Neptune played before delivering havoc and mayhem to the beach.

Where the sand beach ended, where the boulder-strewn point jutted out from a high driftwood bulkhead at the forest edge, walking proved precarious. Raindrops formed a thick slime on the seaweed-coated rocks. Heading toward Point Danger, Venus hopped helter-skelter across the treacherous landscape. Even the driftwood logs wore slippery coats, only slightly less precarious than the slick green boulders. The air hung icy and damp. A lone gull screamed overhead. She worked her way around the point.

Rutledge was nowhere in sight. As she passed the spot where earlier she had discovered the mutilated bear, she spied the driftwood marker standing upright in the sand, and smiled grimly. After removing the remains, Claudia and Dave had stuck the marker back in the sand. She felt a pang of fondness for Dave, a confusing, melancholy feeling. Maybe love.

Reluctantly, knowing she had to go there, she stepped into the forest and began the long climb to the ranger station. The thick forest hadn't escaped the rain; waterlogged conifers shed surplus raindrops, and under her feet a spongy pine-needle carpet offered little traction. In here, the heavy, musty air shed its salt tinge, held a clean top note of evergreen, a pungent concoction that stirred a thousand years of memory.

She climbed slowly, occasionally sliding backward on a slick, mossy outcropping. The sky, barely visible above the forest canopy, darkened into twilight. Perspiring profusely, the familiar feeling of Death's icy fingers squeezing her heart, Venus stopped climbing and rested. Reaching into her jacket pocket, she felt around until her fingers located the tiny vial of pills. She held out her hand, collected a few drops of the clean rain. Swallowing two pills, she drank from her cupped hand, then moved on.

At the ranger station, in the forest clearing, rain and fugitive winds had whipped up a soup of brown pine needles and mud. Sparks's Ford Bronco stood parked beside the ranger shack. This time, the shack was locked from the inside; no padlock hung in the metal hasp. She knocked at the shack's front door. Through a crack in the shutters, rays of soft, artificial light leaked out, but no sounds came from inside, no reply to her knocking.

Daylight had utterly disappeared, the sun gone behind black thunderclouds. She had only a small penlight. She flicked it on to examine a fresh set of tire tracks, aided by the dim light beaming from the shack. These tracks weren't from Sparks's Bronco. She was stooped over, examining the tracks when she heard a vehicle approaching on the gravel road that connected the trail to Highway 101. She looked up at two blinding headlights, feeling like a trapped animal when a poacher's jacklight surprised it at night in its den. Above the two headlights, a cherry light flashed through the darkness and mist.

The driver pulled the car up near the shack, let the engine idle, and rolled down the window. He had a fleshy face and small, suspicious eyes. On the sedan's driver-side door, an imposing insignia was surrounded by gold lettering: *HARBOR COUNTY SHERIFF*. The driver rested his elbow on the windowsill and drawled, "You Venus?"

She nodded. She didn't wonder how he'd identified her, because just then Sparks, a dog-eared paperback book in hand, bounded out of the ranger shack. Before Sparks shut and bolted the door, Venus glimpsed the shack's interior. Shelves lined the walls, loaded with books, like a rural library. Sparks slid into the passenger seat.

Venus went over to the driver, held out her badge. He studied it, then glanced over at Sparks. Sparks nodded to the driver, who turned back to her and said, "Get in."

She slid into the backseat of the patrol car. Sparks said to the driver, "Let's boogie."

The driver turned off the cherry light and spun out onto the gravel road. They drove in silence broken only by the rain's monotonous sound. At the fork, he turned right and headed toward Ozone Beach. After the turn, the driver glanced at Venus in the rearview mirror and said, "I'm Ball. Sheriff Ball."

Sparks glanced demurely over his shoulder, sucked in his thin cheeks, and made a moue. In mock queen tones, he said, "Little Riding Hood get herself all lost and scared in the big, bad forest?"

She stared at him. Sparks continued his taunt.

"Big bad bear come 'n' get you next time."

Ball wore an amused smirk. He said, "Kinda wet out there for jogging."

Silence.

Ball turned serious. He said menacingly, "Care to say what you're doing out here?"

Sparks leaned against the door, watched her, grinning widely. The grin triggered the familiar tic at the edge of his mouth. She looked at Sparks, then at Ball's steely eyes in the rearview mirror. She said, "Looking for *xiong dan*."

Sparks's eyes dilated and his jaw dropped open. He hadn't expected such candor. Ball kept his eyes focused on the gravel road. The windshield wipers did double time, because the rain had started up again, this time with a vengeance. Ball said, "What's that?"

She said, "Gall bladder of bear."

Ball made a horrible face.

She said, "Some people consider it a delicacy. They eat it fresh, and raw."

"For chrissake," said Ball, "don't make me puke."

Sparks passed one bony hand across his facial tic. She'd caught him off-guard with the *xiong dan* remark. He hadn't expected that bluntness. He massaged his cheek hard for a minute, and the tic disappeared.

Ball said, "We're hunting a killer. Maybe you heard. Old Lady Leroux got one through her bonnet." He watched in the rearview for her reaction. When she didn't visibly react, he added, "Know anything about that?"

Her forehead had broken out in a fresh sweat. She knew Ball noticed the perspiration and thought he'd thrown a big scare into her. She wanted to wipe off the sweat but didn't. She watched Ball's eyes in the rearview, didn't answer.

Sparks broke the silence. Reading his watch, he said, "Better hit the gas. We're late."

Ball nodded and put lead in his foot.

Venus said, "Who's your suspect?"

Ball said, "Name of Winters. Used to work at Leroux Timber. Big-shot executive. Friend of the family, of the son. Winters had a fight with Mrs. Leroux and he shot her."

"You got the weapon?"

"Yeah."

"Where'd you find it?"

"In the grass. Back of the airport hangar. He works there. He's the only one ever goes there. But he's not there now. Place is locked up tighter 'n a drum."

Ten minutes later, Ball drove the patrol car into Ozone Beach and asked Venus where she wanted to be dropped off. At Divers' Spa, she stepped out of the patrol car. Sparks rolled down the window and by way of farewell said, "Olson says you're canned tuna, honeybunch."

Ball gunned the engine, peeled off from the curb.

SEVENTEEN

Ball Game

TIMMY answered the door.

"How's my favorite snoop?" she said.

He grinned sheepishly, opened the door wider. He was excited about something.

"We're on the news," he said. "Ozone Beach is on Channel Six. Right after the commercials. Want to watch?"

She followed him across soft Bukhara carpets, through a large foyer crammed with expensive antiques. The hallway had high ceilings, but felt suffocating. On the right, an open door led into a well-equipped gym. The next door along the corridor opened into an aerobics room with pickled hardwood floors and ballerina bars along mirrored walls. Next to that was a closed door with a sign on it that said LAB. Eventually they arrived at their destination, a spacious study, tastefully decorated, bookshelves lining the walls and half a dozen framed diplomas and medical certificates prominently displayed. Chick Divers had earned his medical degree fifteen years earlier, at the University of Washington in Seattle. He had licenses to practice in Washington, Oregon, Idaho, and Montana.

Venus scanned the bookshelves. Mostly medical volumes. A few novels, mostly thrillers. Nothing with a maritime theme, unless you counted *The Night the Tide Turned,* by a Rip Rider.

He'd furnished the study in a bold minimalist style, black leather couches, spare metal Italian chairs, and sleek banks of track lighting. His desk supported state-of-the-art computer equipment, including an expensive digital scanner. Across the room, an enormous television screen threw a moody blue tint on everything, including Timmy. On the screen, some actors dressed as mice munched happily on string cheese, a brand she didn't recognize. Timmy punched the remote and the mice sang. She sat beside him on the couch. While the commercials ran their course, she asked Timmy if Chick had returned yet from the village council meeting.

"Nope."

She asked if the spa had any clients now.

He shook his head, his eyes riveted on the TV. He said, "Spa's closed till June. Except for some of the locals. They come in for massage and stuff."

"Like Park Leroux?"

"Yeah. And Buzz Barnes and Jeannie Winters and some others. I know 'em all."

The news anchor came on the air, a Pacific Northwest classic Nordic blonde. From the Seattle newsroom, the anchor walked her audience through the preliminaries of the Madge Leroux murder story, then turned it over to her colleague, whom, she said, was reporting live from the Ozone Beach village council meeting.

"There we are!" Timmy shouted.

In the dining room of Mercy's Chowder Bar, the reporter interviewed Janice Mercy and Sheriff Ball. Mayor Mercy didn't have much to say. She wore a grim, tight expression, apropos of the occasion. Ball had even less to say, and the reporter had to work him, trying to draw him out.

Ball said that a warrant had been issued for a suspect's arrest. Without naming the suspect, Ball hinted the killer was thought to be a male resident of Ozone Beach who belonged to a radical ecology group calling itself the Pelican Patrol. When the reporter pressed Ball about jurisdiction, the sheriff admitted the United States Department of the Interior had ultimate authority, but said the regional office had granted him permission to issue the warrant. He said Special Agent Oly Olson, of the Fish and Wildlife Division, had granted that permission. That was all.

The anchor came back and narrated some live footage from St. James Cathedral. Here was the body, lying in state. Madge Leroux's coffin would not be opened, the anchor reported solemnly, due to the circumstances of death.

In the background, Venus spotted Father Dylan, Woofy Benson, and Bella, the actress sporting dark sunglasses and a floppy hat, as if her fans wouldn't recognize her famous legs. Bella and Woofy stood musing over a particularly garish, ostentatious floral wreath. She could read Bella's mind. Bella was working out how to chuck the horrid wreath without insulting anyone. In voice-over, the anchor reported that half the city was expected to turn out for Madge's funeral the following morning. Tonight's rosary anticipated large crowds as well. She made it sound like Mardi Gras. Then a sailboat appeared on the screen, her mood brightened suddenly, and she launched into the next news bite.

As the anchor droned on, Timmy said, "I made five dollars today."

"Oh yeah? How?"

"Turned in a report on *xiong dan.*"

She looked at Timmy. He was biting his fingernails, his eyes still plastered to the television screen. She said incredulously, "You wrote a report on *xiong dan?*"

"Yep. I heard you mention it to Mr. Rutledge. I got on the Internet and downloaded some stuff. Want to see my report?"

Timmy pointed to a small desk near a bay window. She went over. On the blotter lay two sheets of manuscript paper, two full pages of careful, hand-printed script, titled XIONG DAN. She picked it up and read:

Xiong dan is like a baggy filled with green slime. It is bear gall bladder, or the bile that comes out of the gall bladder. Asians like to eat *xiong dan.* They believe it cures sick livers and other hot diseases. Japanese, Koreans, and Chinese will do anything to get it, and other Asians too. Because it really works. But it's expensive to buy in Asia, because the bears have been pretty much poached out.

A bear whose gall is drained while it's alive gives a hundred times as much bile as a dead bear. So the Chinese keep thousands of bears trapped in cages and they have a secret process they use to drain them. One bear can produce five pounds of dried gall every year. Dried gall sells for $1,500-

$1,800 a powdered ounce. Now some Asians buy *xiong dan* from American bear poachers.

The poachers kill the bears in spring. Spring is mating season for bears, but the poachers like to kill the bears before they have a chance to mate. That's when the gall bladder is biggest. They kill the four-year-olds, before they can mate. It's illegal in most states, but they kill the bears anyway.

Not only *xiong dan,* Asians like bear paws too. They think bear paw soup makes them vigorous and cleans their blood. Sometimes bear paws and *xiong dan* are traded for heroin from the Burmese triangle. This all happens in a pipeline between America and Asia, but no one has found the pipeline yet. When they find the pipeline, they'll catch the American poachers and put them in jail.

She laid the report on the desk. Timmy looked up, waiting for her reaction. She said, "The Internet's fabulous, isn't it?"

"Yeah. Do you like my report?"

"It's real good, Tim. Did you show it to anyone?"

"Only Chick. He said it was very good, and that it might help catch some bad people. Chick showed it to the mayor. She said I was precoach...precosh..."

"Precocious?"

"Yeah. And she gave me five dollars. I put it in my bank account. I'm saving for a Harley."

She had a sudden urge to grab Timmy, strap him on the Harley, and beat a path out of Ozone Beach, Washington. She wanted to whisk him away from here, to protect him from something, but she didn't know what. She smiled at him and said, "That's nice, sport. I've done some research too."

"On what?"

"Manitous. Manitous don't inhabit this part of North America. Manitous are spirits of the Algonquian-speaking tribes. The Quinault are Salishan. They speak a Salishan dialect. There weren't ever any Algonquian tribes in this part of North America. So there aren't any manitous here."

He shook his head emphatically.

"You're wrong. There's a manitou living in the lighthouse.

Lots of people have seen it. At night sometimes, you can see it flying by moonlight. Cindy Black, she's my friend, she saw the manitou once. She looked out her window one night when the moon was full. And she saw the manitou.''

"It has wings?"

"Big green wings that shine in the moonlight. Besides, there's lots of proof. There's lots of bears around here that get eaten by the manitou. Mrs. Bobbs, she owns a cranberry bog, she says she's seen lots of bears near her bog that had been eaten by the manitou. And there's Mrs. Leroux. The manitou killed her too.''

"They were shot, Tim. With guns. You described what happened to the bears yourself. In the paper you wrote."

He was so nervous he was almost shouting now.

"That's how the manitou works. It always kills the way humans would kill. That way it never gets caught."

"Chick tell you that?"

"And lots of other people too."

"What about Mr. Rutledge?"

He shook his head. "He calls it balderdash. Mr. Rutledge says the manitou is a filament of my imagination."

She sat down beside Timmy on the leather couch. Very gently, she said, "Did your stepmother Carolyn live here with you?"

He nodded. His eyes were aimed at the television, but focused on some far-off memory.

"Do you have a picture of her, Tim?"

"Chick says it wouldn't be good for me to have a picture of her. He says it would just remind me of her deserting us, and that would make me more nervous."

"Did Carolyn and Chick fight a lot?"

"All the time." He rolled his eyes. "Chick used to hit Carolyn when she talked back to him. But I'm not supposed to talk about her to anybody."

"Sure. Ah...what did they fight about?"

"Pelicans. Air pollution. The ozone layer. Stuff like that." His eyes suddenly brightened. "Hey, I have an idea. Want to go swimming?"

"It's kind of chilly out."

He laughed. He seemed almost happy when he laughed. "I mean in the swimming pool. We have a heated indoor pool. Come on."

She thought a swim would feel good now. Take the edge off the fever. Relax her. Maybe relax Timmy too. "Sure," she said. "If you think Chick wouldn't mind."

"He doesn't care. Come on. We have swimming suits, too."

She followed him to the rear of the big house, down a short flight of stairs. There was a wood door, aromatic cedar. Timmy unlatched the door, pushed it open. She followed him inside. She was standing in a small cedar-paneled foyer with a door in each wall. The doors on the right and left led to shower and dressing rooms, the one straight ahead led to the pool. Timmy went into one dressing room, she into the other.

In a chest of drawers, she found fresh towels and a selection of swimsuits. She selected a small one-piece skimmer that she thought might fit. She undressed, stepped into the shower, soaped, rinsed, and towel dried, then pulled on the suit. She took a fresh towel and stepped out of the dressing room. As she passed Timmy's dressing room, she could hear the shower running and she could hear Timmy's voice singing.

The pool room was dimly lit. She looked for a light switch but couldn't find one. She could make out the outlines of the long, rectangular pool. Blue mist rose from it, a heavy blanket on the water's surface. The only lights in the room, she realized, were below this mist, shining upward out of the pool, dimly, through the heavy mist.

The diving board had good spring. She took two long paces and, on the third, dove. Breaking the surface, she nearly collided with a floating object. Long silky hair billowed around the swollen face like pale seaweed. The eyes were wide open and clear blue. The expression on the face still registered defiance. Meredith Blake's body was nude.

BREATHE. PUMP. BREATHE. PUMP. BREATHE. PUMP. No response. She blew harder, longer. *Inflate the lungs. Breathe. Pump. Breathe. Pump.*

When Timmy appeared at the door, she shouted at him to go into the dressing room, to lock the door and stay there. Obediently, he went. She worked on Meredith, but Meredith didn't respond. Covering her with a towel, she left her lying on the hard cold tiles beside the pool. She took Timmy back to the study, and from there placed some telephone calls, the first to the Harbor County sheriff's office.

Ball hadn't returned to Oyster Bay. She phoned Mercy's Chowder Bar. The man who answered the phone identified himself as Buzz Barnes. Barnes said Ball was still there, dining with the village council.

Minutes later, someone threw a switch and floodlights washed the pool area. Chick Divers stood beside Venus, pulling on rubber gloves. He pushed her aside, took over the revival work. Ball and the florid-faced Buzz Barnes stood nearby. Barnes seemed disturbed by the sight of Chick bending over Meredith's nude body, breathing into an unresponsive corpse. Making feeble excuses, Barnes fled to the study, to sit with Timmy. After he went away, Venus and Ball searched the pool area, doors, windows, ventilation shafts. No signs of forced entry nor of a struggle. Near the pool's deep end, on a patio chair, lay a neat pile of clothing, some black underwear, the waitress uniform and the K-Swiss athletic shoes Meredith had been wearing a couple hours earlier, when Venus had seen her through Mercy's window. On a patio table beside the pool, Ball found a sheet of paper with a handwritten message. He picked it up, read it. Chick Divers straightened up. Staring down at Meredith's body, he shook his head. "I don't understand this," he said. "She knew how to swim. But she drowned."

Ball continued reading the handwritten message. He glanced over his shoulder when Chick spoke and nodded. Ball said, "Maybe suicide."

He handed Venus the note. She read:

To Whomever Finds Me:

    I saved the brown pelicans. I shot Madge Leroux. Last Monday night, I took Richard Winters's gun while he was sleeping. I phoned Mrs. Leroux and lured her down to the beach with a phony story. I grabbed her on the beach, bound her hands and feet, then shot her. I dragged her body into my little skiff, rowed out a few hundred yards off the coastline, and dumped it into the ocean.

No one helped me do this. I planned this and executed my plan entirely alone. Richard Winters knew nothing about my plan to murder Mrs. Leroux. Please don't blame him. After I shot her, I panicked and threw the pistol in the grass near the hangar. You'll find it there, if you haven't already found it. But please don't blame Richard. This was my personal contribution to saving the pelicans. That's why I came to Ozone Beach. To save this endangered species. To do this, I had to eliminate the biggest threat to the pelicans' survival. That was Mrs. Leroux, an enemy of brown pelicans and a grave threat to the ecological balance of the Olympic Peninsula.

When her body washed ashore, I knew that eventually I'd be caught, arrested, and tried for murder. I'd really be in the soup, if you get my meaning. So rather than face punishment, I am taking my own life. I have no regrets. I only did what was necessary. May God's pelicans return to roost forever on "Pelican Rock" (I named it that myself).

Peace and ecology,

Meredith Blake, Founder of the Pelican Patrol.

"In the soup?" Venus spoke softly to herself. She stored that mental image. The message was written in bold script with green ink. Venus handed the note back to Ball.

Ball said, *"Whomever?"* and shrugged.

She went into the dressing room, pawed through the bureau drawers, ran fingers along tufted carpets. Nothing. She dressed and walked back to the pool area. Ball stood near the diving board, holding a small object at eye level, examining it. She moved closer to Ball, saw it was an empty syringe, the needle intact. The needle gleamed beneath the floodlights. Ball sniffed at the syringe. Divers went over and inspected it. Divers said to Ball, "Heroin." He shook his head sadly. "I never would've guessed it."

Ball raised his eyebrows.

Divers said, "She had a habit."

Ball said, "Why do you say that?"

"Signs on the body."

"Tracks?"

"No. No tracks."

"Then what signs?" Ball was annoyed.

"The eyes. The shape of the pupils. She'd ingested some narcotic substance before she went swimming. I'm guessing it was heroin, and that she had a habit. An autopsy might support that hypothesis."

"Why heroin?"

Divers shrugged. "It's the trend these days. But educated kids like her don't usually shoot it. That part is odd."

Ball said, "Any heroin sold in the village?"

Divers shook his head. "I seriously doubt it. If anything like that was going on here, we'd know about it."

"Who's 'we'?"

"Village council."

Ball grunted. He said, "There aren't any signs of forced entry. What was she doing here?"

Divers pulled off the rubber gloves. "She'd been coming here to swim pretty regularly. She had free access to the pool in exchange for some favors she did for me."

"What kind of favors?"

"Baby-sitting the boy." Chick looked directly at Ball. "She told people around here that we were lovers. But that wasn't true. She fabricated that. She had a lot of fantasies. All she did here was baby-sit the boy. I gave her a key to the pool room." He indicated a door on the building's beach side. "That door."

Ball pawed through Meredith's clothing. He fished a single key out of her uniform pocket, held it up to Divers. Divers nodded.

"That's it."

Ball palmed the key and the syringe and the "Whomever" note. Chick Divers went into the foyer and came back with a clean white sheet. He placed this over Meredith's corpse. Ball watched him, then said, "I'm sending a deputy, and a man who'll take pictures. They'll pick up the clothing. Don't touch anything till they've finished their work. And Divers?"

"Yes?"

"I want you to autopsy her. Tonight."

Divers dropped the rubber gloves into a wastebasket. Wringing his hands, as if scrubbing for surgery, he said, "Just give me a few minutes with the boy. Then I'll get started."

RAIN FELL in torrents. In front of Divers' Spa, Venus sat in the passenger seat of Ball's patrol car. Ball opened the door and slid into the driver's seat. His potbelly skimmed the steering wheel. Ball started the engine, turned on the windshield wipers. Rain sheeted off the windows. Something made a thudding sound against the window on the passenger side. Venus looked out. Through the sheeting rain, Timmy Divers's face appeared, his fist pounding against the window glass. He shouted, but she couldn't hear what he was saying. She opened the door, pulled Timmy inside the car. He was soaking wet, trembling, his teeth chattering.

Ball watched the boy shiver. Venus held him in her lap and said, "Where's your jacket, sport?"

Timmy said, "Can I go with you?"

Ball smiled sadly and shook his head. "Sorry, son. You go back in there now to your daddy."

"He's not my dad!" An anxious, angry little voice.

Venus said, "Hey, Tim. What say you go back inside, and tomorrow I'll come over and we'll go for a ride."

He began crying softly. Ball indicated the door. She got out, carrying Timmy. "Come on," she said, "it's going to be okay, Tim. I promise."

When they reached the front porch, she wrote Bella's home phone number on a small piece of paper and gave it to the boy. She said, "If you ever want to call me, just call collect. Tonight

I'm at the Driftwood Inn. Any other night, you can find me at this number in Seattle.'' She placed an arm around the boy. ''Okay?''

Timmy relaxed slightly and nodded. She led him to the front door. Chick appeared at the threshold, ushered Timmy inside, shut the door firmly, using two hands against the strong winds.

As Ball put the car in gear, Venus looked back at Divers' Spa. Soft lights shone from the study window where Timmy stood silhouetted, peering out. She waved. He saw her and waved back, a forlorn, listless wave, like someone doomed. The manitou had just claimed another victim, and Timmy was terrified. Ball steered away from the curb, cautiously navigating the rain-gorged streets.

Ball guided the patrol car along Golf Club Lane. Rain pelted liquid bullets against the hood. The windshield wipers strained to perform. At the airfield, Ball swung into the hangar's driveway. The Ozone Beach helicopter stood on the pad, tethered down against the storm. Ball pulled the car up beside the hangar, braked. The engine idled.

For a few minutes, Ball said nothing. He stared at the hangar building, his attention focused on the padlock on the hangar's door. He'd been primed for a big raid, and seemed profoundly disappointed by this suggestive padlock on the door. He hadn't obtained a search warrant for the hangar.

Venus said, ''There's a window on the beach side.''

Ball chewed his lip, considered. After a while, he turned off the ignition, took a flashlight from underneath the dash, and said, ''Let's go.''

The window pried open easily. Ball shifted his heavy weight over the sill, slipped inside. She followed. Ball shone the flashlight on the scene.

Richard Winters's office had been ransacked. The Buddha shrine had been smashed, the young Siddartha kidnapped. They rummaged through debris, piles of file folders and computer print-outs scattered across the floor. Nothing seemed worth finding. The small word processor Winters used for keeping business records was missing. Then she thought of something. She borrowed the flashlight from Ball, shone it into the hangar's interior. Empty. Ball said, "Something wrong?"

"There was an ultralight here. Tandem, built for two."

Ball grunted. "This was their headquarters."

"Whose?"

"They call themselves the Pelican Patrol. Radical ecologists. Far as I'm concerned, they're terrorists. She was a recruit. But Winters is the mastermind." Ball chewed his lips hungrily. "I want that bastard."

"It doesn't make sense," she said.

Ball looked up inquiringly.

She said, "They might pop the old lady. But not Meredith."

Ball said, "You don't buy the suicide?"

She shook her head.

"What's wrong with it?"

"A lot of things. She had too much self-respect to kill herself. She wouldn't have taken her last swim nude. And there are a few other things that bother me, too."

Ball said, "Ever hear of Satan?"

"Bikers."

He nodded. "They're in the area. We're not sure where. They do a lot of drugs. Heroin. Lot of damage, too. Maybe they did this."

He was testing her.

Ball said, "Maybe Satan turned this place over looking for drugs. Maybe they took her out too, and made it look like suicide."

"Why?"

He shrugged. "Contract work. Maybe a drug debt."

"What about Mrs. Leroux? Did Satan do that, too?"

Ball placed a hand gently against his chest, stepped gingerly over some debris, and gazed quizzically at the smashed shrine. He said, "What do you think?"

"She was murdered. By the same individual, or individuals, who murdered Mrs. Leroux."

Ball grimaced, kicked the broken shrine. "Damn pelican lovers."

"What's wrong with pelican lovers?"

"They stink, that's what." Ball's tone was bitter. "They act like prima donnas and they make trouble. They threaten government officials with anonymous notes because they're too goddamned chicken-hearted to sign their own names. They dupe young kids like this Blake girl into joining their guerrilla forces—or they force her—then they decide they haven't got enough public attention. So they plug this innocent old lady and sure enough, they make headlines. What, for chrissake, does all that do toward saving birds?"

She said, "And Meredith?"

"I'm buying the suicide."

"Think she shot Madge?"

"I think the girl was Winters's pawn. She did what he told her to do. I think Winters convinced the girl to shoot the old lady. Then, I think the girl took her own life. Just like she said in the note. Delusions of grandeur. The heroics scrambled her brain. Then she got scared. So she kills herself, becomes a martyr to the cause. Some cause. Who needs pelicans anyway?"

She said, "Where's Sparks?"

Ball looked at her. He said, "He went back up to Seattle. With the Channel Six crew, in the chopper."

"Who flew the chopper?"

"It was the television station's chopper."

Ball studied the tips of his fingers for a while. Then he said, "Sparks says that you're brain-damaged." He watched her reaction, his small dark eyes glinting.

She said, "Let's blow this fire trap."

"BALL?"

"Yeah?"

They were riding back to the village, through the rain.

"What about the complaint?"

"What complaint?"

"The one Madge Leroux filed. Saying that Winters had threatened her life."

"What about it?"

"Who took the complaint?"

"I did."

"In person?"

Ball glanced over at her.

"Over the phone."

"So there was no official affidavit filed against Winters?"

"Who said there was?"

"Maybe I misunderstood. Are you sure it was Madge on the phone, making the complaint?"

"On the phone?" Ball thought a minute, then said, "I won't swear to it, no."

"Who turned in the gun?"

"Barnes. Buzz Barnes."

"Say where he found it?"

"Behind the hangar. In the grass. Like the Blake girl said in the note."

"We'll want the weapon up at HQ. And the other evidence."

Ball nodded.

EIGHTEEN

Squall

ZEN BARKED. A soft, well-modulated, round bark. He barked to direct Venus to where he stood beside Mrs. Liu, beneath the big neon fish near an entrance to the Pike Place market. Venus went over there. Mrs. Liu glanced down at Zen, as if for approval. Zen made a deep, guttural sound. Mrs. Liu smiled weakly. Her husband had fallen ill, she explained, had sent her to meet Venus.

Liu Ping's message, said his wife, was that on the previous Wednesday, a man Liu never met before came into his shop with some bear paws and a fresh gall to sell. Liu Ping told the man that he no longer dealt in the stuff. The man said, well, he had information from a source in Ozone Beach that Liu had ordered a fresh supply, and he was just the delivery boy. Liu, claimed his wife, refused to buy the paws and gall. The man argued with Liu, but when the old Chinaman didn't flinch, he stormed out of the apothecary. That was all Liu Ping knew.

What did the man look like? Mrs. Liu didn't know, except to say that he was young, maybe eighteen, nineteen years old. And Liu said he had lots of freckles. Maybe he was a solo operator, or maybe he worked for someone else, she couldn't say.

Venus said, ''Who's Liu Ping's source down in Ozone Beach?''

The Chinese woman shook her head. ''My husband buys direct from the poachers, see? That's all I know. That's all he ever told me.''

A small crowd had formed around Zen, people admiring the strangely exotic creature. Mrs. Liu held them at bay with her foot as she squirmed under Venus's hard stare. After a while, her voice lowered, she said, ''They will kill us if my husband talks.''

An admirer reached out to pet Zen. Mrs. Liu swatted at him and he backed off. Mrs. Liu coughed nervously, called the dog, and skittered away. Zen sat motionless, refusing to follow her. He wasn't ready to leave. He was busy growling at all his fans. He ignored Mrs. Liu. She came back, pushed through the crowd, snatched up the little dog. He howled. Mrs. Liu leaned in close to Venus, whispered, "There is one more thing. But don't ever tell my husband I told you."

"I won't, Mrs. Liu."

"My husband's source is a woman. A very nasty woman."

People started pawing at Mrs. Liu, trying to get to the dog, demanding to know what kind it was, where they could get one exactly like it. Venus said, "What's her name?"

"I never heard a name. Please, stop asking me questions now. My husband said if you give me a hard time he'll make trouble for you in Chinatown."

"You tell Liu Ping that if I catch him fencing *xiong dan* again his ass is busted. We'll confiscate the shop, we'll take away your home, and we might even take this pooch. Tell your husband that for me, Mrs. Liu."

Gripping the bawling dog, Mrs. Liu plunged through the crowd. Venus watched them for a minute, then ran after them.

"Hey, Mrs. Liu," she called out.

Mrs. Liu was running fast now. Venus broke into a sprint.

"Just tell me what she looks like."

Mrs. Liu felt panic now. She clutched the little dog tighter and ran for their lives.

OUTSIDE the Driftwood Inn, the yellow shadow lurked beneath a street lamp, slicker collar high around his face, sou'wester rakishly low over his eyes. Popeye O'Connor smoked a Gauloise, pretending to be Bogart. It felt good being Bogey, righteous. Like being a Naval Intelligence Officer man, which he was, or 007. When he spotted the Harley approaching, he smiled thinly to himself, flicked the Gauloise into the gutter, and sauntered down Beach Drive, disappearing in the squall.

Venus went inside the Driftwood Inn. She'd seen Popeye but

didn't feel like pursuing him just then. Ingrid Hëll handed her a message, neatly folded. She regarded Venus for a moment, then averted her eyes and shuddered. The message, Venus saw, was from Bella, who'd identified herself as "Mother." This had disturbed Ingrid Hëll, who found it incredible that she and this odd-duck, alien creature had probably entered the world through similar passages. To Ingrid, an immigrant herself, alien birth, including her own, was a strange, unmentionable process.

Soothingly, Venus said, "That's okay. Her voice scares me too."

Ingrid Hëll shivered.

Venus said, "Who's the hunk staying in one-sixteen?"

Ingrid shook her head. She wasn't talking tonight.

Venus returned to 111 and made the call. Bella's voice rang through the phone like mellifluous chimes.

"Venus, why are you phoning me at this hour?"

She read her Swatch. Eleven-oh-three.

"The message said to phone you tonight no matter how late."

"Well, it's after eleven o'clock. You know I am always in bed and fast asleep before eleven, social occasions excluded."

"How was the rosary?"

"Very tasteful. Though I must say, I wish Madge had owned a decent pair of shoes. She had such wide feet. None of my Ferragamos fit her. So we went with the old brogans, and believe me, it's just as well a closed coffin."

"Was Park there?"

"Certainly. Poor lamb handled himself beautifully. You know what I admire most about that young man? He has such a public presence, such grace. He held up beautifully. Dagny really should have been here. When are you coming home, dear?"

"I'll have to stay here overnight, but I should be home tomorrow afternoon."

"In that case, dear, I wish you'd do me a little favor."

"What's that?"

"You know how it is with families and funerals. Park is suffering so, he's completely useless on small details. It seems that Frederick Tapp, Madge's attorney, left some documents at the

Ozone Beach house when he was down visiting Madge last week. Burden telephoned this evening to say the documents had been accidentally left behind. He suggested you might carry them up to Madge's attorney's office. It's nothing urgent. Just some papers."

"If they aren't important, why does Tapp want them?"

"They are part of her estate, and therefore important. I meant that fetching them is not urgent. Honestly, Venus."

"Madge hasn't even been buried yet."

"You know how legal people are. Mr. Tapp no doubt wishes to ascertain that every angle is covered, in case his client has any skeletons hiding. Estate wars can be vicious and bitter. You may learn that sticky lesson firsthand one day."

"Is Madge going to be cremated?"

"Don't be ridiculous. Catholics aren't cremated. They are properly laid to rest. Madge will be buried at Evergreen. A truly divine spot beneath a Douglas fir."

"You're sure?"

"Of course I am sure. Woofy's handling that end of things, and doing a spectacular job. Poor Madge. Hardly a relation in the world. But I must say, the rosary was packed. Those hypocrites always show up for the carrion."

"I'm going to hang up now, Mother."

"Don't forget to pick up the documents from Burden. And if you happen to meet the Harbor County sheriff while you're down there, tell him for me that I think he is a perfect ass."

"Why do you say that?"

"If he had been doing his job, this horrid tragedy never would have occurred. After all the Leroux family has done for Harbor County, you would think the least its sheriff could do is protect poor Madge from those natives."

"I'll relay the message."

"Fine, darling. I'm going to try failing back to sleep now." Bella rang off.

Venus paced for a while, then picked up the phone and dialed O'Connor's room. No answer. She got the long-distance-information operator in Sherman Oaks, California, and obtained a telephone number from him. She called the number, but the line was busy, so she hung up, put on her jacket, and went out into the corridor.

She walked down the corridor to Room 116. She knocked on the door. No answer. Just for fun, she thought to herself, she could try the knob. The door didn't budge. She wasn't surprised. With her little Swiss Army knife, she fiddled with the lock. She heard it click, then a flash of yellow appeared in her peripheral vision. She straightened up, turned. Something hard and cold hit her skull. She saw exploding colors, but didn't remember falling.

NINETEEN

Tumble

THE SQUALL RETREATED, huffing back out to sea, leaving a damp, salty snap in the air. High tide had gained maximum ground, sopping the driftwood line. Moonbeams stole across a human hand grasping listlessly at Neptune's flowing, gelid cloak. Sprawled across the cloak's foamy hem, Venus studied the hand until she realized that it was attached to her. Waves of chill and pain seized her. She tried moving, couldn't. She shut her eyes and brooded over the hazards of wearing black leather.

Heads turn. Wearing black leather, you are instantly respected. You become the Black Pearl, sheathed in a tough protective outer skin that absorbs blows and, just as important, obscures any hint of imperfection. These are dangerous times, and in black leather you present an heroic image vis-à-vis the timid majority. All the world secretly adores a maverick in black leather. Even the most casual passerby flashes you the peace sign, and in perfect strangers, you inspire grateful smiles, for the world is safe as long as you're around to fight the good fight.

Wearing black leather can devastate your opponent. The enemy cannot know that a mere human exists beneath these forceful pelts. Years of wearing black leather has caused you to doubt your own vulnerability. You behave heroically in black leather. As if invincible. But perhaps only hypocrites wear animal skins while pursuing big game hunters. Just for a moment, you wish they'd design a black leather jacket for the heart. Then no part of you would ever break.

A cold wave lashed Venus's face. The next wave tossed her violently against the driftwood bulkhead. She tumbled like a rejected seashell, beached on a mass of barnacles and kelp slime.

The waves released her and rolled back out to sea. The tide had turned. Slowly, painfully, she crawled to her feet.

Whoever did this had wanted to kill her. Threw her on the tide, to create the appearance of an accidental drowning. Thanks to the leathers, only her hands and face suffered scrapes. No immediately discernible broken bones, but blood streamed down her cheeks, and her skull felt cracked. She wiped her face with a bleeding palm. She was a mess. She began walking.

In the lobby of the Driftwood Inn, Venus jangled the call bell. After a while, Ingrid Hëll came out wearing a Japanese kimono. When she saw Venus, her cuts and bruises, she stiffened but didn't say anything. Venus said, "Tell me about the Thais, Ingrid."

Ingrid clutched the kimono close to her bosom. "What ties?"

"The two Asian gentlemen who stayed here last week. Timmy Divers reported them, and they were run out of town."

Ingrid stared.

Venus said, "Who are they?"

Silence. Then, "That is confidential."

"They were Thai government agents, weren't they?"

Ingrid nodded. "Yes," she said. "I suppose they were."

"What were they doing here?"

Ingrid shrugged. "All I know is, they were not welcome here. There is a lot of ignorance in this town. A lot of ignorance."

"Why were they here?" Sweating and chilled, Venus shivered.

Ingrid said, "I don't know the whole story. I gathered they were trying to catch some smugglers. But this village is lily white. There aren't any drug dealers here. I don't know why they came here. Anyhow, the Divers boy had apparently been spying on them, and he reported them to the village council. A rumor spread that the Thais had brought drugs into the village. But no one could be sure what they were all about, because in private they spoke their own language. It's a remarkable sound."

"Like Donald Duck?"

Ingrid smiled sardonically and nodded. "Timmy Divers's description. And so the council ran them out of town. In the middle of the night. They just simply disappeared. One night I saw them go up to their room, and the following morning there wasn't a trace of them. Except for the photograph.''

"Photograph of what?" Venus felt her teeth clench against the chills.

Ingrid went over to a little file cabinet, opened a drawer, and after some dexterous flipping through file folders fished out a small photograph. She handed it to Venus.

"I found it under 'Revelations' in the Gideon Bible in their room. I tried turning it over to the sheriff's office. They weren't interested. I figured sooner or later, someone would want it. So I saved it.''

The fever must have shot up to a hundred and four by now. She might be hallucinating. It was an infrared night photo of the Point Danger lighthouse, and nearby, an ocean-going vessel she had seen before, in another harbor, in another land. The *Barnacle Bill*.

Venus said, "How do you know these men were Thai government agents?"

"Well, they told me they were lighthouse historians, and that they came to Ozone Beach to study the old architecture on this lighthouse out here. But by accident I discovered they were foreign agents. I was cleaning up their room last summer—"

"They were here last summer?"

"Yes. They came here once before, last summer. Anyway, I was cleaning their room. They were out on the beach, doing God only knows what. I saw their wallets on the dresser. One wallet was open. I saw the police badge, and the official papers. I confess that I opened up the wallets out of sheer curiosity. Both men had documents stating in English that they were agents of the Thai government."

"The documents were in English?"

"Partly. The other papers were in another language that must have been Thai. That is really all I know about them."

"Their names?"

"I can't recall. They were complex names." She went over to her registration book, leafed through. "Here they are," she said finally. "Pornchen. Pornchen and Chandrak."

Venus grimaced. "Stupid," she muttered.

"What?"

"Sorry. What about the mustache in Room one-sixteen?"

"Mr. O'Connor?" She seemed surprised. "What about him?"

"U.S. Navy?"

She shrugged. "He's never mentioned the navy. But he is also a regular. For maybe the past five or six years. Every few months he comes here for a few days at a time. I believe he takes the seaweed cure at Divers' Spa. Once he told me he had ancestors from Ozone Beach. I am originally from Stockholm, so I wasn't really interested." She yawned. "I am very sleepy. Maybe you would like some ice for those cuts. Then I would like to go to bed."

Ingrid went away and in a few minutes returned with a small bucket of ice. Venus mumbled some apologies for waking her. Ingrid nodded politely, went into her apartment, shut the door. Venus limped down the corridor to her room.

In the bathroom, she inspected herself in the mirror. The damage appeared superficial, some scrapes across her forehead, a small abrasion above the left eye. That side of her face had swollen and turned deep purple. A generous goose egg decorated her head, spoiling the haircut's swell design. She tossed cold water on her face. It stung. She daubed the cuts and scrapes with ice until the blood stopped oozing and formed clots. She tried running a comb through her hair. A garden rake would have felt better. She stepped into the shower, let steaming-hot water wash over her for a long time.

On the pillows rested fresh chocolate kisses. Ingrid must have come in recently and placed them there. Venus couldn't remember the last time she had eaten. She thought it was crumpets for breakfast. She wolfed down the kisses, then picked up the telephone receiver and dialed the number in Sherman Oaks. This time Dagny answered.

Her sister Dagny lived in Sherman Oaks with her husband, who was a steeplechase jockey. Dagny once described her husband as small but relentless, like a spot of grease on a hot griddle. She came on the line, breathless as usual.

"Trouble," she shouted, "is that really you?"

Venus said yes, it was.

"I heard you were back in the States. Mother said you had contracted malaria. She said you weren't really all that ill, but that she had a terrific time in Singapore. It was so thoughtful of Mother to rush to your sickbed like that. She would never do that for me."

"How are you, Dag?"

"Blissed out, as usual."

"Blissed out," in Dagny's vernacular, meant pregnant.

In her prime, Dagny had enjoyed a long string of torrid love affairs, beginning with the brief liaison with Park Leroux. Like the brown pelican and By-the-Wind-Sailors, Dagny's migrations involved adjusting to prevailing conditions. She had embraced the sexual revolution, copping one of the best seats on that roller coaster. None of her affairs could be deemed even-tempered romances. Each tryst became an exercise in psychodrama, each torch more flammable than the last. She chucked it all after her best friend, Jane, died from AIDS. She married the jockey, who Bella referred to as a Zen fascist, and had been giving birth regularly, about once a year.

"When's it due?"

"Oh...July, I guess. Trouble, why are you ringing me up out of the thinnest of air?"

"You remember Park Leroux, Dag?"

Breathily, Dagny said, "God, what memories that name conjures ..."

"His mother was murdered a few days ago."

"Madge Leroux? My God, I didn't hear about it. Why?"

She told Dagny about the murder.

Dagny listened, then said, "Mother must be devastated."

"She'll survive."

"Hmmm. How's Park taking it? He's made of Jell-O, if you want to know the truth."

"Park's doing fine, Dag. I wanted to ask you about him."

"Ask away. John's asleep, so I've nothing better to do."

"When did you last see him?"

"Let's see. It was just last summer. I was up visiting Mother, and I ran into Park at a garden party at Woofy Benson's. Park was there with his mother and some friends of theirs. We didn't speak very long. I could feel that old spark of animosity, or whatever it is, between us. Of course, I forgave him long ago for taking advantage of my youth and innocence. But Park has never forgiven me for knowing what a total wimp he's always been underneath all the bluster."

"How did he get along with his parents?"

"Coolly, I should say. Park never liked his father. I think he was rather fond of Madge, though. Although I must add that he never really liked anyone but himself. He's a first-rate narcissist. I gather he's doing quite well as a timber magnate. I read about him occasionally in *The Wall Street Journal*. Has he married yet?"

"Sort of informally engaged," Venus quipped.

Dagny said, "Oh? Who's the girl?"

"Actually, maybe 'engagement' is too strong a word. The woman's husband might object to the suggestion."

"Eeeuw. Messy."

"Her name is Jeannie Winters."

"Trouble, you don't mean Richard Winters's wife?"

"The same."

Dagny laughed. "That spitfire? I don't believe it. Park couldn't possibly be interested in Jeannie Winters." Dagny sniffed. "She's way out of his league."

"You know the Winters, Dag?"

"I met them at Woofy's garden party. The one I just mentioned. They were with Park and his mother. I understood that Park and Richard were old Stanford buddies; and that their families go back years. My impression was that Richard Winters came from a very sort of privileged background, but at Stanford he fell into some bad habits, which he'd recently discarded. I was very impressed by him. I had the feeling he was headed for a place on the Leroux board of directors. And he's enchanting to look at. Jeannie was disgusting. Hanging all over Park. Woofy almost croaked, she was so embarrassed. Not to mention Madge.

Madge didn't miss a beat. She always kept a hawk's eye on Park. Mother told me later that Madge offered Jeannie money to keep clear of Park. So she's got her claws in, eh?''

"Maybe. Does Park have a habit?"

"Other than deflowering virginal landscapes?"

"Yes."

"Trouble, you're in such a dark mood. What's the matter?"

"Nothing, Dag. Does Park do heroin?"

"Oh gosh, I don't think so. Although I understand heroin is back in vogue in a big way. But Park got over hard drugs years ago. Alcohol is his nemesis."

"Any more juicy tidbits?"

"Not unless you count the blowout with Madge."

"What happened?"

"I only heard Park's side, understand. This was at Woofy's party. Park was fairly sopped on gin, and his tongue got pretty loose. He claimed, and I emphasize *claimed,* because he was so roaring drunk, that the United States Navy was conducting a secret military operation at the old Point Danger lighthouse. You remember the old lighthouse, don't you? Remember how we used to sit on the beach and daydream about going out there?"

"I remember."

"Apparently Madge bought the lighthouse when the coast guard abandoned it. Then someone from the navy offered her great sums of money, according to Park, to lease the place from her. She refused, and she and Park got into a violent exchange over it. This is according to Park. He begged Madge to lease to the navy, but she still refused."

"Did Park say what kind of military operation it was?"

"No. I don't think he knew, really. He just knew that the navy wanted to lease the place and was willing to pay a bundle. He was only interested in the revenue."

She thanked Dagny and promised to call her again soon. Dagny said, "Give me your phone number in Ozone Beach. If I think of anything else, I'll ring you back."

She gave Dagny the number, then said, "If you notice any brown pelicans heading up this way, call immediately."

"Oh sure, Trouble. I'll keep my eyes peeled."

Before turning out the light, she popped some more medication, then swabbed down the leather pants and jacket. She thought about Meredith Blake, how she looked lying facedown in Divers's swimming pool. She recalled the defiant expression on Meredith's face. Maybe Venus imagined the defiance, maybe murder had played tricks with the corpse. If Meredith had come to Ozone Beach to champion pelicans, her death might not have been in vain. Unnecessary, but not in vain. Venus was ruminating on this point when the phone rang. She went over and picked it up, expecting Dagny's voice.

"I have to whisper," Timmy Divers said. "So Chick won't hear."

"What's up, Tim?" She tried not to sound worried.

"It's about Meredith."

"What about her?"

"I was spying on her."

"Why, Tim?"

"Because she wasn't from here. We're supposed to spy on suspicious people who come here. I saw Meredith stealing some food out of the freezer at Mrs. Mercy's restaurant."

"How do you know it was food?"

"It was a little package, like you get from the deli. Wrapped in white paper. I think it was clams."

"How do you know she was stealing? Maybe she was preparing some chowder for the restaurant."

"She was stealing. I know it. Because when Mrs. Mercy heard about it, she got mad."

"When did you see Meredith?"

"Yesterday, after school. Then last night, I told Chick. He phoned Mrs. Mercy right away. He said she was furious. Chick said we don't want any thieves in Ozone Beach. That they would have to run her out."

"Anything else?"

"No."

"Timmy?"

"What?"

"I never mentioned *xiong dan* to Mr. Rutledge."

"Yes, you did. I heard you."

"Think, Tim. Maybe someone else mentioned *xiong dan,* and you heard them. Maybe you got mixed up."

"Now I remember."

"Who was it?"

"It was Meredith. I heard her talking on the phone. She said she'd tasted some. After she got off, I asked her what it was, and then I looked it up on the Internet."

"Who was she talking to?"

"I'm pretty sure it was Richard Winters. I think I hear Chick. I have to hang up now."

As she settled under the covers, a soft knock sounded on the door. She got up, went over to the door, said, "Who is it?"

"Ingrid Hëll."

She unlocked the door, opened it. Still in her kimono, the innkeeper displayed a plate of sandwiches. On top of the sandwiches she'd made a mountain of chocolate kisses. She offered the plate.

"I thought you might be hungry. After what you have been through."

Venus took the plate from Ingrid. "Thanks," she said. "You're a lifesaver."

When Ingrid had gone, Venus carried the plate over to the maroon love seat, put her feet up on the coffee table, and wolfed down the sandwiches. Before going back to bed, she stuffed the chocolate kisses in her jacket pocket. Later, she would marvel that she'd had the foresight to do this.

The bed felt reasonably soft against her bruised bones, the scrapes and scratches. She lay there, a mass of charcoal blue, feeling the malaria fever rise and ebb and rise again. She'd seen people die from malaria, horrible death. Now, she realized, it might be her turn, here in this Godforsaken burg, in a motel room, alone. The chills returned, creeping up gradually; she began sweating profusely, drenching the bedsheets. Then came the hallucinations again, the incoherent babbling, the cries for help. But nobody heard her. She slipped into a semi-coma, a Hail Mary half finished lingering in the heavy, heavy air.

TWENTY

Angels

VENUS didn't hear the man enter the room. She might have missed the visit altogether had he not leaned over her for a long moment, softly exhaling near her face. Was he studying the scrapes, the clotted cuts? His breath woke her and when she opened her eyes he placed a cool hand gently on her forehead. Then he went away. The next thing she remembered was the hand again, brushing her hair off her forehead, then a cool damp cloth being pressed to her brow. She could only mumble incoherently and through the fever haze saw him smiling gently, in a way she had imagined he might smile at her. Then the wonderful hands raised her sweat-drenched body up out of the sheets. He carried her in his arms into the bathroom and slowly, slowly submerged her burning body in a tub of cool water. He held her there so she wouldn't drown, because she had lost all of her strength and could not hold herself up. He bathed her in the cool water, ran some more into the tub, rinsed her, then, wrapping her in a clean towel, carried her in his arms back to the large room where he placed her on the couch. Then he picked up the phone.

She vaguely remembered the woman entering, and the two of them working quickly, efficiently around the room. The bed was stripped, the fan turned down, hot tea was brought in and jugs of ice water, the bed was freshly made up, and the woman slipped a clean white nightshirt over her body. They helped her to the bed, sat with her, held her hands, fed her ice water while they drank tea to keep themselves awake. The man and the woman spoke softly to each other, but she couldn't make out what they said. Hallucinations got in the way. When the demons attacked, she cried out and the woman held her hand and comforted her.

Sometime during the night, she thought she heard him weeping. She opened her eyes. They sat on the couch, the woman holding the man in her arms as he wept and wept. Like grieving. But not over her. She wasn't dead yet. Tell him to stop grieving! He might be grieving over someone else. She blacked out. The next time she awoke, she heard a conversation, soft whispers.

"Ball has an arrest warrant on you."

"I'm not surprised."

"Why don't you turn yourself in? People will support you."

The man laughed. "Like who?"

"Jeannie. She wants to help you."

"Sure. Like a cheetah helps a gazelle."

"You think the same ones killed Meredith?"

"Sure. And the Thais, too. They got too close. They had to shut them up. Sure, they killed them too."

"Where are you staying?"

She didn't hear his reply, if in fact he answered the woman's question. They spoke in low whispers now and she couldn't hear them. She sank back into darkness. The next time she awoke, daylight streamed through the window and Ingrid Hëll stood framed in sunshine, hands on hips, in the chenille robe. Ingrid said, "So you survived."

Venus smiled weakly, nodded.

Ingrid went away and came back a few minutes later with a tray of hot tea and toast. On the way out, she said, "Richard wants you to know that he did not steal the Buddha. It was a gift, given to him by Mrs. Leroux."

Venus sat up in bed. Maybe that was the last fever, maybe now the malaria would go dormant, never return. Chin up. Let's be optimistic. She tackled some dry toast.

Ingrid grinned tiredly. "Now I am going to bed," she said. She went out, shutting the door softly behind her.

Venus picked up the phone and dialed the front desk.

When Ingrid finally picked up the receiver, Venus said, "You're an angel, Ingrid. A guardian angel."

"My father was a sailor. He also had malaria. He died from it. Now take your medicine and let me sleep."

On the coffee table by the couch, she found a sealed envelope. Driftwood Inn stationery. She opened it and read:

"I came to cry on your shoulder. Mer meant so much to me. I heard you yelling but the door was locked. Ingrid gave me the key. You almost died, you know, but we didn't call Chick. I hope you understand. Mer did not commit suicide. Richard."

If she cooked, she thought to herself, she'd bake him some scones.

TWENTY-ONE

Tide Table

MORNING BROKE bright and clear, the ocean blue and pacific, like its name. Except out near Point Danger lighthouse. Out there, the ocean raged.

Mrs. Mercy was caressing a portable calculator when Venus walked into the chowder bar. No grief, no mourning tears clouded these eyes intent on checks and balances. She didn't notice Venus enter. Venus located a table, fished the tattered, blow-dried remains of Rutledge's handmade choker from her breast pocket, and with elaborate gestures lit it. Around her, patrons stirred uneasily.

Mrs. Mercy sniffed, looked up. That familiar obnoxious odor. Her eyes searched the chowder bar until they came to rest on Venus. She marched over to the table where Venus sat enveloped in billows of acrid smoke. Venus smiled, waved. Mrs. Mercy pulled up short and glared. Venus said, "I hear you're descended from Ennis Ozone, the slave driver."

Taken by surprise, Mrs. Mercy sputtered at first, but then composed herself. Noting that half of Venus's face was swollen black and blue, and that the other half grinned impishly, Mrs. Mercy scowled. She shook a stiff finger at the cigarette dangling between Venus's lips. "Here now. Put that out or I'll put you out."

"I thought this was the smoking section."

"There is no such section in my restaurant. Extinguish that cigarette, if you please."

Nervous titters capered among the diners. When Venus dropped the cigarette into a full water glass, it fizzled out, leaving ashy fluid. She said, "There. Drowned."

Mrs. Mercy paled visibly. But she was a trooper. She recovered rapidly, raised one long arm, extended a finger pointing at the door, and said sharply, "Out. *O-U-T.*"

"I was going to order breakfast."

Mrs. Mercy thought that over. Patrons were gawking. She mustn't be too rude, mustn't appear unreasonable, in spite of fresh tragedy. Of course, any patron would understand her sour mood, having lost her waitress so horridly just last night. Surely they would forgive a little gruffness on her part. But she was also mayor, and a mayor should under all circumstances, no matter how personally painful, maintain poise, composure, a diplomatic air. It was part of the job, it came with the territory. Slowly a tight smile formed on her Day-Glo lips and her head nodded graciously.

"Very well." Cool but polite. "What would you like?"

"Have you made today's chowder yet?"

Mrs. Mercy squinted, confused. "Fresh chowder is never served before noon. Most people don't want clam chowder for breakfast."

"Any left over from last night?"

Amazed, Mrs. Mercy answered, "Maybe just a dribble."

"I'll take that."

"Clam chowder. For breakfast?"

Venus nodded. More titters scampered through the room. Mrs. Mercy relaxed slightly. This apparition in black leather had just demonstrated to one and all that she was thoroughly weird. Nobody in her right mind orders clam chowder for breakfast. Mrs. Mercy played along, for the sake of her audience.

"Very well. One bowl of chowder. Would you care to see the wine list while you're at it?"

More titters, louder.

"Just the chowder, thanks."

Mrs. Mercy went away, and after a few minutes returned with a bowl of steaming microwaved chowder. She set the bowl neatly before her customer, straightened up, smoothed her skirt, and, sucking in her cheeks to control a runaway smirk, strode over to the cash register.

Venus examined the chowder. While Mrs. Mercy had her back

turned, Venus removed a small lump from the chowder, dropped it in a paper napkin, wrapped it, stuffed it into her jacket pocket. She didn't taste the chowder, didn't need to. One glance convinced her that she could identify the added ingredient.

A shadow fell across the table. Venus looked up. Mrs. Mercy said, "I am very sorry, but I'll have to take that away." She scooped up the bowl of chowder.

Venus protested. "But I've just started. Maybe I'd like to finish."

Mrs. Mercy shook her head. "I think it is spoiled. I just remembered, it stood out all night. I had other things on my mind. Would you like something else?"

Venus ordered coffee and a Danish and gawked out the picture windows while she thought about Meredith's suicide note. On her way out, at the cash register, she said to Mrs. Mercy, "Too bad."

Mrs. Mercy arched her brow. "You mean about Meredith? Yes. Tragic."

"I mean, too bad you lied, Mrs. Mercy."

Her eyes popped wide open. "About what?"

"About your chowder." Venus picked up a menu, pointed to some bold print. "It says here that your clam chowder is made entirely of geoduck meat, Idaho spuds, fresh milk, and spices."

Mrs. Mercy nodded frostily. "That's right."

"I found something else in this chowder, Mrs. Mercy. And I don't mean overalls. It's just an educated guess, mind you. Nothing definite."

"I beg your pardon?" Indignant.

"Don't get all puffed up, Mrs. Mercy. It's not becoming. Neither is lying. A mayor should never lie, not even to protect her own constituents. Life is too fragile for lies, Mrs. Mercy. Then again, maybe you didn't know."

"Know what?" A frozen mackerel.

"That your chowder was spiked. Yesterday, somebody laced your chowder with herb balls containing *xiong dan*."

Mrs. Mercy's eyes sprang wider. Her mouth formed one of those churlish, contorted O's. She sputtered, "You are a savage. I want you out of this village. Immediately."

Venus smiled on her way out and over her shoulder quipped, "Don't try to run over me again, Your Honor. It's not hospitable."

Yes, Meredith. It was in the soup.

BURDEN WAITED by the front door, a small manila envelope tucked under his arm. When he saw Venus riding up the drive, he smiled, relieved. He went out onto the porch to meet her, handed over the manila envelope. Tucking it into her inside jacket pocket she said, "Park back from the funeral yet?"

Burden shook his head. "I don't expect him for several hours. He was going to buy a boat this afternoon, after the funeral." Burden made a sour face. "He needs a diversion, so he says, from all the gloom."

"You didn't go?"

"To her funeral?" Burden shook his head solemnly. "Someone had to hold down the fort here. Besides, I prefer remembering Mrs. Leroux as last I saw her. Here in the garden, feeding the purple martins."

Venus leaned against the door jam and said casually, "Know anything about her will?"

"Nothing conclusive. Of course, each of us has his and her guesses."

"Burden," she said, "did the little overnight case ever show up?"

"No."

"Any guesses about that?"

Burden sighed deeply. He nodded. "But this is in strict confidence, mind you."

"Sure."

"The morning before Mrs. Leroux disappeared, she removed a large sum of money from her bank account. Bernadette, our maid, saw Mrs. Leroux place the cash in her little pink overnight case. Then, that afternoon, Mrs. Leroux had a meeting, here at the house, with Mr. Frederick Tapp, her attorney. I gather she was revising her will. I overheard Mr. Tapp phoning in dictation to his office up in Seattle. Apparently, it was an extensive revision. Part of the change involved Mrs. Leroux's son's share of her estate. From what little I overheard, she was apparently docking Park, Junior so much for costs she had incurred trying to protect him.''

''The cash in the overnight case?''

He nodded. ''I had strongly suspected, for some months now, that Mrs. Leroux was being blackmailed in some fashion. Apparently the blackmail was somehow connected with her son.''

''Any ideas who? Or why?''

Burden fidgeted. ''Just a hunch.''

Gently she said, ''What's your hunch, Burden?''

''The Winters woman. I can only guess why.''

She nodded. ''Have you heard what happened last night over at Divers' Spa?''

''Bernadette told me just a little while ago. The Blake girl. Horrible. Bernadette said she drowned herself.''

''Did you know her?''

''She came by the house once or twice. With Park, Junior's friend Richard. A lovely young lady, Meredith Blake. But she chewed gum.''

''Any impressions about her?''

He cocked his head sideways, pursed his pale lips. He said, ''She loved birds. Especially pelicans. I knew that she was an advocate of the brown pelican. She and Mr. Winters. The last time she came here, I seem to recall now, she came alone. Just last week, in fact. She rang the doorbell, and when I answered the door, she handed me a book. The subject was brown pelicans. She asked me to give this to Mrs. Leroux. Then she went away. That was the last time I saw Miss Blake.''

''How did Mrs. Leroux like the book?''

He brightened. ''Oh, she was absolutely delighted with the book. At the time, she was devouring everything she could find about the brown pelican.''

''Why in the world was she doing that?''

''Why...'' Burden paused, smiled. ''Oh, of course. How would you have known? You see, I do know a little secret about Mrs. Leroux's revised will, but it's a secret, mind you. Even her son hasn't learned about it yet.'' He bent over and whispered in her ear. ''Mrs. Leroux was establishing a foundation for the preservation of the brown pelican. Mr. Winters was to be the foundation's sole trustee. It was their little secret. Mrs. Leroux's and Mr. Winters's. Of course, it will all come out in the open soon.''

''I thought they were bitter enemies.''

Burden straightened up again. ''They had been, once upon a time. Mr. Winters had greatly insulted Mrs. Leroux, and she had fired him from his position with the company. Then just a few days later, Mr. Winters came to the house and apologized to Mrs. Leroux. He said that although he still believed Leroux Timber's policies were endangering the ecology, he should never have behaved in such an uncivilized manner toward Mrs. Leroux. He had insulted her over some company policies he took issue with, which concerned the company's position toward conservation issues. At any rate, Mrs. Leroux accepted the apology and offered Mr. Winters his job back. He requested a leave of absence, which Mrs. Leroux granted. Then, somehow the conversation turned to birds. They were both bird fanciers.

''To make a long story very short, Mr. Winters offered to fly Mrs. Leroux out to the old lighthouse, to see where the pelicans roost in springtime. This was last December.''

''But the pelicans don't roost until March or April. What would he be showing her out there?''

Burden shrugged. ''Perhaps evidence of the birds having been there. The gist was, Mr. Winters wanted very much to preserve that site as a sanctuary, and on this trip, he apparently convinced Mrs. Leroux to champion his cause. Mrs. Leroux returned from that dangerous excursion giddy with enthusiasm for pelicans.''

''He'd converted her?''

Burden nodded. ''After that, to other causes as well. She grew very fond of him, as if he were a second son. For Christmas, Mrs. Leroux gave Mr. Winters an antique Buddha passed down in her family from generations ago, when her ancestors helped colonize Burma.''

''Burma, or China?''

''Burma. I am quite certain about that.''

Of course. Now the puzzle came together. She nodded at Burden, and he continued.

"In recent months, Mrs. Leroux had examined her company's policies and had concluded that they disregarded the environment. She instructed Park, Junior to implement a string of new policies which she hoped would promote conservation. Park, Junior was not in the least bit pleased, just between the two of us, but I gather he obeyed his mother. When it came to business, young Park could be obedient."

Burden coughed lightly. "Pardon me, Miss, but what is the matter with your face?"

She'd forgotten. She touched it lightly, felt the rough scrapes, imagined how unpleasant she must look. She tried smiling, but it hurt. "Oh that," she said breezily. "I fell down, that's all. It's nothing."

"Certainly, Miss. One other thing I wanted to mention. This village thrives on rumor mongering. Someone even went so far as to circulate a glossy brochure around the village, claiming the Leroux Corporation was planning to exploit the lighthouse. You mustn't believe half of what these villagers tell you."

"That's what Bella told me."

"Lady Bella is very insightful. No, according to the revised will, Mrs. Leroux was planning to donate the lighthouse back to the Department of the Interior. The foundation her will is establishing is meant to provide funds for upkeep of the sanctuary, and to study the pelicans' migration patterns along the Pacific Coast. A most worthwhile project, I thought."

"Burden," she said suddenly, "who knew about these plans?"

"Only Mrs. Leroux and Mr. Winters. And her attorney, Mr. Tapp, learned about the plan just a few days ago when he came down to make the revisions in her will."

"And you."

Burden made a sheepish face. "One overhears much more than one ought. But one is discreet."

"Was the revised will signed?"

"I had worried about that, to be honest, and took the liberty of telephoning Mr. Tapp's office. I was told that while the revised will was still being prepared, Mr. Tapp did not wish to risk any hitches, so he had Mrs. Leroux sign what he called an holographic will, a handwritten document which does hold up in the courts. I was relieved to learn that Mrs. Leroux's wishes will be carried out."

"Tapp took that document to Seattle with him?"

Burden pursed his lips. "The holographic will?"

"Yes."

Burden stared pointedly at her jacket, at the pocket where she had tucked the small manila envelope. She patted the pocket. Burden nodded slightly. She felt the stiff envelope through the leather. She reached inside, zippered the pocket, then snapped the buttons on the leather jacket. Burden smiled. As she walked down the porch steps, he said softly, "It's a pity, really."

She turned, looked at him. "What, Burden?"

"That she had so many enemies. People treated her like a shrew. It took a chap like Mr. Winters to see that all Mrs. Leroux needed was a little moral goosing. She was always a gentle lady at heart."

AT THE CORNER of Lighthouse Lane, near the post office, Venus located a telephone booth. She fed it her Sprint code, pressed some buttons. When Wexler's secretary came on the line, she asked to speak to the boss. The secretary said, "Who's calling?"

"Venus."

"Oh."

Silence. Then some muffled sounds. Then she was pretty sure she heard some muffled laughter. Then the secretary came back on the line and said, "Mr. Wexler is [giggling] in Hawaii. Call back some other time."

Then the secretary hung up.

From the Seattle directory assistance operator, Venus got the phone number of the offices of Tapp, Tapp, and O'Toole, Attorneys. She programmed the Sprint code again. When a female voice answered, she said, "May I please speak to Mr. Tapp?"

"No," said the female voice. "You can't please speak to him."

"Why not?"

"Because he's in Rio. Attending a legal seminar."

"How about the other Mr. Tapp?"

"He's in Rio too."

"O'Toole?"

"He went along for the sun and the girls. Why don't you call back next week?"

Venus said, "It's pretty important. I'm calling about Mrs. Leroux's revised will."

"Who's this?"

Venus told her. The voice replied, "Well, I don't know anything about that. All of Mrs. Leroux's papers are locked up in a safe deposit box, and that won't be opened until Mr. Tapp returns next week. So you'll just have to wait like everybody else."

"Oh?" said Venus, trying to sound offhand. "Who else is interested in Mrs. Leroux's will?"

"Her son, for one. Guess you can't blame him. He stands to inherit a fortune. And then Mr. Winters, that hunk from Ozone Beach. He's called here so many times I'm actually sick and tired of hearing his voice. I don't care how pretty he is. I have told him I don't know how many times that Mr. Tapp is in Rio and won't be back until next week. Then today at the funeral, he had the nerve to walk right up to me and—"

"Richard Winters was at the funeral?"

"Sure. Why not?"

"By the way, who are you?"

"Shirley. The firm's paralegal."

"Shirley, did you happen to speak with someone named Bella this morning?"

"Oh, now I get it. You're her kid. Did you pick up the documents?"

"I have them right here in my pocket."

"Hey, well, thanks a lot. We really appreciate your taking time to do that."

"I'll bring them in this afternoon or tomorrow morning. No later than tomorrow morning. Meantime, I could fax a copy."

"Don't bother. We need originals. Mr. Tapp told me over long distance that we absolutely need to have the original document. (Snorting.) How can the kitchen inventory be that crucial, anyway?''

"Why'd you go to the funeral?"

"Representing the firm. The bosses are in Rio, remember?"

"You go to the rosary too?"

"Negative."

"You studying to be a lawyer?"

"Sure. Ten years from now, half the population will be lawyers and the other half will be doctors. Then murder will be legalized and everybody will be gainfully employed." She cackled.

"Why don't you get out while you're ahead?"

"Don't rain on my parade." She hung up.

TWENTY-TWO

Jelly Roll Hell

THE CRANBERRY BOGS behind Mrs. Bobbs's house wore a bumper crop of scarlet berries. Flooded from the rains, the bogs lay deserted this morning. Mrs. Bobbs, a widow who lived alone, smiled as she locked the back door of her wood-frame cottage. She'd planned an afternoon at Oyster Bay, combing the factory outlets with her daughter Marvine. Humming, Mrs. Bobbs slid into her new blue Chrysler, started up the engine, and backed out of the drive. She drove off down the highway.

She hadn't been gone from home ten minutes when two adult female bears poked their heads out of the woods behind Mrs. Bobbs's bogs. Sniffing the air, they moved cautiously forward. When they had tested the territory with their own presence and met no enemy, they grunted. Four younger bears, including a pair of yearling cubs, scampered out of the thicket and fairly dove into Mrs. Bobbs's flooded scarlet bogs. But this was not their lucky day.

They had come from the beach, where, near a picnic table not far from the jetty, they had gorged on a huge pile of jelly doughnuts. They ate until their stomachs swelled, then scampered across the park to make dessert of Mrs. Bobbs's cranberries. No sooner had they arrived and splashed into the bogs than, one by one, they grew woozy and fell into a stupor.

Much later, the bears awoke to the gentle wafting aroma of freshly baked jelly doughnuts. If their senses had not been muted by the spiked jelly rolls, the captives would have realized that they lay shackled inside great wire pens running in a row along one side of a huge room with sleek silver walls. In this prison, the bears lay woozy, confused by bright overhead lights and by

their ennui. Once, a cub tried shaking off the restraints around
her legs, but soon grew tired of struggling, lay down, and rolled
over on her side, softly panting, terrified but helpless.

Eventually, when the hypnotic wore off, the bears scrambled
to the bars of their cells and peered out. They saw then that other
tenants shared this prison, for lining the opposite wall of the silver
room were other pens, with other bears inside them. Twenty-five
in all, not counting the four-year-old male now shackled to the
butcher table, terror in his eyes.

The senior tenants, although alive, sat haggard and laconic,
weakened into a powerless stupor from a constant diet of heroin-
laced jelly doughnuts. Catheter tubes hung from each bear's ab-
domen.

Across the brightly lit room, a woman wearing a white
butcher's jacket, white mask, and surgical gloves slit the belly of
the drugged four-year-old male bear. He struggled to no avail; his
energy subdued by iron restraints. The pain seared his belly, but
he could only lie there as the knife was drawn across and then
suddenly plunged into his bowels. The woman cut out the ago-
nized creature's gall bladder, held it high, admired its plumpness,
its freshness. Then she noted with satisfaction that the young bear
had stopped breathing. Now the dismemberment work would go
swiftly. When she had finished carving up the young bear, his
head rested on the counter beside her. His fur had been skinned
off and hung on a hook. Methodically, she wrapped each part of
the bear in white paper, taped each parcel with butcher's tape
then carried them over to a massive freezer. She placed the parcels
inside the big icebox, among other stacks of white parcels. This
young male's gall bladder, harvested whole, she placed in a sterile
glass container. Then she returned and carved up and packaged
some more.

When the female cub moved again, the woman looked up
sharply. The cub, noticing the woman, lay very still. The woman
glanced at her wristwatch, then resumed carving, but soon the
female cub grew restless, began making noise. Too much noise.
The cub bared her teeth at the woman. The woman said, "So you
want more tranquilizer, do you?"

She went away and returned shortly carrying a rifle with a silencer and a tranquilizer dart. She loaded the cartridge and dart into the gun. Standing at the opposite end of the long room, she raised the barrel of the gun, aimed it at the female cub, and fired. Soon the cub lay still. It did not wake again for hours, and then rain was pelting against the roof and so the sound of her whimpering and fussing did not leak outdoors, did not attract attention. The cub growled, and the woman brought the gun again, and the bear went back to sleep.

While the captives slept, several humans entered the room, donned white lab coats and surgical masks. One by one, the sedated bears were removed from their cages. Twenty-five bears from twenty-five cages. Each sedated bear was transported by a gurney to a surgery, where the woman, acting as surgeon, and several assistants went to work. The catheters, placed in the bears' abdomens, pierced the gall bladders. Bile was drained from the gall bladder into glass bottles. As each bottle filled with green bile, a surgery assistant labeled it and stored it in a large refrigerator. It would be dried or delivered fresh, depending on the client's preference. Each sedated bear was then returned to its cage. This procedure continued until every bear had been catheterized and drained. The tubes were left inserted for future drainings.

These new additions, captured in Mrs. Bobbs's cranberry bogs, produced more bile than the older, more sickly creatures. They had been a windfall for the poachers, an entire family, six in all: two adults, two four-year-olds, two yearling cubs. The spiked jelly doughnuts had sedated them so effectively that the poachers were able to take them alive. Alive was better. Alive made the job of harvesting fresh bile and whole, fresh galls easier, more precise. When they could work in the slaughterhouse, no messy traces got left behind in the woods. No gut piles, no evidence at all. They could take their time draining bile from live creatures, harvesting whole galls, taking fresh sex organs and paws. That would bring a pretty penny.

When they had completed the day's work, the operating personnel cleaned up the surgery and checked to be certain that all their prisoners were securely locked up inside their cages. They'd be drained again, and again, over the next few months, then slaughtered and carved up for bear paw soup and other lucrative delicacies.

The woman went into a large kitchen, checked that the jelly doughnuts were cooling nicely and that the ovens had been turned off. The other laborers left by the back exit. The woman, more brash, removed her surgical mask, cleaned up a little, brushed her hair, shut out the lights to the slaughterhouse, and walked out the front door of the Upper Crust Bakery, locking it securely behind her.

TWENTY-THREE

Blackmail

THE POST OFFICE was closed. Trixie's Agate Shop, Heard's grocery, the snakey lingerie shop, Mercy's Chowder Bar, every shop in Ozone Beach was closed. The door to the Bell Buoy Lounge was locked. Venus rapped knuckles against the glass. This was Thursday, in the fourth week of March. She tried to recall American holidays. She couldn't recall any that fell on this day, unless they'd recently made a fortnight out of April Fool's Day.

Jeannie came to the door, peeked out. When she saw Venus, she rolled her eyes, unlocked the door, and opened it about two inches. She meant for her to come in, but not to drag anything in with her. Venus squeezed inside. Jeannie locked up again. Venus said, "What's the holiday?"

"Satan rumors. We're on alert."

Jeannie's hair was racheled, framing her face, emphasizing full, sensuous lips painted pale lilac. She had been sitting at a table near the bar, working on a gin fizz and a stack of "balance due" notices a mile high. She went over to the bar, mixed another gin fizz, and took a near-beer from the cooler. She came back, shoved the stack of "balance dues" aside, and uncovered an ashtray. She handed Venus the near-beer, sat down, and rummaged through the paperwork until she located a pack of something menthol. She lit a cigarette, braced it between her teeth and the lilac lips, and said, "Satan rumors make me nervous."

"How about murder?"

Jeannie glanced up quickly. "Meredith? I heard it was suicide."

Venus said, "Where's Richard?"

"How would I know? That's your job. I'm your client."

"Not yet." Venus pulled on the near-beer. She said, "Why didn't you go up to the funeral?"

"Madge's funeral?" This amused her. "You kidding? They would have tossed me out on my sweet ear. I'm not a member of Seattle's elite, in case you hadn't noticed. Anyway, we weren't all that close. Madge and me." She chortled.

"Maybe you weren't that close. But maybe something connected the two of you."

"Like what?" Drolly.

"Extortion."

She made a face. She didn't say anything, just made a sour face. Venus took a deep breath, leaned forward and growled, "Listen, Jeannie, I've had enough of Ozone Beach, Washington, to last the rest of my life. I've had it with these narrow-eyed paranoiacs who think every tourist is a communist or a Hell's Angel or some kind of espionage agent. I'm sick and tired of the lies and deceptions and the trigger-happy bigots who slink around these faux-trendy sidewalks just drooling to shoot someone for trespassing. I've had it with two-faced hypocrites who are so scared of their own shadows that they'll protect a lunatic murderer just because the killer is one of them. Ozone Beach is a gentrified pit of filthy sleaze and lowlife scum. I'm sick of this burg."

Jeannie grinned over her cigarette. "You're in a bright mood today."

Venus said, "Spill some beans, Jeannie. Or else there's big trouble for your soon-to-be-former husband."

Jeannie shrugged. "You ask, I'll spill." Confident and cooperative.

"Where's Richard?"

"I told you, I don't know. The last time I saw him was yesterday morning, when he left the condo for work. I haven't seen him since, haven't spoken to him. There was a message from him on the answering machine at the condo. Last night when I got home. But he never came home, never phoned."

"What did the message say?"

"Just that he needed to talk to me. Urgently. Oh, and that his gun was missing. He thought I might have it. But I don't, and I don't know who does.''

''Where's the ultralight?''

She seemed surprised. ''It's not in the hangar?''

Venus shook her head.

''Then I don't know where it is. Richard must have taken it with him. He has a pickup. He can fasten it to his pickup. And the pickup's nowhere in town. I've looked on every street. In every driveway.''

Venus said, ''The Pelican Patrol.''

Jeannie smirked. ''That dumb name. Meredith probably coined the term. It sounds like her.''

''Not Richard?''

''Listen, Richard has a Stanford education. He wouldn't come up with such a dorky name. And he and Meredith were the only ones around here, by the way, who were obsessed with pelicans. So if there was such a group as the Pelican Patrol, it had to be Meredith's idea. The smartest thing she ever did was to commit suicide after murdering Madge. She saved herself a lot of grief.''

''What if I told you that Meredith was on friendly terms with Madge Leroux?''

Jeannie balked. ''I'd say Meredith was plotting against the old lady, pretending to be her friend.''

''Carolyn Divers?''

Jeannie blinked. Her mouth twisted into a snarl. She said, ''Basket case.''

''Tell me more.''

''Maybe I don't want to.''

Venus growled, ''Don't be coy, Jeannie. I don't like coy. Do you want Richard cleared of the murder charge?''

''He's as good as cleared now, with Meredith's confession. All I want now is for you to find him. I have some papers he needs to read and sign.''

''He could be charged as an accessory. Anyway, the charges against him haven't been dropped yet. Now, spill, Jeannie. Carolyn Divers.''

''Oh sure,'' she said sarcastically. ''Next you're going to tell me Richard murdered Madge and Meredith too. What does Carolyn have to do with the time of day?"

"Spill."

"Oh, all right. She was a bird doctor. From California, I think from down around L.A. She came up here to do some research about six years ago. She met Chick, our local doc. They got married and she stayed. Then, a few months after they were married, Carolyn found this little boy abandoned on the beach. She took him home. They adopted him. That little snoop, I hate him."

"Where did the adoption take place?"

She sniffed. "I don't think it was exactly a legal adoption. Don't quote me on that. You know how rumors make the rounds. I think Timmy was one of these boat people who wash ashore. Or something. He turned up here one day, and Carolyn just took him home. She was like that. Real saccharine."

"What else about Carolyn?"

Jeannie placed a finger on one side of her nose. She squinted, concentrating. She said, "Carolyn was the first person to spot the flamingos. I mean, pelicans. I always get them mixed up."

"Think of the Pelican Patrol."

"Shut up. Can't you see I'm trying to be helpful? And wipe that fake smile off your stupid face. Can you manage that?"

Venus managed it and Jeannie calmed down. She said, "Yeah, pelicans. So Carolyn, being the goody-goody she was, reported it to some government agency. I suppose to your office, I don't know. Then before you know it, the island was declared a wildlife sanctuary. That made all the locals happy. We felt we'd all had a hand in saving the lighthouse from becoming a creepy columbarium. Just the thought gives me the willies." She shivered.

"Madge Leroux's columbarium?"

She nodded. "Rumor was, Madge planned to convert the old lighthouse into a burial vault called 'Eternity at Sea' and sell little cubicles for people's ashes. Sick, huh?"

"Maybe that's all it was. Rumor. Maybe someone was trying to discredit her."

"Maybe. Anything's possible. Anyhow, Park was only joking the other night. About the neon thing? He has a rotten sense of humor. So back to Carolyn. Not long after she spotted the pelicans, she left here.''

"Where'd she go?"

"She went nuts, that's where. Chick said he had to commit her to a psychiatric hospital."

"Based on—?"

"That she was nuts. He didn't need evidence. She was a basket case, clear as I'm sitting here. Chick had one hell of a time trying to control her. She must have been a real wildcat. Chick said they used to fight all the time. Chick would come to council meetings all scratched up. Like a bear had attacked him. It was mortifying for him. Being a doc and all. Anyway, a couple years ago, Carolyn started getting really depressed. She was never very happy living in Ozone Beach. It was quite an adjustment, coming from L.A., I'll give her that. So she got pretty depressed and then I guess, from what Chick said, she just cracked up. So he had her committed to a hospital up in Seattle. But I heard she got out pretty soon after he committed her. The laws are that screwed up.''

"Know where she is now?"

Jeannie shrugged. "I heard Montana. With some cowboy."

"She still use Chick's last name?"

"How the hell would I know? Listen, if you want to know all about Carolyn Divers, why don't you find Richard and ask him? They were pals, at the very least. Maybe she slept with him, I don't know. Anyway, I don't see what Carolyn Divers has to do with anything. I must admit, though, it's pretty damn bizarre that the Blake bimbo came to Ozone Beach to find Carolyn and ended up in bed with Carolyn's old man. Now, that I find interesting."

"If we could find Carolyn Divers," Venus said, "maybe she could back up Richard's innocence."

"Well, good luck. That's all I can say."

"When exactly did she leave Ozone Beach?"

"How the hell do you expect me to remember something like that?"

Venus finished the near-beer, placed the bottle on the table amid the piles of bills. She said, "Where do you think Richard might have gone?"

Jeannie lit another cigarette, blew smoke out thoughtfully. She said, "Maybe Seattle. He has friends up there. But I don't have any addresses. Maybe Yakima. He has some ultralight buddies over in Yakima. Anyhow, that's your responsibility, not mine."

Venus watched Jeannie smoke. While she smoked, she stared sullenly at the stacks of bills.

Venus said, "Who would want to murder Meredith?"

"It was suicide, remember?"

"Or maybe Meredith had discovered something illegal was going on in this village. Maybe she was one of several people to discover it. Like Carolyn Divers. And Madge Leroux. Maybe Carolyn was murdered too, by the same killer."

Jeannie smirked to herself. She inhaled some smoke and said, "That's an elaborate idea. Stupid too." She leaned her head back and laughed. "Something illegal in Ozone Beach, Washington? In this puritanical burg? Like what, for instance?"

"Smuggling. Between the West Coast and Asia."

Jeannie's tongue found her cheek. She said, "Oh now, cut me a break, will you? We're not that cosmopolitan here in Clamville."

"That's exactly why Ozone Beach would be the perfect location for a black market operation."

Jeannie looked up, surprised. "Black market what?"

"Animal organs, paws, and gall bladders."

Jeannie allowed this to sink in, then said, "You want to know what I think?"

Venus nodded.

Jeannie said, "I think you're totally weird."

The glass panel on the Bell Bouy's front door shattered loudly. They looked up to see a well-manicured hand reach in, unlock the door. Dressed in funereal black, Park Leroux stepped inside. Jeannie winked at Venus and quipped, "Park's like that. When he needs a drink."

Leroux carried a small pearl-pink overnight case. He walked over to Jeannie, slammed it on the table, sending stacks of bills flying. Jeannie stared at the overnight case, then at Park. Park growled, "Open it, Jeannie."

Jeannie blinked a few times, then leaned forward stiffly and unlatched the overnight case. She looked up at Park and said pleadingly, "I know what's in here…"

"Take it out, Jeannie."

She reached in, fished out a wad of hundred-dollar bills. Crisp, new bills, like the bills she had tried to give Venus. She placed them carefully on the table. Leroux said, "How long have you been taking Mother's money?"

Jeannie smirked weakly. Park raised an arm, swung wide, smacked his open palm hard against Jeannie's face, and shouted, "You little bitch!"

Jeannie felt her face, the spot where Park's hand had come down so hard. A red welt rose on her cheek. She said, "Your mother wanted me to stay away from you, Park. I told her what I did with my personal life was none of her business. She offered me money, Park. I never asked for it, she practically forced it on me. She gave it freely, Park, of her own choosing. She called it 'investing' in my future. As long as I stayed away from you." Jeannie smiled thinly. "But you know I can't resist you, Pookie…"

Park leaned down, whispered in Jeannie's ear, "You're worse than a whore."

Jeannie sobbed. Park laughed bitterly and called Jeannie some more names. Jeannie covered her face and bawled. Park strutted around the barroom, tugging at his belt, cocking his head imperially. He said, "I'll ruin you, Jeannie. I swear to God, I'll frigging destroy you for this. You'll wish you'd gone to hell, Jeannie, I'll make it so bad for you." He grabbed her, jerked her up out of the chair.

Venus said, "Better cool it, Park."

Over his shoulder, Leroux sneered, "This is private business. Blow kid."

Venus said, "Hey, Park. It's me, Venus."

Leroux's grip loosened on Jeannie. Jeannie backed off. Park

studied Venus's face for a minute, then said, "You're Dagny Diamond's little sister... Hey, Trouble."

Venus smiled, reached out to shake his hand, trying to divert him from his temper tantrum. Jeannie fled to a couch in the corner, sniveling. Venus said, "How was the funeral?"

Leroux slumped into Jeannie's chair. Darkly, he said, "Frigging somber. Your mother was there. And that Woofy Benson. God, I hate Father Dylan. Always fawning over me."

Jeannie cowered on the couch, sobbing softly, talking to herself. Explaining her behavior to herself. After a while, Leroux glanced at the pink overnight case and fury re-entered his eyes. Venus said, "Where'd you find it?"

"In the trunk of her Mercedes." He glanced across the room at Jeannie. "Did you kill her, too?"

From the depths of the lounge came Jeannie's voice, small and meek, a full octave higher than usual, "Would I bite the hand that fed me?"

Leroux growled, "Maybe she had cut you off."

Silence.

Leroux said, louder this time, "Did you kill my mother?"

"I had other ways of getting revenge." Low and throaty.

"Oh yeah? Like what?"

"Like making it with you, Park."

"You frigging bitch..."

Park lunged at Jeannie. Venus moved to intervene just as the gun went off. Leroux folded, slumped across a table, dropped to the floor. His eyes bulged. Venus leaned down, loosened his shirt collar. Behind her a tiny voice said, "It was self-defense."

She'd struck him near the groin. A bad wound, not fatal. He would retain the ability to deflower virginal landscapes.

Venus phoned the sheriff's office and the volunteer fire department. While they waited for the ambulance and the law, Jeannie bent over Park, soothing him, murmuring sweet nothings into his ear. Leroux grimaced up at her, already planning how he'd retaliate.

THE AMBULANCE screamed away from the Bell Buoy, headed for the airfield. Leroux would be flown by helicopter to Oyster Bay, there admitted to a hospital. The same helicopter, from Ball's department, would carry Jeannie and Ball to Oyster Bay, where Jeannie would sign a statement. She'd probably make bail, Ball said, if Leroux pressed charges.

At the airfield, Venus said to Ball, "Have you seen the autopsy results?"

"Yeah," said Ball. "Like I said, suicide. She shot up, overdosed, then drowned."

"I wanted to ask you something."

"Shoot." The chopper pilot started the engine. The blades began whirring slowly.

"Yesterday evening," shouted Venus over the noise, "when you arrived at Mercy's Chowder Bar for the television interview."

"Uh-huh."

"Was the village council meeting still going on?"

Ball thought this over, then said, "Nope."

Jeannie leaned forward, poked her head out the chopper door. "Why do you want to know that?" she asked in that high-octave voice.

Ball placed a finger to his lips. Jeannie got the message, leaned back. Venus said, "Who was there when you arrived?"

"Barnes. Ted Tennant. And the television crew. No one else."

"Janice Mercy wasn't there?"

"She came in behind me. I'd say by ten minutes. Then, later on, this lady here," indicating Jeannie Winters, "came in with Dr. Divers. Then we had supper. We were still at supper when you called us over to the spa."

"Sparks?"

"Yeah. He was there too. Then he left with the TV crew."

She nodded. She said, "You find Winters?"

"Not yet. But I will."

TWENTY-FOUR

Death Trap

CHICK DIVERS opened the door. He wore the white hospital coat and the stethoscope. When he saw Venus, he made an annoyed groaning sound.

"What do you want?"

"Finish the autopsy?"

He leaned against the doorjamb. "Why should I tell you?"

She shrugged. "Why not? Anyway, Ball's already told me that you finished."

Chick nodded. "It was suicide. There was every indication she killed herself."

"Drowned?"

He nodded.

"No sign of a struggle?"

He shook his head.

"What about drugs? Any sign of drugs?"

"She'd shot up heroin. Overdosed."

"Sure it was suicide?"

He sighed wearily. "What are you getting at?"

She said, "Just a thought. Maybe I'm way off. I just thought maybe Meredith could have been drugged, then drowned. And I was wondering about the fact that she was nude. I was wondering if she had taken all her clothes off thinking she was going to do something other than swimming."

"Such as?"

"Shower. Or sex. Maybe having sex with someone. Maybe that's why she was nude. And someone murdered her."

He said, "You have a twisted mind."

"Is Timmy home?"

Chick nodded. "The boy is fine. Stop worrying about him."

"You contact her father? In La Jolla?"

He nodded. "Family has been notified." Curt, cold.

She said, "Anyone else have a key to the swimming pool?"

He shook his head. Then he backed into the house and shut the door.

COOL sunlight bathed a placid ocean. A gentle spring breeze tick-led the waves, and the waves lapped listlessly against the shore. Venus walked north along the beach toward Point Danger. On the horizon, a small fleet of hake fishers trailed deep nets, scraping for the bottom fish. She noticed how hypnotic the ocean's roar could be. She wondered if the natives of Ozone Beach existed in perpetual trance. She wondered if Neptune was a hegemonist, expanding his empire to embrace this coastal village. Neptune might use the ocean's roar to lull the natives, then take control of their village, make them his robotic slaves. Maybe Neptune was behind the trouble in Ozone Beach. Maybe the manitou really existed, working as Neptune's secret agent.

Rutledge wasn't home. She walked up to Point Danger. Rut-ledge was there, sitting on a giant driftwood log, watching Mr. and Mrs. Seal and pups splash in a tidepool. Rutledge looked contented, smoking one of his homemades. When he saw her approach, he waved. She danced across the driftwood bulkhead and scooted out onto the log beside Rutledge. He said, "What about the jerky?"

"Heard's doesn't carry it."

"Could've brought some from Seattle."

"Next time. I had to utilize the poncho, old chap. It's a goner. Sorry." Rutledge shrugged. She said, "I'll replace it."

He grunted. "Grog's on ice."

She said, "Timmy gave me your message."

He scoffed. "Lot of good it did."

"You hear about Meredith Blake?"

"Girl from California?" He nodded. "She didn't belong here. In this village. Like the other one. She was from California too."

"Carolyn Divers?"

"Like her. People like them don't belong in Ozone."

He studied her bruised and swollen face. "What happened t' you?"

She told him. He spit into the ocean. "Landlubbers," he snorted.

She said, "Hardly anyone around here has mentioned my condition. Like they don't see the scrapes and bruises."

Rutledge grinned. "Small towns, you don't ask direct, you get it secondhand. That's the way in small towns. Then again," he mused, "maybe word's gone round about your trouble on the beach. Maybe everybody knew all about it."

"This is supposed to be a tourist resort, right?"

He nodded.

Venus said, "From everything I've been told, the villagers support themselves on tourism."

"Cranberries, too. Mrs. Bobbs, she's got the biggest bog. But two or three other'ns grow cranberries too."

"But supposedly it's tourism that supports Ozone Beach. Am I right?"

"Yep."

"But this is a rotten, unfriendly bunch here. This is no way to attract tourism. I think tourism is a front. I think the locals have other ways of supporting themselves."

Rutledge pulled on his beard and stared out across the water to where the ocean raged around the big rock and the lighthouse. Venus continued, "I think a smuggling ring operates out of here. Animal organs traded for drugs, and cash. I think most if not all of Ozone Beach's citizens know about it. They're silenced by fear. And by hush money. Big hush money. I have another theory, too. I think Carolyn Divers was murdered, and for the same reason Mrs. Leroux and Meredith were. And two narcotics agents from Thailand. I think they were all murdered by the same killer, for the same reason."

"I thought it was suicide."

"Meredith? She didn't drown herself, Rutledge. Meredith was murdered."

He started to say something. She raised a hand. "Hear me out."

He pressed his lips together. She went on. "Carolyn Divers, then the Asian men, then Mrs. Leroux accidentally or willfully came upon the operation. They were murdered to prevent them from blowing the whistle. They were all outsiders who got too snoopy. There might have been others too, innocent tourists who accidentally stumbled upon some evidence of illegal activity. You know what else I think?"

"Nope."

"I think the heart of the operation is on this beach and up in these forests. Poachers harvesting fresh galls. Bear, elk, maybe other species too. Selling to Asian traffickers, for cash, and maybe a little heroin as a bonus."

Rutledge rose slowly to his feet, walked over to where the seal family frolicked in the tide pool. He yelled at them and they lurched away, padding down to the tide line. Venus went over, stood beside him. He said, "You ever see a By-the-Wind-Sailor?"

She crouched down at the edge of the tidepool. Some By-the-Winds had found these reviving waters. She said, "Asians eat them. In salads." She hoped she'd remember to tell Richard Winters that.

They walked south along the beach, toward Rutledge's cottage. From shallow waters, the fugitive seals honked victoriously, bellying back into the tide pool. Rutledge plucked tobacco off his tongue, studied the tobacco shred, flicked it away. He said, "Go on back up to Seattle. Come back next summer, in tourist season. It's safer then."

She pointed to the lighthouse on the horizon. She said, "I'm going out there."

"Don't play Cap'n Courage."

Rutledge stopped walking, turned. His eyes scanned the beach, the driftwood bulkhead, the forest edge. He had seen something, or heard something. Suddenly he lunged at her. "Look out!" he shouted. He shoved her down onto the sand.

From the forest came sounds of gunshots. Rutledge fell, grasping his arm where a bullet had grazed him. Venus drew her gun and sprinted toward the woods. Rutledge shouted, "Come back here. That's the poachers!"

"Go home," she shouted over her shoulder.

She turned in time to see an adult black bear, terrified, scampering across the driftwood logs: the real target of the gunfire.

Paralleling the bear, Venus stepped off the driftwood bulkhead into a stand of Douglas firs. Sunlight filtered through the boughs, dappling shadows over rich black earth. She climbed the steep escarpment, eventually reaching an old logging trail that veered off from the main path deep into the woods. At the trail's entrance, she stopped, listened.

A soft breeze. Ferns brushing against tree bark. A woodpecker at work. Crickets. Some gulls in the distance, and the ocean's dull roar. High tide. The winds must be picking up. In the fir stands, on her left, a shadow moved. She slipped off the trail into a confusing shadowland of maidenhair and salal, crouched under the soaring conifers, and waited. To reach her, the stalkers had to cross the trail. She had the advantage. Her gun was ready.

Minutes dragged by with no movement, no sound from the sylvan thicket. Then, across the path, she heard the underbrush rustle, saw something move. She aimed her pistol, barely breathing. Silence. Then, more rustling, this time farther down the escarpment, on the small path leading to the beach. A retreat? No. Maybe encirclement. Poachers work in gangs, always two or more. Or, it might be a wild creature. She blinked. Drops of sweat dripped from her brow. The pills weren't working after all, the stubborn fever impervious to the Hindi's prescription.

Behind her now, a terrible, familiar noise. Hounds. Not one hound, but five or six at once, rushing through the underbrush, working up a horrid yelping chorus. She leaped to her feet, flung herself against an evergreen tree, and clambered up its trunk. Halfway to the thick boughs, her pistol fell to the ground. The hounds moved in a pack, their blood red eyes and vicious fangs appearing first, then their lean, rippling bodies. Hounds trained to flush out bear could rip a human apart in seconds. From her poor hiding place, she held still, barely breathing, looking downward, but she wasn't prepared for what happened next.

Baying sickly, the pack raced past her, driven mad by the scent of bear. One after the other, they scrambled down the escarpment toward the beach. Soon from the forest appeared the men, moving rapidly, four armed hunters racing through the underbrush after the hounds. From where she crouched on a high branch, she could not make out their identities, or even hope to describe them later on. They disappeared down the escarpment. They hadn't seen her. She crouched in the boughs, waiting.

Ten minutes later, they returned, pushing through the underbrush, hounds at their heels. They had lost the bear. Somehow it had escaped. As they passed below her, she held her breath. The hounds sniffed curiously around the tree, but the hunters hurried them along. The hounds followed obediently, still hungry for bear. She heard a frustrated male voice say, "He took the bait. He'll be back for more."

Minutes later, in the distance, an engine sounded. She heard the vehicle backfire, the engine gunned, then silence. She worked her way down the tree branches and had just located her pistol in a salal bush when a low, almost whispered growl sounded behind her. She turned. He was enormous, ancient, with wise black-button eyes. When he snarled, his teeth appeared. Very white, very pointed. Still thin from hibernation, the bear was hungry, foraging for food.

He lumbered toward her. Slowly, in the same rhythm as the bear, she backed into the path, scanning over her shoulder for another tree. She couldn't go forward to the tree she had just left. He stood beneath it now, sniffing the bark, watching her in peripheral vision. If she could find a taller tree, maybe she could outclimb it. Bears can't climb very high. But she saw no branches low enough to grab.

He watched Venus, curious, wary. Licking his paws, he stepped into the path, into a shaft of sunlight, and warmed himself in the sunshine, his wet nose sniffing the air, all the while keeping her in peripheral vision. Now the forest grew quiet again. The old bear cocked his head, took two steps toward her, and paused. His haunches quivered. In her steady grip, the measly .38 Smith &

Wesson felt like a bad joke. She aimed the pistol at the bear's skull. She'd never shot a bear before. She didn't want to shoot him, but would if he attacked. His nose wriggled, glistening.

A noisy bumblebee zoomed out of some blackberry vines and circled the bear. He reached up, batted it with his paw. The bumblebee teased him, landing first on his ear, then on his tattered backside. He rolled around, playing tag with the bumblebee. After a while, the bumblebee buzzed out of sight, and he turned his attention back to Venus. Her finger felt the pistol's trigger. The bear shrugged. She stood very still. Through beads of sweat, through the stark scent of danger, her senses heightened. She smelled chocolate.

Slowly, she reached into her jacket pocket, fished out some chocolate kisses. Avoiding direct eye contact with him, she unwrapped a kiss, tossed the chocolate nip a couple yards away, on the ground. The bear's nose wriggled, sniffed. He lumbered slowly toward the kiss, his nose inquiring, exploring. He sniffed the chocolate kiss. A cranberry-colored tongue appeared between his lips, between the sharp teeth. The tongue scooped up the kiss. She eased her hand back into her pocket, pulled out some more kisses, unwrapped them, tossed them across the path, this time a little farther away. The bear sniffed each one, snatched them up. Then, as if he'd forgotten she was there—his own pretense to save face—he turned and lumbered toward the escarpment down to the shore.

THE RANGER shack doors wouldn't give. Bolted from the inside. With a fist, she pounded on the front door. No response. She pounded again, then yelled, "Open up, Sparks." His Bronco stood beside the shack, also locked.

Silence. She listened for a few minutes, then yelled again. "Sparks, open the door. I need to talk to you."

Silence. On the ground, in the damp pine-needle carpet, she saw fresh tire tracks, not from the Bronco, and knew this was the path the poachers and their hounds took out of the park. Sparks wasn't answering. No sound came from the shack. As she headed back toward the logging trail, more shots rang out. She slid down the escarpment, scrambled down through the forest underbrush, reaching the beach in about five minutes. The gunshots had sounded from down here, down below, on the beach again. She scaled the driftwood bulkhead, sprinted across the beach, following the bear's tracks in the wet silver sand. She saw him in the distance, lying in a heap on the tide line. She ran faster, looking right and left for signs of the men, the hounds. They must have taken another trail back to the beach. Now she had reached the bear. She bent over him. The old creature had been blasted through the heart, his paws chopped off, and he had been savagely disemboweled.

She flew into a rage, pummeling the wet sand, thrashing at the wind, yelling at the ocean surf. Her fury echoed off the ocean, but the dense forest sucked in her terrible ravings, and soon silence blunted her spirit. She hated the forest for its silent aloofness.

RUTLEDGE sat smoking a cigarette on the porch steps. "Go on inside," he said to Venus. "Man in there wants to see you."

She went inside Rutledge's cabin. The man was tall, slender, with copper-colored hair and a thick, red handlebar mustache. She had never seen him without the yellow slicker and the sou'wester. Popeye. Now he wore a naval officer's uniform. A hint of gun holster peeked out under his jacket when he pulled his hands from his pockets and produced the silver handcuffs.

"Jack O'Connor," he said smoothly. "United States Navy." He clipped the handcuffs on her wrists loosely, to show he was a gentleman. "I'm taking you into custody."

"What for?"

"For kicks," said O'Connor. "That's what for."

He was better looking without the rain gear. On the way out, O'Connor said, "I'm taking you in for interfering with a government investigation."

Rutledge sat on the porch steps. Venus said, "How's the arm?"

"Okay. Just a nick." He showed it to her.

Bitterly, she said, "Thanks a heap, old timer. You really did me a favor."

Rutledge grunted and watched O'Connor lead her down the porch steps. She'd be better off, Rutledge told himself, under arrest. Safer. Safer than if she stayed in Ozone Beach.

O'Connor gripped her elbow, steered her along the beach to the redwood steps, up the redwood steps to a white sedan parked in front of Mercy's Chowder Bar. He opened the passenger door. She slid in. He shut the door, locked it, went around to the driver's side, got in, and started the ignition. Pulling away from the curb, Venus said, "Are we driving all the way back to Seattle together?"

"No."

Navy's helicopter stood beside the Ozone Beach Bell Jet Ranger at the airfield. O'Connor helped her up. Her Harley had already been loaded into the chopper. This annoyed her more than anything else. O'Connor gave the signal and the navy chopper's pilot lifted off. Thirty minutes later, the chopper landed at Sand Point Naval Air Station in Seattle. Twenty minutes after that, she sat in a comfortable leather chair in O'Connor's spacious private office. Olson was there, too, and he was ticked off.

TWENTY-FIVE

Barnacle Bill

IT MUST HAVE BEEN her lucky day. O'Connor took the brunt of Olson's wrath. Livid, Olson snarled, "You think you're some hot shit, don't you, O'Connor?"

O'Connor grinned pleasantly, pressed a button on his desk. "Michelle," he said calmly, "send in our guest, please."

Olson growled, "Take those cuffs off my agent."

O'Connor stood, swished around the desk, bent over her, and removed the handcuffs. Venus could smell his expensive peppery cologne. She rubbed her wrists. They felt stiff. Olson growled, "Did you have to do that to her face?"

She said, "I fell on the beach, Olson. He didn't do it."

She wasn't ready to tell O'Connor that she knew he'd dumped her on the tide. Olson muttered under his breath. Back at his desk, O'Connor smirked behind folded hands, then the door opened and Venus understood why he looked so smug.

Wexler walked in, his complexion the color of coconut meat. No leis, no Hawaiian tan. He wasn't smiling.

Venus said, "Aloha."

Olson snapped, "Shut up, Venus."

Wexler nodded at O'Connor, walked over to Olson and said quietly, "I'd like you to wait outside."

"What—" Olson protested.

"Do as I say."

Olson rose slowly, lumbered to the door. There, he turned and said, "I told her to stay out of Ozone Beach." He went out, shutting the door softly behind him.

Wexler stood near Venus. She could hear his stomach rumbling. Maybe the puny airline meal. He hadn't been in Hawaii at all. He'd been on a flight from Washington, DC, to Seattle. Surprise, surprise. Wexler said, "How's the fever?"

She shrugged sullenly.

Wexler's ice blue eyes flickered. He walked over to a chair and sat down. Wexler wore his favorite khaki suit, a button-down oxford shirt that matched his eyes, and desert boots. A man of habits, he had worn variations of this style ever since she'd known him.

Wexler furrowed his brow. A shock of snow white hair fell across thick black eyebrows, softening them, smoothing the furrows. His attention turned from her to O'Connor. O'Connor said to Wexler, "Shall we begin?"

Wexler nodded.

O'Connor leaned back in his chair and said, "There's no point in playing games. We're at a crucial stage. The situation is serious. Your agent has been interfering."

Wexler said, "In all fairness, I think you owe us an elaboration on what you mean by the 'situation.'"

O'Connor nodded, and that smug, superior expression returned. He stood, walked around to the front of his desk, leaned against it. "For several years now," he began, "I have been in charge of Navy's intelligence operations along the Washington coast. As you may know, we have a nuclear submarine base over at Bangor, and since we began that project, Navy has maintained a presence in the waters here off the coast, to protect our subs. But we have other interests along the coast as well.

"For instance, Rain Dance, a classified operation that peripherally involves the Point Danger lighthouse. Now, before you get too worked up, let me explain that the operation itself poses absolutely no danger to wildlife out there. But Rain Dance has always been a secure operation, it's never been made public, never even leaked out. That's how secure this operation is, and we cannot and will not tolerate any interference whatsoever, from your agency or from those villagers down there."

He walked around Venus's chair, made a complete tour, ending up near her right elbow. She watched him in her peripherals, but her eyes focused on Wexler. He appeared irritated, definitely not delighted to be at O'Connor's party. O'Connor said, "Maybe you're wondering what sort of operation we would conduct on a federal wildlife sanctuary."

Wexler glared at O'Connor the way a big cat eyes its prey just before it attacks. Wexler would love to pounce on O'Connor now, tear him to shreds. But Wexler was a civilized man, with infinite patience.

O'Connor said, "We have secured all the necessary permissions. We are certainly under no obligation to reveal the nature of the Rain Dance operation to Interior, or to anyone else, for that matter. Except the president."

He paused here for dramatic effect. Venus shivered at his closeness. He continued, "To put your minds at ease, let me assure you that Rain Dance has the blessings of the congressional committee that oversees classified military operations. That's really all I'm at liberty to reveal at this time. However, just for your peace of mind I will tell you this much: Rain Dance does not involve a lot of equipment. In fact, we have very little equipment on the island, all of it located inside the lighthouse, where it could not possibly interfere with the pelicans. I've been out there myself many times to monitor the project, and have seen pelicans roosting in the windows of the lighthouse. They're quite content with our presence out there. The pelicans are not being harmed. We aren't interfering with the sanctuary in any way whatsoever. In fact, the operation requires only one man to visit the lighthouse, and he goes out only once every three or four months. So you see, Rain Dance isn't hurting anyone, or anything."

Venus said, "Who's the one man?"

"Who goes out there? Me, of course."

Wexler said, "Is that all?"

"No." O'Connor raised a rigid finger. "Just one more point. These deaths which have occurred in Ozone Beach. The timber heiress, Mrs. Leroux, and the young lady who worked at Janice Mercy's restaurant. They are absolutely not related to our business. So here's the deal. You stay clear of the area for the next forty-eight hours. Then after that, you can go in there and do your job. And sometime soon, we'll call a meeting to clear up jurisdiction out there. Agreed?''

Wexler stared at O'Connor. "Forty-eight hours for what?"

O'Connor grimaced. He didn't like revealing secrets. He said, "We are preparing to apprehend a submarine of unknown origin that periodically operates off the coast here, out just beyond the light. Until we've got them in custody, I can't have you out there interfering. I'm asking for forty-eight hours, that's all. Then we can sit down again, iron things out."

Wexler stood up, motioned for Venus to rise. She stood, her mouth already open to protest O'Connor's offer of a deal. Wexler flashed her a sharp look. To O'Connor, he said, "Okay. Is that all?"

O'Connor looked at Venus, then at Wexler, and nodded.

IN THE ELEVATOR, Wexler said, "You have blood in your ear."

To Olson, he said, "Go on home, champ. It's late. I'll meet you at the office tomorrow. Then we'll talk."

Olson glowered. At the curb, he shuffled his feet, dallied. He started to say something, changed his mind. He turned and skulked away.

Wexler said, "How's Bella?"

"Magnificent, as usual."

"Would she mind unexpected company?"

"You ever ride a Harley, Wexler?"

"Ah, sure. I can handle that."

"I have a delivery to make on the way."

They stopped at the offices of Tapp, Tapp, and O'Toole. The paralegal was working late. She unlocked the door, accepted the parcel from Venus, promised to lock it in a safe immediately and leave it there until the Tapps returned from Rio.

The paralegal was tall, statuesque, model material. Nothing like her voice over the phone, Venus thought. The paralegal said, "Sure, I'll lock it up. But I still don't see what's so all-fired important about a kitchen inventory."

Venus said, "That is a handwritten will you're holding. Lock it up and throw away the key till Tapp comes back."

The paralegal clasped the manila envelope to her small bosom. "God," she said breathily. "Oh God. Now I get it." She ran to a wall safe, opened it, and with Venus and Wexler witnessing, thrust Madge Leroux's holographic will deep inside the safe, closed the door, and spun the lock.

During the ride to Bella's, through the crisp evening air, Venus let Wexler wear the helmet with Benny Goodman in the headphones.

TWENTY-SIX

Sharpei

BELLA had a lap pool installed in the north wing of her castle. Her Chinese shar-pei, Pansy, often swam in the pool, but Bella rarely dipped. She said chlorine spoiled frosted hair. The lap pool wasn't deep enough to dive into, but you could drown someone in there, if you used muscle. Venus inspected the water before sliding in.

From the recreation room next door came throcking sounds of Ping-Pong paddles hitting little hollow balls. She could hear the balls bounce on the table, the paddles throcking them. *Bounce. Throck. Bounce. Throck.* She could hear Bella's symphonic laughter and Wexler's deep masculine baritone egging Bella on. Bella had given Wexler a personal tour of the castle. They had paused in the rec room for a bit of sport.

Bella and Wexler had met before, briefly, when Venus had introduced them at an awards ceremony in Washington, DC. Venus was receiving a "Special Agent of the Year" award, but Bella and Wexler forgot all about that when they came face to face. *Enchanted* was the word Bella frequently employed to describe that moment. But then, Bella described numerous moments and countless introductions as enchanting, so Venus had taken it all with a grain of salt.

She glided lazily, hoping Bella and Wexler would not decide to join her in the pool. She wanted to be alone. To think. *Bounce. Throck. Bounce. Throck.* In a few minutes, they went away, leaving Venus and the shar-pei alone in that wing of the house. Pansy snoozed at poolside, curled up inside a life ring. Venus worked up into serious laps, let her brain rest a while, let her body do all the work. The subconscious appreciates physical exertion. The subconscious prefers to mull and compute in private, while the body is busy elsewhere. She gave her subconscious twenty-five minutes of utter privacy, pushing her heart and lungs to the max. No corpse came to get her this time.

At dinner, Bella spoke of pleasant things, as Bella always did, being allergic to unpleasantness at the dinner table. Anyone who raised untoward topics at Bella's table would not be invited back. Wexler seemed to intuit Bella's rule, even to appreciate this quality of hers, and maybe a few other things about her: Venus had noticed earlier, while Wexler and Bella flirted over cocktails, that Wexler had trouble keeping his eyes off Bella's million-dollar legs. Bella noticed it too, and at the dinner table she seated Wexler perilously close to them, where, should he drop his napkin, he might enjoy a quick tour. Wexler fell, no, *leaped* into the trap, for it seemed to fit with his own plans. Venus felt mildly miffed. Maybe it was childish, but she didn't like this Oedipal third-wheel feeling.

Over the Remy Martin, Venus managed to slip a word in between flirtations. To Wexler she said, "I'm ready to hear your explanation now. Why you brought me back to the States."

Life is full of little distractions, and now Wexler wasn't inclined to professional matters. One of Bella's lovely hands slowly smoothed the folds of her Mizrahi skirt, and Bella's dazzling smile had Wexler hypnotized. Venus poured Wexler more cognac and used it to lure him into the living room. On the couch, Wexler mentally rubbed knees with Bella, and began, "The note I received last January, from this Pelican Patrol...I didn't take it very seriously at first. Then two weeks ago, while you were still in the hospital in Singapore, I received a phone call from someone on the congressional committee that oversees classified military operations. He asked to meet with me. When we met, privately, understand, my informant told me that according to his files, an operation called Rain Dance had been active for six years or more, having gone unnoticed by the committee, having never been investigated nor given the green light. There was no evidence of a secret presidential order—in fact, no evidence of any funding for the operation. Understandably curious, he contacted a friend in Navy Intelligence. You'll be interested in the response he got."

He sipped the Remy, smiled at Bella. He reached out and was on the brink of patting her knee when he thought better of it. Instead he smiled and said, "This business talk must bore you."

Bella gushed, "Nonsense. You are absolutely fascinating, Jerry. Do please resume your story."

Wexler's hand fell softly on her knee. Pat. Pat. There. Maybe now he could concentrate. He said, "My congressional informant could find no one in the upper echelons at Navy who knew of an Operation Rain Dance. So he went back to his records and read them over. He discovered that in fact, the only information the committee had ever received about this Rain Dance came from a civilian source. A woman living in Ozone Beach had written several times, asking the committee to look into a secret project called Rain Dance, which she claimed was a military operation off the Washington coast. Because no one had ever heard of the operation, her letters got filed. No action was ever initiated, no investigation ever conducted. That was about three years ago, just about the time pelicans were first reported roosting out on the rock at Point Danger."

Venus said, "Did your informant mention the woman's name?"

"He told me in confidence."

"If I say the correct name, will you just nod?"

"Venus," Bella chirped, "that isn't kosher."

Venus said, "Carolyn Divers."

Wexler nodded.

"This meeting was just two weeks ago," he said. "I showed him the note that I'd received from the so-called Pelican Patrol. At that point, I found it auspicious to bring you back to the Pacific Northwest. I needed you on the scene, but was not at liberty to divulge details yet. Now, you must be wondering why I appeared so uninformed today, in O'Connor's office."

Venus said, "Almost docile."

Bella chirped, "Jerry, docile? I hardly think so, dear."

Wexler liked that. To Venus, he said, "We think O'Connor

invented Rain Dance. He's been using the lighthouse for smuggling *xiong dan* and other illegal animal parts. Now, O'Connor surely has partners in this operation, and surely they suspect that you're onto them. You're very close, Venus, to rounding up that international poachers' ring you've been tracking for three years. O'Connor apparently wants to complete one last transaction out at the lighthouse. Then they'll have to relocate their operation somewhere else along the coast. He figured if he kept you out of Ozone Beach for the next forty-eight hours, they could complete the current transaction, and then get out of Ozone Beach for good.''

"We'll pull a raid," Venus said. "Make this their last deal."

Wexler raised a cautionary hand. "Only if we avoid unnecessary risks."

"Risks!" Venus sprang to her feet. "What risks, Wexler? How can you talk about risks when these bastards have already—"

"Venus, I do not permit the use of that word in my home," Bella murmured.

Wexler said, "You're sure of your facts?"

"Positive. I am certain that the three women were murdered by the same person, or persons, because they had discovered the poaching operation." She told Wexler about the two Thai government agents. "Chandrak and Pornchen never told me they'd been coming over here to Point Danger, never mentioned any American leads. Maybe they wanted to score the arrests, be heroes."

Bella said, "Perhaps they were in on it. Did you ever think of that, darling?"

"Mother, Chandrak and Pornchen were my colleagues—"

"I rest my case on the salmon camellias..." Bella trailed off.

Venus continued, "They'd come close to cracking the operation. They weren't run out of town. I believe they were also murdered. I can't prove it yet, but I'm sure they were murdered."

Wexler said, "Does Sparks fit into this?"

Venus shook her head. "No. Sparks is shiftless and lazy and territorial. But he's not a part of this."

"How can you be sure?"

"I know, that's all. He doesn't fit the pattern. He's no poacher. He's not that ambitious. And he cares about wildlife, in spite of his shoddy attitude. You know what he does, Wexler? You know what Sparks does on the job? He reads. He spends most of his time at the office in the library. When he's down at the park, he holes up in the ranger shack with stacks of books."

Wexler stared at her.

"It's true, Wexler. Sparks is no more dangerous than a fly."

"Or," quipped Bella, "a mosquito, perhaps?"

In the distance, the telephone rang. She heard Stephen answer the phone. She heard him raise his voice, shout into it, then Stephen came into the living room and said, "For you, Miss. Long distance, collect. The connection is very poor, but the voice sounds very young, like a child."

Venus was already moving toward the telephone, her brain on full alert now. If she had a fever, she didn't feel it because a cold chill had gripped her heart. She raced down the long hallway, Pansy barking alongside, nipping at her heels. In the foyer, she collided with Bella's driver, who had just returned from Wexler's hotel with his luggage. She leaped over the luggage, grabbed the telephone receiver, shouted into it.

"Timmy, is that you?"

"Venus?"

"What's up?"

"The manitou is trying to get in the house. And Chick isn't here. I'm scared. It's trying to break into the house through a window."

"Where's Chick?"

"He went to a council meeting. He's been gone a long time. I'm really scared."

"Are all the doors locked?"

"Yes."

She tried to sound calm, but she knew that everything was wrong and that time was running out.

"Timmy, listen to me. There is no such thing as a manitou. What noises are you hearing?"

"I don't hear it. I see it. Out the window. It's walking around the house, trying all the windows, trying to find a way in. I tried to phone Mr. Rutledge, but he wasn't home."

"Where are you now?"

"In the den."

"I'm going to call Chick. Then I'll call the sheriff up in Oyster Bay. Then I'll come right down. Meanwhile, Tim—"

"What?"

"I'm going to call a friend of mine. A Mr. Burden. I'm going to ask Mr. Burden to come to your house and watch television with you until Chick gets home, or I get there. I want you to let Mr. Burden in when he comes, Tim. But no one else. Okay?"

"All right. Are you coming right now?"

"I'm leaving now. I mean it. Don't let anyone else in the house, no matter who they are, no matter what they say. Do you understand?"

"Yes. The manitou is looking through the window."

"Can you see the face?"

"No. It's dark out there. Only when the eyes blink. I can see it when the eyes blink."

"Go to the window and shut the curtain. Then come back to the phone."

"Okay. I shut the curtain. I'm still scared."

"Listen, Timmy. I'm going to help you stop being scared. We'll get you off the phenobarb and the fingernail biting. You'll start feeling like a normal kid. I'm going to help you be happy and relaxed. I don't ever want you to be afraid again."

"Chick says it's healthy to be afraid. He says that if you're not afraid, then there's something wrong with you."

"I'm on my way, Tim."

"Venus?"

"Yes."

"I know why the manitou is after me."

"I told you, there's no such—"

"Because I wrote that note."

"What note?"

"To your boss. In Washington, DC. Me and my friend Lola over at the post office. We wrote the note because we found out about the poachers using the lighthouse. We read it in one of my stepmother's notebooks. We were afraid to tell anyone here, even the sheriff. So we sent the note. We made up the part about the Pelican Patrol. There isn't any Pelican Patrol. And now the manitou is after me because I squealed.''

"I'll be there soon, sport."

SHE HUNG UP. She pawed through Bella's digital telephone directory, located the Leroux's phone number in Ozone Beach. She called Burden, told him what to do. Burden agreed to go immediately. She phoned Mercy's Chowder Bar. No answer. She let the phone ring twenty times. Still no answer. She got the operator on the line, told him there was an emergency, asked to be put through to Divers' Spa, but to stay on the line. He placed the call. No answer. She explained to the operator that a child was in danger, told him to keep trying the number. When the boy answered, she told the operator to keep him on the line, keep talking to him. The operator said he was very sorry but that he wasn't permitted to do those things. She yelled at him to bend the rules just this once, then hung up. She was heading out the front door when Bella and Wexler intercepted her in the foyer.

"Where are you going in such a rude hurry?" Bella demanded.

"Ozone Beach. No time to talk..."

Bella grabbed her arm, held it in her familiar steely grip. Wexler said, "O'Connor's extremely dangerous."

She almost shouted at him. "Who got me into this, Wexler?"

Quietly he said, "Okay, Venus. What about backup?"

Her mind raced. These plans had been forming in her brain for years. Now they emerged, organized, precise. "It's what? Nine-thirty? We'll plan the raid for three A.M. Get Olson and Dave. Have the team meet me in the park at the ranger shack. Sparks knows where that is. Have them meet me there at one o'clock. No, make that midnight. Bring everyone who's available."

Wexler nodded. Bella cried shrilly, "Venus, I will not permit you to become involved in this questionable scenario. Close the door at once."

Pansy growled and nipped her ankles. "Mother," Venus said

firmly, "an eight-year-old child is about to be kidnapped. Maybe even murdered. Yes, probably murdered. Unless you let go of my arm..."

Bella loosened her grip. Pansy backed off. Bella cried, "I am going with you. Stephen, get my coat and umbrella."

Venus said to Wexler, "Don't let her out of this house. Do anything, just don't let her out. I'm going to take the chopper down, leave it at Oyster Bay. Do I need permission?"

"You've got it. I'll call for a pilot to meet you at Bumbershoot."

"Find Dave," she said. "We can't pull this off without Dave."

Wexler nodded somberly. "I'll get that team down there."

"My little April fool," murmured Bella proudly.

BURDEN had tacked a note on the front door of Divers' Spa. "Miss Diamond, Came right away. Rang bell, but no response. Tried doors and windows without success. Hope the boy's all right. If you need me, I am up at the house. Best luck, Burden."

She was smashing a den window when Chick Divers rolled his car into the drive. He ran over, shouting, "What's the idea? What are you doing breaking into my house?"

"Timmy's in trouble. Open the door, Chick. Hurry."

Chick unlocked the front door. She shoved past him. The house was dark. Chick turned on some lights. She went into the den. The television set was on. The late movie tonight was *The Incredible Shrinking Man.* On the coffee table stood an empty Coke bottle and a half empty plastic carton of Oreos. She went over to the little desk. The report on *xiong dan* wasn't there. She asked Chick about it.

"I destroyed that," Chick said.

"Why?"

"The boy was behaving too proudly. He needed a lesson."

She said, "You're a sick man, Chick."

Chick tore at his hair. "All this killing has to stop!" he cried. "It isn't right to murder people. It's a terrible thing. And now they've got Timmy."

She searched the house, Chick at her heels. No sign of forced entry. The evil manitou must have convinced Timmy to unlock the door. Chick, nearing panic, cried suddenly, "It's Satan! It's those goddamn bikers! They've taken Timmy." He buried his head in his hands. "Oh God," he sobbed.

"What points to Satan?"

"Nothing. Nothing. I don't know. Just an idea I had. I heard they're coming back. But why Timmy?"

"Satan doesn't have Timmy, Chick. Maybe years ago, someone here in this village used the gang to fence contraband, then double-crossed them. That's why they set the village on fire back then. But I doubt Satan is coming back here."

"But, the reports—" Chick cried desperately.

Venus said, "Rumors. That's all. There's no real evidence that the gang is coming back here. Satan doesn't have Timmy, and you damn well know that. And I'll tell you something else, Chick. Black market traffickers are a lot like poachers. They'll cut their own children's throats if they have to, to save their own necks. Think about that, Chick."

Divers rushed sobbing from the house, dove into his car, and squealed off into the night. Venus didn't have to follow him. She knew where he was going. She gave him a half hour lead, then mounted the Harley and headed up the dark gravel road into the park.

TWENTY-SEVEN

The Raid

RAIN FELL, and in the clearing the pine-needle ground cover proved treacherous, slick and spongy beneath Venus's feet. Standing beside the ranger shack, Venus checked her Swatch. Four minutes to midnight.

Dave arrived first with a team of deputies from Oyster Bay, including three state game agents, four of Ball's deputies, and Ball himself. Behind them, from DOI, came Dot Johanson and Claudia; then, a few minutes later, another DOI agent, Eric Sweetwater, with Olson and Sparks. Altogether, fifteen.

She'd gone down to the beach earlier and located where the bait was set this time. At the base of the stone jetty, she found the pile of jelly doughnuts and, underneath them, an electronic trip wire that would signal the poachers. Carefully, she removed a sample doughnut, bagged it. She guessed that when Claudia analyzed it, she'd find traces of narcotics.

They would be out soon, the poachers, in their lookout posts, waiting for the alarm to spring, waiting for their prey. They'd try to take the bears alive, slow them down with the spiked jelly doughnuts, tranquilize them with guns, load them into cages, and transport them by truck to the slaughterhouse, where they could make a clean operation of the butchery, or cage them until they were drained to death. That was how this operation worked, unless their prey resisted. If a bear resisted, the poachers killed it and butchered it on the spot, left a gut pile behind. The poachers would be heavily armed and would resist arrest.

She briefed Dave, who moved through the woods briefing the teams. She gave him a map she had drawn, indicating the site of the jelly roll bait, the old logging trail leading from the forest to the beach just north of the jetty. The map showed the bears' escape route, through the park, through Mrs. Bobbs's cranberry bog. She had drawn a map of the village too, where she suspected they would discover the slaughterhouse.

Olson had paired off with Eric Sweetwater. They came up through the woods, in the rain. Olson said, "Before all hell breaks loose out here, I want to apologize for being such an incredible ass..." He fumbled for words, unaccustomed to apologizing. "Not just about this, I mean about everything. I think I've finally bottomed out of this depression. If only...I mean...I didn't know about Wexler's plans..."

She looked at Olson, saw the pain in his eyes, the shame and remorse. "Hey," she said softly, "it's okay. Just lose the gender jokes and we'll be pals again." Olson reached out, took her small hand in his, squeezed it.

Venus said, "Where the hell is my carbine?"

Dave handed the gun to Venus. She was checking the sight when Dave said, "What color dress you wearing Saturday night?"

She lowered the carbine, thought a minute, said, "All I got's white. Why?"

Dave smiled secretively, murmured, "Just wondered."

She said, "I hear you're a big-shot movie star now." A little banter might take the edge off.

He chortled. "They wanted local color. A real live wildlife agent to add credibility to their improbable plot."

"What's it about?"

Dave winked. "Top secret."

Venus groaned. "Don't tell me. I'll bet the working title's *Leek Soup*."

"Oops." Dave laughed. "I'm busted."

She felt that strange emotion again, like love, maybe mixed up with something she couldn't define. Dave leaned over and kissed Venus gently on the mouth.

"You're my best pal, Dave," she whispered in his ear.

Dave smiled. The kiss had felt right, like starting things off on the perfect note.

Venus read her Swatch. "Let's go, guys."

The teams fanned out into the park and waited in the rain. Venus paired off with Dave. They moved cautiously down the old logging path, slid down the steep escarpment. Where the forest ended, at the topsy-turvy driftwood bulkhead on the beach, they crouched, waiting. It might be minutes, or hours. It all depended on the bears.

An hour later, the rains let up and only a fine mist fell on the beach. Fog rolled in off the ocean and then a fat moon pierced the mist, played peek-a-boo with the fog, shedding intermittent shimmering light on the undulating tideline. In a few minutes, from the direction of the cottages came a family of bedraggled bears, rain-soaked, lumbering along the tideline. Venus and Dave exchanged glances. He pressed some buttons on a digital phone, put it to his face, spoke softly. "Okay," he said. "On the beach."

The bears moved single file, led by an adult male, then two adult females, then three cubs at the rear. Gingerly, they padded onto the jetty, scampered over the boulders, all the while sniffing the ground. In a few minutes, the male adult made a grunting sound. He had located the jelly doughnuts. The others circled the bait. They plunged into the sweet rolls, gorged. Then the adult male scampered to the tide's edge, stood on his hind legs, and began twirling, dancing a slow ecstatic waltz. The others soon joined him, the two female adults also dancing, even the cubs, trying the rhythm on for size. As they danced in the moonlight, they swatted at the foamy tide water, raised their front paws high above their heads, their noses to the sky, feeling the cold salt water rain down.

Rain Dance.

From the forest edge, like phantoms, six men emerged aiming shotguns at the euphoric dancers. No hounds yet, just humans. Sensing them, the adult male turned. Then a great blinding light washed the jetty. The poachers' jacklight blinded the bears. Sightless, startled, they froze. The men aimed their guns at the bears' heads. They weren't going to take them alive tonight. Tonight they meant to kill on the spot, harvest fresh organs. Dave, seeing this, said, "Shit," and got on the phone. Venus fired one shot into the air. The startled bears scrambled blindly up the beach, and then the hounds appeared from nowhere, in a horrid baying pack, and raced after the bears. Dave spoke into a portable loud-speaker, "You're surrounded by federal agents. Put down your weapons. Come out of the woods. Place your hands over your heads. You're under arrest."

"The hell we are," shouted one of the men.

Ball shone a spotlight on the poachers and cursed. He could see them now, and he recognized them. There was Heard's boy, the kid with the clamshell lips who worked at the grocery. There was one of Ball's former deputies, and there was a schoolteacher from the village elementary school. There was a man Ball didn't recognize, and then there was Chick Divers. The kid from Heard's grocery aimed an AK-47 toward Venus and Dave and fired.

Bullets sang off an ancient cedar. Then the whole forest went to war, chaos everywhere. Bullets flew, zinging off trees. The bear family, terrified, scrambled up on the stone jetty, then back again into the waves. In the shallows, the hounds bayed wildly, then in the distance, a blast, like dynamite, went off, a slick diversion while the poachers found a hole in the dragnet and slipped through it into the park forest. The hounds fled with their masters.

The team scrambled after them. Thrashing, pounding on wet earth through the forest, they chased, dodging gunfire. The poach-ers knew these woods better than the team, knew all the intricacies of the park. They headed toward Mrs. Bobbs's cranberry bog. When they reached the bog, they took cover behind Mrs. Bobbs's cottage.

Inside her cottage, Mrs. Bobbs crouched below a window, only daring to peek. A few minutes earlier, she had turned off the all-night movies, said her prayers, and gone to bed. Then came the sound of gunfire. Then these dark figures splashing through her bog, heading for her cottage. Who were they, with their terrible guns? What did they want? Mrs. Bobbs trembled violently.

The team moved into the forest surrounding Mrs. Bobbs's cran-berry bog, and the battle escalated. Near the bog, Venus and Dave

got separated. From the forest edge, Venus had a clear view of
the cottage. Someone fired a direct shot at the kid with clamshell
lips, and he fell beside the cottage. Another poacher made a run
for the woods, sprinting through the bog. Somebody's expert aim
brought him down with a leg wound. He fell, howling, into the
bog. Sparks and one of Ball's deputies plucked the fallen man,
handcuffed him. Then somebody else went down near the bog—
one of the team. Venus fell to the ground, crawled alongside the
bog, ducking bullets and exploding shotgun shells, sliding through
the muddy ground until she reached him.

Dave. His chest was gone. Bullets zinged above her head. Ve-
nus held David close, hugged his body to the ground, lay over it.
He wasn't breathing. *Come on, David, breathe. Dave, come on,
Dave. Breathe, goddamn it.*

Olson, in a rage, flew out of cover, splashed into the bog, and
went straight for Chick Divers. Stunned, Divers aimed his gun,
but Olson had moved too fast, too boldly. Olson fired. Divers
lurched backward, hit the cottage wall beside the window where
Mrs. Bobbs stood paralyzed with fear. Divers clawed the cottage
wall and slid to the ground, dead. Within minutes of Divers's fall,
the battle subsided.

Venus cradled Dave in her arms. Then Olson came over with
Sparks and Claudia, took Dave from her, carried the dead man
away, sloshing through the bog. Venus fell to her knees beside
the tainted scarlet waters, and wept. Across the bog in a thicket,
a young bear cub, terrified, sat in frozen bas relief.

TWENTY-EIGHT

Bon Voyage, Timmy

BALL HAD Mrs. Bobbs flown to Oyster Bay, to the hospital and then to her daughter Marvine. The Heard youth, wounded but conscious, told Venus where to find the slaughterhouse. It was where she'd guessed, at the Upper Crust Bakery. Ball and Olson, with the team, kicked down the front door, went in, found the terrified caged creatures, and the grisly remnants of slaughter. The freezer had been emptied, the fresh galls removed from their hooks. Olson cursed.

Venus said, "They've got Timmy. They're going to deliver the galls, and they've got Timmy with them."

Olson, Ball, and the others fanned out through the village. Venus jumped into a deputy's car, peeled off from the curb. This time, Olson didn't try to stop her.

Venus parked the car half a block from the airfield, stole through darkness across the tarmac. There might still be time to save Timmy. She looked around. The airfield was deserted, but the village's helicopter sat on its pad. The pilot's door was locked, but the Jet Ranger's passenger door was unlatched. She climbed in. This Jet Ranger could hold up to six passengers. Two of the rear seats had been removed, to accommodate several large wooden crates. There were labels on the crates. Canned salmon. Yakima apples. Probably somewhere a little crate of Chateau San Michelle Beaujolais Sauvignon, to complement the bear paw soup. Venus peered out the window.

In the darkness, she could barely make out the airstrip, golf greens, and the hangar Richard Winters once shared with the Siddartha Gautama. There might still be time. She worked quickly, jostling the crates around to make a small space for herself. Her hands trembled and she choked back the tears and rage. *Dave. Come back, Dave.* She crouched in the nest for maybe fifteen minutes before she heard voices.

They grew louder, more distinct. There was a cheerful, well-articulated voice. There was an arrogant, cocky voice. And there was a small, angry voice. The one voice in all the world she'd hoped to hear.

The passenger door swung open. The cheerful voice said, "Here now, Timmy. Mustn't talk like that. Strap in, now. That's a good boy."

Something landed on top of Venus. A package. Hard, very cold. She let it slide off her. More hard, cold bricklike packages. Frozen. She endured the barrage silently. Just before the engine started up and the blades rent the air, she heard Timmy say, "Are we really going to kill the manitou?"

The cheerful voice replied, but Venus couldn't hear the response. Then the cheerful voice again, louder, closer: "Now, these fresh galls should go on the rear seats, like this." A clinking sound, glass containers. "Strapped in, for safekeeping."

A moment later, the chopper's blades whirred. The Jet Ranger lifted off the pad.

"Blessed Jesus," said Venus silently. "Here we go."

The chopper churned smoothly in the calm night air. She crouched in the cold nest, listening to sordid conversation. The chopper pilot said, "Reach back there, Jack, and see if I remembered the salmon."

Grunting sounds, then O'Connor's voice, "It's there."

"Fine. Who's meeting us this time?"

"Lok Toy himself."

"Why not Pan?"

"Pan got into some trouble up in Seattle. He's being detained by Immigration."

"We need to clear out the bakery, Jack. Let's do that this morning, as soon as we get back. We can move the animals to my farm, until we find a new site."

"Okay. When we get back on the mainland, I'll phone Chick. I wonder why he hasn't been answering my page."

"How long had Winters been working with the Thais?" The pilot.

"I don't know. I just saw them together that one time." O'Connor.

"I was never fond of Richard Winters."

Silence. Then O'Connor's voice, "It's just four-thirty. We'll be a few minutes early."

"Kiss me, Jack, honey." The pilot.

"Not in front of the boy."

"Prude." Taunting.

"I've seen people kiss before." Timmy.

No response. Then: "I had no choice with Meredith. No options. Really, Jack, she was on to us. Come on, honey, don't be mad—Anyway, I didn't particularly enjoy it."

Silence.

A few minutes passed. Then the pilot said, "Reach back there and check the paws. Have the paws defrosted?"

Rummaging. Venus reached inside her jacket, felt the butt of her pistol. More time passed, maybe a full minute, before she felt the cold round spot against her temple. A large hand gripped her shoulder, jerked her up out of the crates. The only light inside the chopper came from the forward control panel. In this light she saw the gun held to her head. She saw O'Connor's red handlebar mustache and his sparkling white teeth. O'Connor said to the pilot, "Stowaway."

In the passenger seat opposite the pilot, a child's head bobbed and Venus caught a glimpse of that familiar chocolate-colored hair. The pilot nodded suggestively to O'Connor and tilted the chopper. O'Connor held the gun steady at her temple, unlatched the cargo hold door, opened it. The pilot turned then to face her. Day-Glo lips formed a malicious snarl. Mrs. Mercy said, "Jump."

O'Connor helped her along.

Venus freefell into the black gulf and down.

TWENTY-NINE

Watchman, What of the Night?

DROWNING in an inkwell. Cold, flowing, choppy India ink. Bobbing like a cork, then, clutched in strong, wet fingers, sinking like a stone, down below the water's surface. Down there, demons play tug of war with your equilibrium. Venus struggled, but when she pushed up the demons pulled her back down, deeper into the inkwell. So this was drowning, gulping black saline ink, sinking, sinking, sinking. Very tired, very cold, very relaxed.

Venus gasped and thrashed and retched. In the distance, something made a throcking sound. Bella's Ping-Pong game. No. Helicopter blades. Moving away through the black velvet abyss. She floated now on the choppy black surface. Alone. Left to die. To drown. Alone. Treading, she vomited black ink and forced herself to stay awake. Then, from the darkness, somewhere in the distance, came her own voice, crying like a child's.

No, a child. Crying. Calling out. A tiny voice in the far distance. Somewhere through the pre-dawn blackness. There is always one last act to perform before that final, utterly peaceful rest. One last heroic effort. Nobody ever said dying wasn't work. *Wake up. Wake up. The boy is drowning. Timmy.*

She thrashed, sure that her head was above water, but her eyes saw only blackness. Clouds obscured the moon. She could hear the tiny voice but could not locate it in the darkness. She called out to him, but he didn't hear her. He shouted nonstop, in panic. She started swimming, making circles, widening the circles each time she thought she'd completed a lap. Futile maybe. She kept swimming. Timmy's voice seemed farther off now, weakening. She shouted to him again. Silence. Maybe he heard her. Desper-

ately, she ploughed on through the cold black ink, hearing no
sound but her own futile echo.

Then heaven's angels ripped apart the black clouds and poured
a shaft of golden sunbeams over the drowning Earth. The path to
heaven lay before her, paved in liquid sunshine that poured forth
from God's brilliant eye. The golden path undulated beneath her
tired, cramped, crawling body. Instinctively she knew hope lay in
a psychic connection between her spirit and the Big Light. Pawing
through the liquid path, numbed by cold, she grew sleepier. The
path lay before her, lovely and smooth, but this work was too
tiresome. Too tiresome. If death is like this sleep...

"Venus! Here I am!"

She opened her eyes. Across the golden shaft of liquid light
she saw a small dark bobbing object. It had a mouth. The mouth
moved, calling her name. Timmy. She shook off the sleep and
swam toward the only other living creature in the world.

Timmy grabbed, flailing. Treading water, she held him in an
armlock. Choking, sputtering, but he was alive. He shouted,
"Look! Up there. The big light."

Brilliant. Definitely the finest first-order Fresnel ever imported
from Paris. She'd tell Rutledge that someday, if she didn't fall
asleep first. Timmy shouted, "The chopper. It's going to crash!"

The big light had turned from them to capture the Bell Jet
Ranger, blinding it. The chopper tried flying out of the light, but
the big light had already done its work. The chopper veered,
tipped, treaded air, spun again. The bright beam had mesmerized
the great moth. The chopper made another sloppy U-turn. Too
steep. It tipped over and fell out of the light into the inky abyss.
Drowned.

The big light swung back and bathed her once again in hope.
Timmy clung like a sack of stones. She struggled, crawling, drag-
ging Timmy along the path of light. The golden path led to a wet
black shore. But the shore seemed very distant. She swam, but
the cramps in her legs, in her side, were too much. I'm very sorry,
she thought. I just have to give up. She began sinking, pulling
Timmy down with her.

The big light illuminated the ocean depths. She and Timmy

sank down, down, into Davy Jones's locker, and there witnessed unbelievable sights. Electric blue-winged creatures swam past them, batting yellow eyes. A long red eel slithered past, followed by a school of orange fish shaped like pears. A fourteen-foot octopus waved and applauded. There was more. Much more. But she had no time to gawk. She had to breathe air. She thrashed at water with her cramped legs, rose slowly to the surface. She came up choking, spitting, retching. Timmy, still in her grasp, Timmy was asleep. She shouted up at the big light, a silent scream. Then a big green dragonfly swooped down into the path of golden light.

The manitou.

It glided gently along the golden path, purring as it flew toward them. It was as if the green-winged dragonfly had parked on the big lantern, spied them, and was coming over to investigate. Well, that was all right. Let it come. It was beautiful. And it had a voice.

"Reach up!" shouted the dragonfly. "Grab the bar."

She reached up and on the first try grabbed the bar.

"Hold on!" shouted the dragonfly.

She held on with one hand, still clutching Timmy, limp Timmy. The dragonfly flew high above the shaft of golden light, purring softly, gliding gently, navigating the black nothingness, then swooped, losing altitude. The dragonfly shouted, "Now let go!"

She didn't wish to let go.

"Let go!" the dragonfly shouted again.

She let go, pitched onto a bed of pebbles. Timmy landed on top of her. The impact caused him to retch. He vomited up seawater and opened his eyes. She clutched him to her and fell asleep.

RUTLEDGE stood over the crumpled heap, his mouth forming words, his finger pointing at something. "'…'N' right over there," Rutledge was saying, "is where those sailor boys carved their captain's name." He shone his flashlight at a boulder. She focused on it. On the stone was neatly carved:

Captain Alfred Alan Danger, Master Mariner
Who Saved His Crew from Death's Wet Fingers
This Rock Is Dedicated to His Name.
                                    Danger's Faithful Crew
                                    Her Majesty's Ship,
                                    The Clipper Myrtle.
                                    17 April 17—

The date had worn off. Rutledge helped her to her feet. She staggered along behind the old man as he carried Timmy up the steep, rocky cliff. At the base of the lighthouse, the ground lay flat and soft. Grass. She fell upon it, spread-eagle on her back. Grass had never felt so alive, so supporting. Some minutes later, Richard Winters appeared, standing over her, smiling that capricious smile. Rutledge stood beside him, holding Timmy in his arms. Rutledge said, "Ever seen a pelican up close?"

Winters said, "Too early, old timer."

"The hell it is."

The lightkeeper led them to the lighthouse door. On a deep windowsill near the door roosted a sleek brown-silver bird with wings the size of a small airplane's tucked up at its sides. Its long beak preened a fluffy white belly. One beady red eye peered warily at the motley crew. Rutledge said, "She's got a lame wing. Don't get too close."

Winters whispered, "Look, Meredith. They're back."

Inside the lighthouse, Rutledge warmed Venus and Timmy by a potbellied stove that he stoked with logs and kindling. He poured her a cup of hot, steamy liquid, said, "Have some grog. We're out of jerky."

"The chopper..." she said, weakly.

Rutledge stared. "Went down."

"Rescue?" She could barely form words.

Rutledge said, "There was a ship out beyond the buoys. Maybe half a mile beyond this rock. *Barnacle Bill.* They launched a small vessel, but too late. That chopper sank fast. And now the ship's gone. Reckon that's the last I'll ever see of the old *Barnacle Bill.*" He grimaced, shook his head. "I had to make a choice, see, of where to shine my light. I chose to shine it on you and the boy. Time I got back to the chopper, she'd gone down. Disappeared." Then ruefully, "'Course, my light might've blinded 'em."

He didn't look sorry about it, either.

Proudly, like a homeowner, Rutledge showed them around the old lighthouse. In the small galley, frozen galls and paws were neatly stacked on freezer shelves. In the pantry, Venus found the lagniappe: a cache, a hundred kilos or more of powdered gall, wrapped in heat-sealed plastic bags, each package weighing about half a kilo. Winters said, "This is exactly how I found it. Carolyn told me it was here, but I didn't really believe her. Then Mer wanted me to fly her out here, then the Thai agents—"

"Chandrak? You saw them?"

He nodded. "Only once. They came to the hangar last summer, tried to pay me to fly them out here. I couldn't. The weather was awful. I never saw them again. They told me they were lighthouse historians, but Ingrid told me about finding their papers."

"You weren't working with them?"

Winters made a face. "Who said I was?"

"Just a rumor."

They climbed the steep spiral brass staircase, Timmy, recovered and energized by adventure, in the lead. As Venus climbed, she thought about Ozone Beach, that toney tourist mecca, that environmentally correct, crime-free community. They didn't need a police force in Ozone Beach, no sirree. Ozone Beach exported its own brand of evil, feeding animal organs through its pristine mainline. No one in their right mind would ever suspect the Village of Ozone Beach was the center of vicious animal slaughter, a murdering ground. Nor could a right-minded person imagine that the prim mayor of Ozone Beach had repeatedly committed such horrid, grisly crimes. Habits are terrible, nasty things.

Behind her, Venus heard Rutledge mutter, "Landlubbers."

At the top of the lighthouse, the first-order Fresnel, magnificent jewel, washed the mainland shore. Timmy shouted, "There's the village. I can see the village from here."

Winters touched Venus's arm. When she looked at him, he said, "Feel like riding tandem?"

The big green dragonfly swooped into the path of light and followed the fluid golden waves to the mainland shore. She clung to her seat as Richard swooped and glided over the village. Below, she saw searchlights aimed at the Upper Crust Bakery. She saw that crowds had formed on Lighthouse Lane, in front of the bakery. Winters leaned over, shouted in her ear, "So that whole block of storefronts was just a cover?"

Venus nodded. "It's all a slaughterhouse."

Or was. No more hypnotic jelly rolls would waft sweet scents from the Upper Crust Bakery. No more torture, no more slaughter would take place behind the pristine village façade.

Now that the big light had plumbed ethereal Pacific waters and driven the evil spirits far, far out to sea, perhaps a renewed serenity would visit the ceremonial rock, and on the mainland shore, a black bear could find peace in the cool evergreen forest. Then maybe Dave, Dave the peacemaker, hadn't died in vain.

EPILOGUE

Singapore Slings

THE MALAY waiter placed two Singapore Slings delicately on a tray, swung on his heels, and wound through elegant crowds across Raffles's manicured lawn. Reaching Venus's side, he deftly handed her a fresh Sling without spilling a drop. Venus sipped through a long straw and said, "Another mango juice, Tim?"

Timmy glanced up from where he had curled into a rattan chair, reading a lesson book. Beside him, in another rattan chair, Reuben sprawled, smiling lazily at the boy. Reuben's feet rested on a low glass table, and the waiter had to walk around the long way to deliver his Sling. The waiter stood by for Timmy's decision.

"No thanks. Can I go swimming now?"

Across the pool, Khm stood among a group of friends, drop-dead stunning in a red sarong trimmed in liquid gold. Venus traced Khm's sensual curves as she answered the boy. "Go on, Tim. Just don't splash anyone."

When Timmy had dived into the pool, Reuben said, "What happens to the boy now?"

Venus's eyes scanned the grand lawn, the orchid garden, the harpist in her long blue gown, plucking stars out of the sky, making them sing. She felt good back on this turf, like she belonged here. Her brain functioned like an Asian's, she thought. Or, maybe it was a regressive British Empire gene back somewhere in Bella's ancestry...

She said, "We're still trying to locate Carolyn Divers, but we're fairly certain she was murdered too. Meanwhile, you'll never guess who managed temporary custody of Timmy. Here's a hint: She has magnificent legs."

Reuben held a hand to his face, whispered, "Not Bella?"

"And Wexler's got the congressional committee investigating Rain Dance. They begin taking testimony next week. They'll conclude Navy knew nothing about O'Connor's setup. He manufactured Navy's involvement to cover his tracks."

"What's your theory?"

"O'Connor happened upon Mrs. Mercy's operation, joined up with her. He didn't have to do much, just protect her pathway to the *Barnacle Bill,* protect her base in the lighthouse from snoops like Carolyn Divers and Meredith Blake. And then Richard Winters and poor old Madge Leroux. He'd even recruited the local post mistress, who thought she was performing some patriotic duty by tipping off O'Connor whenever a suspicious stranger came into the post office. She had no idea the naval officer was mixed up with the poachers. She phoned him as soon as she saw me."

Reuben shook his head. He said, "So it was a conspiracy between Chick Divers and the Mercy woman?"

"Divers and some other locals poached for Mrs. Mercy. Divers had figured out how to catheterize the bears to drain their gall. We don't plan to tell Timmy about that until he's much older, much calmer. Sparks, our agent down there, knew Chick was poaching but was too terrified to report him. But it was Janice Mercy who ran the operation, and she also committed the human murders. That was her forte. That, and butchering. She ran that slaughterhouse, and it didn't surprise me when Chandrak's and Pornchen's remains were found there. Maybe that's where Carolyn Divers ended up, too."

"God." Reuben covered his eyes.

Venus smoothed the skirt of her white linen sundress. She felt good wearing a dress, for the first time in her life. Bella might even approve. Venus continued, "I wasn't absolutely certain about Janice Mercy until Meredith laced the chowder to tip us off. Meredith must have learned a good bit about the smuggling from Carolyn Divers when they met in California. I think that's why she went to Ozone Beach, to help Carolyn break open the smuggling operation at the lighthouse. Carolyn must have accidentally discovered it while studying the pelican migration. I later learned from a friend of Meredith's that Meredith hadn't actually been Chick Divers's lover. I gather he wasn't much interested in sexual activity. But Meredith had gotten cozy enough with him to correctly identify his role in the operation. Then she figured out Mrs. Mercy was the brains behind the operation.''

Reuben shook his head. Across the pool, Khm laughed at someone's remark and her laughter floated like brilliant music through the garden. Venus said, ''Khm is the most exotic creature I've ever seen.''

Reuben glanced appreciatively at his wife. After a while, he said to Venus, ''So you discovered the slaughterhouse in the back rooms of a bakery, of all places?''

Venus nodded. ''But the mistake Janice Mercy made was bringing a package of freeze-dried gall-laced herb balls to the chowder bar. She must have been planning to take it up to Seattle to fence. Or maybe she took the stuff herself, I wouldn't be surprised. In Asia, they say once you've ingested bear gall your temperament turns surly. Then somehow the package of herb balls got mixed up with packages of frozen clams, and Meredith found it in the chowder bar's freezer. That's when Timmy reported Meredith for stealing 'clams.' Then, before she was killed, to tip us off, Meredith put some herb balls in the chowder. When Janice Mercy made Meredith write the fake suicide note, before she drowned her, Meredith tipped us off by referring to being 'in the soup.''' Venus sipped the Sling. She said, ''Khm certainly looks happy.''

Reuben grinned. ''So am I. But, Venus, how do you explain this Satan gang's involvement?''

Venus scratched her head. The haircut had grown out just enough to feel unruly, a blond ruff going nowhere in particular. Khm's hair, on the other hand, flowed like black silk to her waist, and she could wear orchids in it without fearing the competition.

Venus said, ''They weren't really involved. We've known for a long time that smugglers don't care what they deal in, as long as it's lucrative. Poachers work the same underground network as drug traffickers. At some point in the past, Janice Mercy had probably needed a fence. Satan had dealt drugs. They'd already have a well-rehearsed distribution system. But the idea that they were coming back to hit Ozone Beach again was probably just another small-town rumor. That village was rife with rumor.''

Reuben said, ''But no one in the village ever went to the authorities? No one ever reported the illegal activities to the police?''

Venus shook her head. ''Most of the villagers knew about the poaching, but they never squealed. Life in Ozone Beach was too comfortable. Squealing on the mayor meant everything would change. Ozonians don't like change.''

Reuben said, ''So what actually happened to the timber queen? How was she murdered?''

''Both Madge and Richard Winters had been on Mrs. Mercy's hit list since they went out to the island. They might know something they shouldn't. When Madge Leroux went beachcombing that night, just as her son had reported, Janice Mercy saw her heading for the beach. This was Janice Mercy's opportunity to get rid of Madge. She nabbed Madge on the beach, took her out to the lighthouse, and shot her out there. She had tied Madge up with Rutledge's old hemp rope. Then she tossed the body into the ocean, figuring it would never wash ashore. After all, Carrie Violet's body never washed up.''

''Who was Carrie Violet?''

Venus smiled. ''That's another story, for later. Anyway, Madge did wash up onto the mainland. That discovery, along with the letter Timmy and Lola sent to Wexler, brought attention to the village, the kind of attention Janice Mercy didn't need. The .38 caliber weapon used to kill Madge Leroux was the same one Ball found near the airport. Janice Mercy had tossed it there, planning to implicate Richard Winters in Madge's murder. She had stolen the weapon earlier from the hangar at the airfield. Some fibers from her clothing were found on the gun's barrel. And her fingerprints matched some on the syringe. Sloppy work.''

Reuben reached out, touched her arm. ''Hey,'' he said, ''who's that over by the bar?''

His entrance had caught everyone's eye. Even Khm paused

mid-sentence to watch the dark-haired man with aquamarine eyes enter Raffles's garden. He must have already checked in at the desk because he carried no luggage, only a small box of Frango Mints. His eyes discreetly scanned the crowds until they met Venus's. Richard Winters strolled toward her, smiling mischievously.

Reuben's jaw dropped as the stranger raised Venus from her chair, pulled her close, stroked her funny hair. The Frangos fell to the grass, forgotten, and before Reuben could say "malaria," Richard's two nice hands pulled Venus's face up to his own and placed an intoxicating kiss on her mouth.

"I wonder if this is the scones man," Reuben mused silently. She'd left out this part.

Venus didn't see the waiter walking toward them, carrying a telephone. The waiter stopped short behind her, averting his eyes from the public display of affection. When it was over, he held out the phone. "Long distance, Miss," intoned the waiter. "A Mr. Wexler."

Take 2 books and a surprise gift FREE!

SPECIAL LIMITED-TIME OFFER

Mail to: The Mystery Library™
3010 Walden Ave.
P.O. Box 1867
Buffalo, N.Y. 14240-1867

YES! Please send me **2 free books** from the Mystery Library™ and my free surprise gift. Then send me 3 mystery books, first time in paperback, every month. Bill me only $4.19 per book plus 25¢ delivery and applicable sales tax, if any*. There is no minimum number of books I must purchase. I can always return a shipment at your expense and cancel my subscription. Even if I never buy another book from the Mystery Library™, **the 2 free books and surprise gift are mine to keep forever.**

415 WEN CJQN

Name	(PLEASE PRINT)	

Address		Apt. No.

City	State	Zip

FREE BOOK OFFER!

Dear Reader,

Thank you for reading this Worldwide Mystery™ title! Please take a few moments to tell us about your reading preferences. When you have finished answering the survey, please mail it to the appropriate address listed below and we'll send you a free mystery novel as a token of our appreciation! Thank you for sharing your opinions!

1. How would you rate this particular mystery book?

  1.1 ❑ Excellent   .4 ❑ Fair

    .2 ❑ Good   .5 ❑ Poor

    .3 ❑ Satisfactory

2. What prompted you to buy this particular book?

_____

_____ (2, 7)

3. What are the most important elements of a mystery fiction book to you?

_____

_____ (8, 13)

4. Which of the following types of mystery fiction do you enjoy reading? (check all that apply)

14 ❑ American Cozy (e.g. Joan Hess)

15 ❑ British Cozy (e.g. Jill Paton Walsh)

16 ❑ Noire (e.g. James Ellroy, Loren D. Estleman)

17 ❑ Hard-boiled (male or female private eye) (e.g. Robert Parker)

18 ❑ American Police Procedural (e.g. Ed McBain)

19 ❑ British Police Procedural (e.g. Ian Rankin, P. D. James)

5. Which of the following other types of paperback books have you read in the past 12 months? (check all that apply)

20 ❑ Espionage/Spy (e.g. Tom Clancy, Robert Ludlum)

21 ❑ Mainstream Contemporary Fiction (e.g. Patricia Cornwell)

22 ❑ Occult/Horror (e.g. Stephen King, Anne Rice)

23 ❑ Popular Women's Fiction (e.g. Danielle Steel, Nora Roberts)

24 ❑ Fantasy (e.g. Terry Brooks)

25 ❑ Science Fiction (e.g. Isaac Asimov)

26 ❑ Series Romance Fiction (e.g. Harlequin Romance®)

27 ❑ Action Adventure paperbacks (e.g. Mack Bolan)

28 ❑ Paperback Biographies

29 ❑ Paperback Humor

30 ❑ Self-help paperbacks

6. How do you usually obtain your mystery paperbacks?
   (check all that apply)
   31 ❑ National chain bookstore (e.g. Waldenbooks, Borders)
   32 ❑ Supermarket
   33 ❑ General or discount merchandise store (e.g. Kmart, Target)
   34 ❑ Specialty mystery bookstore
   35 ❑ Borrow or trade with family members or friends
   36 ❑ By mail
   37 ❑ Secondhand bookstore
   38 ❑ Library
   39 ❑ Other _____ (40, 45)

7. How many mystery novels have you read in the past
   6 months?
   Paperback _____ (46, 47)   Hardcover _____ (48, 49)

8. Please indicate your gender:
   50.1 ❑ female   .2 ❑ male

9. Into which of the following age groups do you fall?
   51.1 ❑ Under 18 years   .4 ❑ 35 to 49 years
    .2 ❑ 18 to 24 years   .5 ❑ 50 to 64 years
    .3 ❑ 25 to 34 years   .6 ❑ 65 years or older

*Thank you very much for your cooperation! To receive your free
mystery novel, please print your name and address clearly and
return the survey to the appropriate address listed below.*

Name: _____

Address: _____ City: _____

State/Province: _____ Zip/Postal Code: _____

In U.S.: Worldwide Mystery Survey, 3010 Walden Avenue,
P.O. Box 9057, Buffalo, NY 14269-9057
In Canada: Worldwide Mystery Survey, P.O. Box 622,
Fort Erie, Ontario L2A 5X3

098 KGU CJP2

WWWR98D2